MRS. BENNET'S MENOPAUSE

Lucy Kate King

PREFACE

Mrs. Bennet, the mother of Jane Austen's beloved heroine Elizabeth, is "a woman of mean understanding, little information and uncertain temper.When she was discontented she fancied herself nervous.The business of her life was to get her daughters married, its solace was visiting and news."

This description, appearing in the opening chapter of "Pride and Prejudice", does little to endear her character to the reader. The first two qualities may be due to her lack of perception and education: defects that render her mildly disagreeable. But the third makes the reader wary. It foreshadows a fitful, irascible and unreasonable woman, without steadiness or sweetness of nature.

The juxtaposition of "uncertain temper" and "nervous" with "the business of her life was to get her daughters married", reveals the stresses upon her. Living in a household dominated by hormonal young ladies is trying enough, to know she must get those daughters married increases the pressure and, for a lady of Mrs. Bennet's limited resources, the situation becomes almost unbearable.

As the story unravels, there is seemingly little improvement; she is perverse and attention seeking, making demands on all who come near her. There are constant complaints of flutterings, tremblings and palpitations, which Mr. Bennet describes as "her nerves". These emotional agitations, after twenty-three years of marriage, have become his "long time friends". His wife's days are mainly spent on her bed or *chaise longue* where she cries, "What a dreadful state I am in. Nobody can tell what I suffer".

The author's final observations on Mrs. Bennet are interesting. "I wish I could say, for the sake of the family, that the accomplishment of her earnest desire in the establishment of so many of her children produced so happy an effect as to make her a sensible, amiable and well-informed woman for the rest of her life; though perhaps it was lucky for her husband, who might not have relished domestic felicity in so unusual a form, that she still was occasionally nervous and invariably silly."

Is it then to be inferred that Mr. Bennet would rather have her foolish, unpleasant and ignorant? This would tally with his nature—"a man of sarcastic humour and caprice"—but is unlikely, since he values the sense and amiability of his two eldest daughters. Perhaps "in so unusual a form" refers to his finding that an alteration in her nature would be so great a surprise that he would have to adjust his own disposition in coming to terms with it.

Does the fact that she is "occasionally nervous" mean she still suffers from her nerves or that she suffers anxiety from time to time? The author implies that he would find this easier to live with than a shift in her personality: 'better a devil you know approach.'

It is Jane Austen's use of the word "silly" that bears closest scrutiny. A dictionary definition gives us three possibilities:

—lacking common sense.

—unworthy of serious concern.

—in a stunned, dazed or helpless condition.

The first is untrue in that she has the common sense to see that in the context of the time, her impoverished daughters must marry to secure their futures. The maxim to which she and other necessitous mothers adhered in the early nineteenth century, was succinctly put by the author when she described matrimony as "the only honourable provision for well-educated women of small fortune and however uncertain of giving happiness, must be their pleasantest preservative from want."

The second may be Mr. Bennet's view of his wife, but she is fully aware of, and has impressed upon her girls, the urgent need to marry well. Lizzy and Jane note its importance often in their conversations together. It is the dilemma of Austen's novels that marrying for love is often in conflict with marrying for improvement of fortune. The two eldest Bennets are fortunate to combine both, but Lydia marries for love (albeit her husband Wickham weds her for Darcy's money). Mrs. Bennet, then, whether foolish in all other areas of her life, is deadly serious in getting her girls wedded as wealthily as she can.

As for the third definition, it would appear to describe the effects of the menopause exactly; "stunned, dazed and helpless". All women will nod in recognition as they pass through their own mid-life years; in whichever century they live or country they inhabit. Past child-bearing and probably in her mid-forties, the likelihood of Mrs. Bennet being menopausal is high. The frequent dippings and soarings of her spirits are possible indications of 'The Change'. Although there was a lack of medical knowledge at the time of writing and the subject is unmentioned in the novel, Mrs. Bennet would have been a man not to have experienced the symptoms and a mute not to have discussed them, at least with somebody close to her. Yet there is no direct reference, conversation or explanation of her irrational and insensitive behaviour.

The author's protrayal of this difficult woman is unquestionably negative, but she omits to tell us why. Or does she? Literature of the period allowed scarce acknowledgement of bodily functions between neck and knee; a delicate cotton-muslin of secrecy was drawn over the menstrual cycle and its aftermath. Such was the convention of the day. This left Jane Austen little room to manoeuvre.

Having no direct allusion to the issue from the author, we can only analyse her subtle text, read between the lines and draw our own conclusions on Mrs. Bennet's behaviour. While her every action is driven by the urge to get her daughters married, her conduct in achieving that exposes her probable menopausal situation. Jane Austen relates the journey, carefully dropping clues like Hansel and Gretel in the forest, marking the path of the post-menstrual. It is possible that the author drew heavily on her own mother who, according to Margaret Drabble's research, "seems to have been something of a trial, hypochondriac and ailing". This exacting, wearisome parental presence may have consumed much of her daughter's patience and tume. Out of a sense of duty and loyalty the author would probably have borne such a charge with little overt criticism. However, the many flaws and few attractive features in Mrs. Bennet when played out against this knowledge, may be looked upon more generously if we believe Jane's commission was accompanied by compassion. Perhaps Elizabeth Bennet's mother is a creature more to be pitied than blamed?

L.K.K.

Prologue

It is a truth universally acknowledged, that for ladies of a certain age, the onset of the menopause is no fun. At such a time, a woman's total preoccupation is with her treacherous body and there is little humour to be found in this condition. By day she is at the mercy of hot flushes and, during the nocturnal hours, by night sweats. Mood swings render her savage and exhausted. Palpitations halt her in mid-stride and wash her with fear. A look in the mirror serves to underline fading looks with fading confidence. Her struggles to maintain some semblance of control manifest themselves in sharp barking at those nearest, or manipulating events in the wider social circle.

This situation, in all its aspects, was most unwelcome to Mrs. Bennet. Married for twenty-three years and with five growing daughters, she had had but one wish, to see all of them married, preferably in financial comfort. The entail of her father-in-law's will instructed that only a male heir could inherit the Longbourn family home. The years of Mrs. Bennet's fertility had not produced the expected son and with each successive girl, the future had grown bleaker. Although never tacitly acknowledged, the blame for this circumstance, or at least the responsibility, fell increasingly on her. And despite the maternal pride she felt when observing her married offspring; Jane, Elizabeth and Lydia, there was a natural frustration at the very existence of Mary and Kitty who remained at home.

Having little money to attract suitors, the Bennet girls had but their looks, wits and talents to recommend them. Love could only come second in importance to that of financial security. The manipulation of social circumstances in the small parish of Meryton in order to engineer the meeting of suitable partners was a constant challenge; there were so few eligible bachelors. Besides, other neighbours had single daughters equally of an age ripe for marriage and so offered not inconsiderable competition.

Mary Bennet was a worthy daughter but rather solemn in nature; a kind observer would find her serious, an honest one, dull. Kitty was easily-led and this had often been exploited by her sister, Lydia, a bold and headstrong young woman with a keen interest in the opposite sex well beyond her years, leaving Kitty with a legacy of forwardness and shallow understanding.

Mr. Bennet often remarked on the uncommon foolishness of his daughters, but did little to control them, avoiding confrontation by retiring to his study to find relief in reading, away from the inevitable feminine raised voices. A generally good-humoured man, his appearances at the meal table lent an air of affability to scenes of tension, and while his two eldest were particularly fond of his dry wit when they lived at home, it now seemed singularly unappreciated by Mary, Kitty and his wife.

It was a period of frustration on more than the family front for Mrs. Bennet. To her dismay and annoyance she found that her own wellbeing was under threat; she was, as she whispered in church to her sister Mrs. Philips, "undergoing The Change". She felt overheated in chilly rooms, unable to sleep when exhausted, her once-lustrous hair leaving her head at every combing and her once-smooth face running to wrinkles. The trim figure she had been so proud of resembled a stack of round cushions and her uncertain temper grew more uncertain.

So Mrs. Bennet joined the greying millions of menopausal women, from Eve onwards, who avoided gazing into any reflecting surface from a pond to a plate glass shop window. A mirror, albeit surrounded by a pretty gilded frame, still told her a thoroughly unpleasant truth; she was at that age where an indoor bonnet was now an obligation.

Chapter I

After morning service, as soon as she had shaken hands with the Reverend Johnson, Mrs. Bennet drew her sister aside, to the edge of the gravel path.

"Oh sister, I am quite unwell."

"The Change?" Mrs. Philips whispered, her eyebrows raised in enquiry.

Mrs. Bennet nodded, looking down in embarrassment.

"My poor sister. I surmised as much; the symptoms are certainly apparent. How are you feeling?"

"Oh I cannot describe what I am suffering," replied her relative then promptly went on to do so.

"The sudden heats, then chills and feeling so faint I have to take to my room. And the palpitations. My nerves are inflamed. I am so anxious about every thing, from decisions over meals to which shawl to wear. Indecision is my constant companion. My memory is unreliable. Every day seems so difficult. I am quite brought down."

"And what of the nights?" asked Mrs. Philips.

"Even more troubled; so hot I throw off every one of the covers. I find I am perspiring all over and have to rise and then completely change my night attire. Then there is the matter of sleep itself. No real rest, tossing and turning until dawn. I tell you sister, there seems to be no end to these burdens."

"And is Mr. Bennet proving sympathetic at this time?"

"Mr. Bennet? Mr. Bennet! Oh that I could say he is. By day he tries to shake me into a better humour, with his dry comments on my nerves and how often they show up like tiresome visitors. At night he retires to his own room so knows nothing of what I suffer. And as for the girls, Kitty is so clumsy she cannot be trusted to carry a cup of tea upstairs, while Mary tells me that all my troubles are a test to strengthen my faith and the cure is to read Fordyce's sermons."

"There there, dear sister. All will be well. We shall speak further, but let us be quiet now on this subject, for here comes Sir William and Maria Lucas. Good morning, good morning. And Mrs. Long too. Well, well and how are the family?"

The churchgoers moved past, exchanging news or walking on, top hats rising, bonnets nodding, hems brushing the late morning dew. The gravestones stood like old grey soldiers in silent homage to the living who gave them little heed for it was a chill day and the mist was unlikely to lift. It was difficult to discern the church spire and even the bells sounded muffled. Ahead, the village houses straggled into the distance like a set of aging teeth, their pretty bow windows obscured by low cloud.

"Mrs. Bennet, Mrs. Bennet. I urge you to join us as soon as may be. The girls and I are catching a chill standing here waiting while you gossip," called her husband who was waiting further along the path. Kitty was hopping from foot to foot, her black boots tapping the ground, her face pinched white with cold and impatience. Mary bore her usual air of piety and resignation. Both had their hands thrust deep into muffs.

Mrs. Bennet glanced towards her family, turned once to wave farewell to her sister, then quickened her pace. They walked under the lych-gate together, and down the lane to Longbourn.

"Mama," began Kitty. "Mama,may I walk into Meryton this afternoon?"

"Certainly not," said her father. "it is Sunday." He added quickly, "nor tomorrow either, unless chaperoned. I will not have you meeting with any young man who may happen to be there."

Kitty looked irritated. "If you mean the officers, well I'm sure I have no wish to do so. Or at least, no officer like George Wickham."

"George Wickham? George Wickham indeed. I should hope that he is unique. It is enough that your sister had to marry such a man," said Mr. Bennet.

"Papa!" began Kitty in protest, but her father cut her short saying heavily "No, Kitty, you should take heed from Lydia who now has to live with the consequences of her rash behaviour."

Mrs. Bennet broke in: "Do not be so harsh on Lydia. She at least has the status of being a married woman and besides, she is no longer a financial burden to us."

"Not a burden? Perhaps my dear you should ask Lizzy and Jane how solvent the Wickhams are now. They continually run from their creditors and always in the direction of Derbyshire. And when finally the goodwill of even Bingley is exhausted, they progress to Pemberley. It is only Darcy's love for Lizzy that opens that door to such a profligate couple."

"It is a point to be remembered that 'to marry in haste is to repent at leisure'," said Mary, a young lady often given to deep reflection.

"Oh Mary!" exclaimed her sister and her mother, one in dismay the other in irritation.

Mr. Bennet interrupted to say, "While grateful for your advice, Mary, perhaps your contribution could have been better timed."

As the walk home neared its conclusion, Mr. Bennet added, "There is one positive element I can observe on Lydia's choice, now he is safely at a distance. It affords me some amusement to consider my three sons-in-law on the matter of fiscal generosity. Bingley opens his purse often and to the public gaze, Darcy is even more bountiful but prefers to do so unseen, while Wickham is totally generous with other people's money and mainly to himself." And chuckling loudly, Mr. Bennet walked into his home.

Hill the housekeeper met them in the hall to assist with bonnets, capes and tippets. After hanging the garments in the hall cupboard, she picked up a letter lying on the table.

"Please sir, this came for you while you were out."

Mr. Bennet glanced at the handwriting, which was flourishing in style and completely unknown to him. He took it with him to his study saying "Do not disturb me until dinner."

The housekeeper turned towards her mistress.

"And when would you like dinner served, ma'am?"

"Oh, around four, Hill. Ensure the mutton is tender and the pigeon pie well-seasoned." She hesitated and said "But perhaps we should have pork cutlets today. No, the mutton, it will go further. And if a large piece, we can have the pie tomorrow. As for the apple loaf, you may use more of the apples from those stored in the barn."

"Yes, ma'am."

"Oh and do remember to warm the plates. That will be all, I think, for the moment."

"Yes ma'am", replied Hill, bobbing a curtsey and leaving.

"Might Mary and I have something now please, mama?" begged Kitty. "We could toast some bread by the drawing room fire."

"You may, Kitty, but do not use an excess of butter. And only one slice each. I declare I have little appetite myself and you would do well to limit yours, if you are to obtain a narrow waist. I'm sure your father will not pay out for new gowns this season."

"Oh mama, I'm sure I do not eat as much as Mary. And besides, with Jane, Lizzy and Lydia gone we are not so expensive a household."

"That's as may be Kitty, but Mr. Bennet tells me there were poor yields from the farm this year so our income is reduced. We shall all need to be careful this winter."

Mrs. Bennet retired to her room feeling exhausted. She took up her quill pen to make an entry in her journal.

> *Sunday February 10th.*
>
> *Worrying time in church - could not concentrate on the sermon. Thought I was the only sinner until I saw Sir William's eyes closed;- praying or sleeping? Lady Lucas was smiling to herself—probably musing on the prospect of her daughter turning me out of Longbourn when Mr. Bennet dies. Humiliating!*
>
> *Noted Mrs. Long and daughters seated in the front pew (of course); they resembled a row of complacent pigeons. Mr. Long was squeezed into the corner, as stick-like and feeble as ever. All their velvets cannot make up for the plainness of their features. As for Mrs. Long's voice: - fortissimo contralto! Warbling and wobbling. Completely drowned the choir.*

Dreadful moment when assailed by a sudden hot sweat. Longed to rush outside. Just gathering the courage to leave, when it faded. I dread these flushes. The final hymn, 'Oft in danger oft in woe' summed up my condition, exactly.

While considering her next sentence, her thoughts turned to her current situation. Here she was to the world's eye a figure to envy, for her two eldest girls were recently wedded to wealthy young men. The whole village had turned out to see them married at a double ceremony, with the sun shining and the brides' faces radiant in the flower-decked open carriages. Her youngest daughter was also married. At such memories she felt full of pride and gratitude, all other cares forgotten.

But two problems soon assailed her once more; the worry of her remaining daughters being still unwed, with the cold fact that should Mr. Bennet die the family would be turned out of their home. The second problem was more immediate; she was in that condition whereby though past childbearing, she was assailed by so many alarming symptoms that she was suffering day and night. This had been the debilitating truth for the past two years. Each morning she woke in hope that the troubles were gone; each new day as it unfolded, showed that they were not. The discomposure of her spirits was a constant and unwelcome companion. Her only relief was to seek intervals of rest during her day. She put her journal aside, drew the curtains, lay down on her bed and closed her eyes. Just as she was beginning to drift into sleep, there was a knock upon her door. It was Kitty.

"I've brought you some tea mama, and Mary has found the lavender water," she said. The rattle of china cup and saucer then the crash as it was clumsily placed on the bedside table, made her mother frown. Mrs. Bennet recognised the kindness of her daughters, so made no complaint, even while observing the tea slop over the cup and drip on to her hand worked lace mat. She said with as much gratitude as she could summon, "Thank you, girls. You do not yet have Jane's soothing quiet ways, but your hearts are in the right place." When the girls left, she poured a small amount of fortified wine into the tea, sipped it, then fell back among the pillows.

At dinner next day Mr. Bennet produced the letter and asked the family to guess the sender.

"Lizzy!' cried Kitty.

"Jane!" said Mary.

"Is it my dear Lydia?" asked his wife.

"That, Mrs. Bennet, is extremely unlikely, since Lydia has not yet put pen to paper since her marriage, unless to beg money, of which this letter contains no hint, I am pleased to say. No, this is from a man whom I have yet to meet but who is related to a cousin of ours."

"Cousin? I'm sure we know all the cousins of my sister's families, the Philips and the Gardiners," said Mrs. Bennet.

"You forget my side of the family, my dear. There is the personage of Mr. Collins to consider too."

"Mr. Collins!" exclaimed his wife. "Why should we give any account to Mr. Collins now? Since Charlotte Lucas trapped him, we have no interest in Mr. Collins."

"That is a pity, since he has a younger brother who would like to make our acquaintance."

This aroused great astonishment and Mr. Bennet had the pleasure of being keenly questioned by everyone at once.

"Why have we not heard from this young man before?" asked Mrs. Bennet.

"If you recall Mrs. Bennet, we have had no communication with that branch of the family, their residing in so far off a county and my father's will being what it was. It was this Mr. Collins' older brother who made the first overtures, when he called here last year."

"Despicable man! I would that he had never left Kent at all. His visit here only upset us all, giving me false hopes of his marrying Lizzy, but it all came to nothing," Mrs. Bennet cried.

"One can hardly blame a man for good intentions. To do him justice, Mr. Collins did make an offer for our second daughter and received rejection."

"Foolish and headstrong girl! When was a mother's advice so abused?"

"But mama, Lizzy is so much happier with Mr. Darcy than she would ever have been with Mr. Collins" protested Kitty.

"Well, well Lizzy has made a much finer match it is true," Mrs. Bennet mused. "How Sir William and Lady Lucas must continually envy me." She smiled in satisfaction. Then her brow furrowed. "How cunning it was of the Lucas family to waste no time in ensnaring Mr. Collins! Not two days after proposing to our Lizzy he was telling us in his simpering manner that he had been accepted by Charlotte and she had made him the happiest of men! But Charlotte Lucas is the poorer for it, since she lives with Mr. Collins' insufferable pride every day. Moreover her world is constantly dominated by his patroness, Lady Catherine de Bourgh. Do you know she has refused to meet her nephew Mr. Darcy since he married our Lizzy? Such impertinence!"

It was difficult for Mr. Bennet to follow the leaps and twists of his wife's thoughts, so rather than exert his intellect to voice his rebuttals he took up his customary stance and ignored them.

"Shall I continue?" he asked his listeners.

His daughters' genial expressions encouraged him, while his wife glowered in maternal indignation, remembering the slighting of her second daughter.

Mr. Bennet coughed, adjusted his glasses, held up the letter and by the light of the candles read:

'Brompton Park, Rochester, Kent.

3rd March.

Dear Sir,

It is in the spirit of conciliation that I write to you, since I have been made aware of the coolness existing between you and my brother after his

own marriage and that of Lady
Catherine de Bourgh's nephew to
your second daughter.'

"Ah yes," broke in Mrs. Bennet, "how angry she was with Lizzy when she came here. She must still be furious that Mr. Darcy did not marry *her* daughter. I wonder Mr. Collins dare go near Rosings ever again being the cousin of such a tainted family."

Mr. Bennet paused in his reading while his wife vented her anger, waited until she needed to take breath, then resumed.

'You may well wonder at my next
words, since William was
unsuccessful in his mission when he
came to Longbourn. It is evident that
the entail in my father's will has
caused much grief for your family,
but it is here that I plan with your
benediction, to redress this fault. As a
clergyman and relative, I feel it is my
duty to bring peace into this world
where I am able and I trust these
overtures of goodwill are not
unwelcome. It is incumbent on me to
smooth the feathers ruffled by recent
matrimonial events, if you are kindly
disposed.

I flatter myself that you will be
pleased to hear my proposals when I
visit your house, which I would hope

to do next month, on Tuesday, April 10th in the forenoon.

My respectful compliments to your family, from your friend and well wisher,

Charles Collins.'

"Well, well. So a second Mr. Collins is to visit Longbourn," reflected Mr. Bennet. "If you have no objection Mrs. Bennet, I shall reply with a welcome."

"But papa," declared Kitty "he may be worse than his brother! Another pompous and silly clergyman. I hope you will not expect *me* to entertain him."

"You will do as manners and your parents tell you," said her mother sharply. "Yes, Mr. Bennet, write at once."

Mary remained silent.

Chapter II

Punctual to his date and time, Charles Collins arrived and was received with civility by the Bennet family. He was like his brother heavily built, but much shorter, with a grave manner and a habit of pressing his palms together as though in constant prayer. He looked with approval when shown around the house, which would have delighted Mrs. Bennet if she had not been so aware that all the property, including the furniture and the house would transfer to the Collins' estate when Mr. Bennet died.

At dinner, with monotonous solemnity, Charles Collins said the grace, which went on so long that the gratitude Mrs. Bennet usually felt at such moments was chased away by the concern that the food was growing cold. The daughters continually glanced up until, at last, he was done. After a mere first mouthful, his resounding voice began, "How delightful to be among such a family. I find your daughters' beauty far exceeds the reports I have heard of them, Mrs. Bennet."

"Why thank you sir. They are not without looks or talent, though I say it myself. Kitty sews and draws well, while Mary plays the piano and reads religious works with a diligence that is admirable."

Mary glanced at her plate, quietly pleased. Kitty scowled for she had no desire to attract Mr. Collins' special attention.

The clergyman continued, "I am very sensible to the hardship the entail has bestowed on my fair cousins. I wish to make amends for such an instruction and hope that this may be addressed during my stay," said the visitor, smiling and nodding to both parents. He went on to compliment Mrs. Bennet on the dinner but added that the food was served a little too cold for his taste. Kitty opened her mouth to protest, but was silenced by a look from her mother. When Hill entered to clear the dishes, Mrs. Bennet whispered, "Please ensure the apple loaf is piping hot and covered."

Mr. Bennet asked him about his living and was told, "My dear sir, I can assure you that there is much to recommend that area of Rochester where I reside. In actual fact, the living is nearer Chatham than Rochester and is situated close to the docks. It is not as grand a parish or residence as I would wish, but it is within the diocese of Rochester and I am able to visit the bishop frequently. Some parishioners rail against the constant ebb and flow of sailors who alight on the quayside, but I find there is ample opportunity to offer religious papers to such men as they pass by on their way to the town.

"And do you find they are receptive?" asked his host.

"I flatter myself that like the sower, some seed will fall on fertile ground and will bear fruit. I deem it my mission to save such souls that are in danger. It is my daily and solemn duty to distribute those pamphlets that will save them. I press these papers upon them, and here I flatter myself, with an air of loving concern. I accompany these moments with an earnest gaze, aiming to share the light of salvation. Those tracts that may fall from the sailors' hands, which I am sure do so accidentally, I scoop up again to redistribute."

"That is interesting, Mr. Collins" Mr. Bennet observed.

"In my clerical position I feel it incumbent upon me to spread the word. One day my patron the Bishop of Rochester was so good as to compliment me on my zeal, when he saw me chase after two seamen who had unknowingly dropped my papers on the street."

"And did you manage to gain their attention by running after them?" As he spoke, Mr. Bennet ran an appraising eye over the clergyman's rotund physique.

"Well, to strictly adhere to the truth, not quite. It seems they did not hear my calling and disappeared into a tavern. I am certain they would have eagerly read my papers had they kept them."

With a mixture of servility and self-importance, Mr. Collins continued to relate his religious experiences, which reflected in varying degrees on those around him. Mr. Bennet was highly entertained, Mary fascinated, Kitty irritated, while Mrs. Bennet glanced frequently at the clock hoping the next hot flush was not showing itself. She sipped often from her water glass, avoiding the wine and hot dishes with some regret. It was difficult to appear the calm, agreeable hostess while at the mercy of the next warm wave of perspiration. Her attention to the general conversation was therefore incomplete. She wished only that the meal was appetising, the hospitality welcoming and to avoid the notice of her debilitating symptoms by guest and family. She wanted rather than expected her daughters to make a positive impression on Mr. Collins, for Mary stared at the tablecloth and Kitty stared at the window. She need not have been so concerned over the matter of being a focus of attention herself, since Mr. Collins in passing dishes, proved less than accomplished. He twice knocked over his wine glass while flourishing his napkin in expressing his views.

"The bishop has most graciously" he began. In nodding his head as if in obeisance to his temporal lord then flapping the napkin to show his humility at the remembrance of that religious audience, he clipped the edge of the wine glass sending the contents scattering across the white cloth, which then sank with reddening misery into Mrs. Bennet's best table linen.

"My dear Mrs. Bennet, I am most profoundly-''

"Think nothing of it, dear sir, it was but an accident. Hill, please mop up the spillage." This involved a small operation whereby the cloth was raised in the area by having a saucer poked underneath, the red wine sponged out from above to weaken its staining and to keep it from reaching the wood below. The whole procedure took several minutes, accompanied by the incessant apologies of Mr. Collins and the clatter of cutlery, china and glass as he moved articles this way and that.

Mr. Bennet and the girls were not as anxious as Mrs. Bennet for the sole reason that it would be she who knew the soaking of the cloth in salt then cold water for several hours, followed by steeping in warm soapsuds and ultimately the wringing out of this sizeable piece of linen, would take up much of the next day. And if the weather were not fair, the drying indoors would add another. She glanced out of the window to see dull skies yielding to rain. This, she grimly surmised, would set back the final ironing of the tablecloth to the middle of the week.

Hill, methodically, laid the table again. She and Mrs. Bennet exchanged glances, but refrained from uttering any words of rebuke.

"Sir, now we are settled again, think no more of it. Please help yourself to the dish of lamb," said Mrs. Bennet with a bleak smile.

Mr. Bennet asked him "Pray sir, could I trouble you for the gravy? It lies just at your elbow. And while we are engaged on the subject, may I ask your views on when you consider the ideal time for dinner might be, in the diocese of Rochester?"

"Of course, sir," answered his guest. "I pride myself that in the matter of dining etiquette, I own no man my master. The bishop, I note, dines at the hour of seven. While I have habitually dined at three thirty (my frugal repast prior to dinner being but a small piece of bread and cheese to break my fast of nine of the morning), I have recently taken to dining at the same hour as my most reverend senior churchman."

"And do you not find the wait between nine and seven, a test of your constitution?" asked his host.

"Indeed no, I see it as a struggle for the soul. It is a test of my faith."

"And does your housekeeper not mind preparing, serving and clearing a meal so late?"

"My housekeeper? Well sir, she has, I hope, the humility to see where her duty lies. Though to be strictly accurate, it would appear that since the dinners are now later, there has been a certain distancing in her manner. Perhaps her age is telling against her (she is nearing three score years and ten). It would be as well to look to the future, whereby a younger woman would be employed. Of course it would naturally follow that the running of the house would be much smoother if there was a wife to manage such matters."

"Have you anyone particular in mind?" asked Mrs. Bennet.

Here Mr. Collins looked thoughtful. His glance fell on the single females at the table.

"Perhaps there might be something settled in that direction at no distant point," he ventured.

While his mouth would offer no more information, his countenance reflected the emotions of his mind; excessive generosity and selflessness. While he was thus employed, he playfully wagged his finger at Mrs. Bennet to indicate he would disclose no more at present. Unfortunately, the motion brought his elbow in contact with the gravy boat, which spilled a sudden brown puddle on to the tablecloth.

"Mr. Collins!" cried Mrs. Bennet.

The second mopping up operation prevented further discourse and the desserts were consumed in silence.

After dinner was over, the ladies withdrew to talk over the coming of Mr. Collins and what it might infer.

"Do you suppose Mr. Collins is here to make an offer of marriage, mama?" asked Kitty with a fearful face. "For I may tell you at once I have no interest in him whatsoever."

Mary looked down and started to blush.

"Why, Mary, surely you cannot be considering yourself to be Mr. Collins' bride?" enquired her sister in astonishment.

"Hold your tongue, Kitty," said her mother more sharply than she meant to. "Lizzy lost her chance of marriage by being too outspoken. Would you let another opportunity slip?"

Kitty retorted "But Lizzy married a man ten times Mr. Collins' consequence. She would not have done so had she taken that first proposal."

Mrs. Bennet dabbed at her forehead with her handkerchief.

"Do not answer back, Kitty. This evening I am feeling most unwell."

Mary, relieved at no longer being the subject of attention, asked "may I offer some lavender water to cool your brow, mama?"

"Yes, yes," she replied, caught between irritation and exhaustion.

As Mary went for the tincture, Mrs. Bennet rounded on the younger girl.

"You will do as I instruct you, Kitty. Should Mr. Collins wish to ask for your hand, you will oblige your parents by accepting."

"Mr. Collins is a conceited, pompous, narrow-minded and very foolish man. To accept any proposal of his would mean a lifetime of misery," said Kitty with some spirit.

Meanwhile, in the dining room, Mr. Collins was making clear to his host the reason for his visit.

"My dear sir, although it is on a matter of some delicacy, that I approach you regarding the purpose of my sojourn here, it is with a certain degree of confidence. I trust the directness of my speech will not be the object of your censure when you have heard my profound and philanthropic proposition. Indeed, having made the acquaintance of all those younger members of the Bennet household who reside at Longbourn, the proposal may be viewed almost in the terms of a panegyric. But I digress.

"The entail of my father's will has caused too much enmity between our families and as a man of conscience it is incumbent upon me, as the remaining single son, to make amends. This would be the charitable action to take and shows no little degree of disinterest and condescension on my part. I have therefore determined to act without self-regard and with true generosity of spirit, to settle the estate of marriage upon one of your fair daughters."

"Indeed?" was Mr. Bennet's astonished reply.

"Yes, Mr. Bennet. I am resolved. I came here a single man and plan to leave with the status of an affianced gentleman. One of the Miss Bennets in particular, strikes me as a woman who would make a suitable, useful sort of wife for a clergyman." Here Mr. Collins smiled smugly to himself.

"And even if I have no objection, you are assured of my daughter's willingness to have you?"

"Oh yes, sir. Believe me, I have already seen a definite favouring of my suit, though under your roof but six hours."

"And what would that have been, sir?" asked his host.

Mr. Collins chuckled to himself then said, "A glance here, a soft smile there. We lovers can read the signs, you know. There is a certain strength of feeling already established between us."

Mr. Bennet hid his surprise and poured his guest another glass of port.

*

The next morning Mary hovered near Mr. Collins' window and while she waited, the dewy grass wetting her boots, she read Fordyce's sermons. Her interest in the visitor had been the subject of much contemplation the previous evening when alone in her room. The urge to indicate her feelings towards him in some way was tempered by her philosophy that "every impulse of feeling should be guided by reason." She wrestled with these notions for a full hour before deciding that, "any exertion should always be in proportion to what is required" - another of her maxims. She meant to impress him with her knowledge. The hundred strokes of her brush had made her hair shine and though it was secured in a style of some severity, it gleamed in the early sunlight. She anxiously polished her spectacles and, finding Mr. Collins did not emerge, sat on the garden bench to wait.

During this time, Kitty had taken a walk with her mother to Meryton in order to call on Mrs. Philips. Their disagreement of last evening was forgotten in the brightness of the morning and their mutual delight of a visit to a dear relative. Kitty had persuaded her mother that fresh air would lift her spirits. It was not so great a distance and their arrival was met with Mrs. Philips' warm smile.

"Some tea my dears?" said the aunt as they stepped in to her warm hallway. "The morning is certainly sunny but the air is chilled. Come in by the fire." Mrs. Philips busied herself with unlocking the tea cupboard, taking out the caddy, boiling the kettle and warming the teapot. It was poured into china cups and then enjoyed with no little gratitude on such a cold morning. Once the tea was finished, the elder women sent Kitty away to the parlour to look over dress patterns while they talked.

"I shall sit away from your fire, sister, though it is a comfort in this cold weather. I hope I cause no offence, but I find fires raise my temperature to an unbearable degree."

"How are you today, my dear?"

"Oh sister, the night was as bad as ever. How feverish I was and how troubled in my thoughts. Such sufferings, such ill usage as I have borne. So much worry about myself. You do not know what I suffer. Such tremblings and flutterings. I am over-wrought and quite used up. This Change will be the death of me. I am utterly fatigued and at death's door."

"No, no, dear sister. Nobody ever died of being tired," Mrs. Philips laughed. "All this is but fruitless alarm. Now, good news! I have been spending some time in study looking over remedies for your condition." Here she brought down from her shelf a thick, leather-bound volume. "Let me show you the abundance of draughts that may ease your discomfort. Smelling salts will stop your faintness. Rhubarb will aid a disordered stomach and I shall make you a "reviver" from my own recipe."

"What is in your reviver?" asked Mrs Bennet with some unease.

"Aromatic vinegar and lavender water, plus a twist of bitter herbs."

Mrs. Bennet turned down her mouth.

"Of course you may go to the apothecary and buy rheum rootstock, but as it comes from the Far East, I fear it will be very expensive."

"And what would be the cost of that?"

"Three shillings an ounce, I believe."

Mrs. Bennet looked shocked but after a brief reflection, she replied in a determined tone,

"Well I shall consult Mr. Bennet and see if it may be purchased for I am sure I have been suffering too long. It may be better to take the druggist's ingredients, than a home-made draught."

Mrs. Philips did her best not to look offended, but her face showed how much she felt the slight. Seeing her sister's discomfiture, Mrs. Bennet relented and spoke in a softer manner.

"Meanwhile, perhaps I shall try your reviver if I may."

Mrs. Philips smiled.

She went to a cupboard next to the hearth and brought out a small phial of brown liquid. She poured some into a little spoon and gave it to her sister. Though scarcely to be judged delicious, its taste was not wholly unpleasant and was rendered even more palatable by the glass of fortified wine that was next sipped by both.

"Now, tell me all the news here in Meryton."

"Well my dear, the regiment is returning to the town, probably by the end of the month. The officers will be most welcome at the shops, assemblies and evenings, will they not?"

She continued, "Lady Lucas' second daughter will be of age in March and it is expected she will be given a ball to celebrate. You will most likely see Reverend Collins and Charlotte there, if you are also invited."

"Well that will be soon enough" said Mrs. Bennet. "Ah sister, if I could but see all my daughters happily settled I should be content. It is incumbent on me to forward those marriage prospects. And it is with this in mind that I wish to advance their education. Kitty and Mary are in need of some further tutoring. Mr. Bennet and I are hoping to engage a master or governess to educate them as soon as may be. Would you know of any suitable person?"

Mrs. Philips frowned in thought and gave her full attention to the matter.

"I know that old Mr. Stamford has retired; he tutored my family you'll remember. There's Miss Watson, but she does not care to travel and indeed I believe she is fully engaged this term, even if your daughters went to Aldenham to be taught there. Allow me to make some enquiries in the town."

"Thank you. I shall be very obliged to you."

Kitty was called for and the maid, who assisted them into their capes and gloves. They left amid the usual flurry of last minute thoughts and sending of messages to those loved ones not present. Evening was falling fast on mother and daughter as they walked briskly homeward. Although it was still chilly, being early spring, the song of a thrush as they turned into the country lane leading to Longbourn, lifted their spirits.

Mrs. Bennet felt the crisp air on her cheeks and thinking of her sister's remedies said "I feel perhaps a new chapter beginning, Kitty dear. All may yet be well."

Kitty glanced at her mother is some surprise. This was the most optimistic that Mrs. Bennet had been in months.

"Yes, Kitty, do not look so amazed. I feel better than I did yesterday. A walk out and my sister's company have restored me a little."

"Perhaps it was just the remedy you needed, mama."

The improvement in Mrs. Bennet's humour was short-lived however, for on their arrival at Longbourn, Charles Collins was in the hall pursued by an earnest Mary who was calling after him in an agitated voice.

"Mr. Collins, Mr. Collins, I implore you to listen."

"Indeed Miss Bennet I can see no sense in continuing our conversation." He shouted these words over his shoulder at Mary as he made his way to the front door, just as Mrs. Bennet and Kitty were entering.

A collision occurred.

"Oh, my most profuse apologies. It seems there has been an extraordinary misunderstanding. I was only- ."

Mary broke in "Oh, mama, I am so glad you are returned, I have something to tell. It concerns Mr. Collins and myself-"

"Madam, I assure you, there has been nothing untoward. Indeed as a man of the church, it would be most—"

"Mama, I would urge you to speak privately—"

Mrs. Bennet and Kitty were both alarmed and intrigued. It was Mrs. Bennet who took charge of the awkward situation.

"Kitty, please accompany Mr. Collins to the drawing room and ask Hill to bring tea there. Mary and I will converse in the library. I will send for your father to join us."

Kitty was piqued; she had no wish to be alone with their visitor and wondered what subject they could possibly converse upon that would last more than two minutes. She liked him too little to care for his approbation and was resolved to offer no conversation as they left the hall. She led the way into the gloomy drawing room and sat stiffly at a small table while Mr. Collins, appearing more ill at ease than she had ever seen him, paced the floor. He pulled distractedly at his cuffs, ran his fingers through his hair and fidgeted with his waistcoat buttons as he spoke.

"Miss Bennet, events have somewhat precipitated my forthcoming announcement. I had hoped to pursue my path at a more leisurely pace, but this is now impossible since even as we speak…."

Before he could go further Kitty interrupted, "Mr. Collins I beg you to cease while we are alone. I believe my father may be joining us soon." She fervently hoped this would be the case.

Mr. Collins looked as anxious as he felt at the prospect of a second person witnessing his utterances. His eyes were drawn to the door. One of the room's occupants hoped Mr. Bennet would immediately enter, the other desired with all his being that he would not. Mr. Collins pulled a silk handkerchief from his pocket and wiped his brow. Then collecting himself, he put his hands together in an effort to become calm. This gesture only made him look as if he were about to pray for a departed soul.

"No, no, Miss Bennet, permit me to continue. I have been aware for some time, albeit a short period in actuality, that a wrong must be righted; but then love can hurl one headlong into a circumstance that places one beyond what would be normally expected and formal etiquette would order."

Kitty began to wonder if the words were making any sense to the speaker, let alone herself.

"My dear lady, what I am trying to say is, the parish needs a useful kind of girl."

Kitty looked blank.

"I mean that your personage would be most useful in my present living."

Kitty wondered if he was advertising for a kitchen maid.

"If more clarity is needed, I must endeavour to make plain my sincere and abiding feelings for you. Almost as soon as I entered the house I singled you out as the companion of my future life, a true soul mate." and here Mr. Collins began an awkward movement that suggested he was genuflecting before his church altar.

"You see before you a man ready to throw himself at your feet."

All Kitty could see was a man who appeared to have the cramp.

"At least, I would throw myself if my joints would allow. It seems I can go no lower."

Kitty thought he had gone low enough already in her estimation.

"My dearest Miss Bennet—may I be so bold as to call you by that sweetest of Christian names—Kiss Mitty? Oh dear, oh dear, of course I mean, Miss Bitty Kennet. Oh dear, was ever man so lost? It must be the spell your beauty casts, dearest Miss Bennet."

Kitty jumped up, determined to end this farce. Mr. Collins made as if to catch her hand to prevent her leaving, but only succeeded in clutching the air, then fell forwards on to the *chaise longue,* his face buried from sight. He raised his head.

"Miss Bennet!" he shouted at her departing figure "Miss Bennet—will you marry me?" The cushions were jostling with his floundering limbs for occupation of the seat. He struggled to turn himself to a sitting position. In so doing he found himself looking at a pair of tall, black boots. He glanced higher. He was staring into the stern face of Mr. Bennet.

"Well Mr. Collins, when you have collected yourself, what have you to say in answer to the charge of trifling with both my daughters' affections? Sir, I have but two at home and wonder if you would have played so fast and loose with all five if they had been present? You are not only here as a guest, but also as our cousin. Above that, you are an ordained man of the cloth and as such, in a position of trust. My family welcomed you with great civility into our home and it seems we have nurtured a snake in our bosom. You have apparently made overtures to one daughter proposing marriage while having come but a mere half-hour from an earnest intimacy with the other. I am astonished and dismayed, sir. I urge you to pack your bags and be gone."

The clerical gentleman rolled himself upright, scattering the cushions. He opened his mouth to reply. Seeing Mr. Bennet's furious features, he halted, straightened his clothes, brushed his hands rapidly down his black sleeves, flicking off some imagined dust from his cuffs and smoothed his hair. He considered, quite accurately, that a reply at this particular moment would be singularly unappreciated.

Mr. Collins to his credit raised his chin and giving a brief nod to his host and a bow to his hostess, walked up to his room in a dignified manner, coat tails flapping in the ascent. The effect was a little marred by a slight slip on the top step, causing him to grab wildly at the newel post. He missed his footing and found himself spinning around only to halt at last with the unfortunate result of facing down into the thunderous features of Mr. Bennet once more, while his daughters giggled behind their father, in the hall below.

A few minutes later, Mr. Collins emerged from above with a valise in one hand, his cape folded over his arm. He descended the staircase with as large a degree of composure as he could rouse.

Mr. Bennet had retired to his study and the girls to their rooms. Mrs. Bennet stood alone in the vestibule, looking up at him as he stood on the last step.

"Oh Mr. Collins, pray do not bear us any ill-will. This surely is a misunderstanding."

"Mrs. Bennet, I can assure you that my character is as unsullied as it was heretofore. Your husband has exhibited great confusion in his parental wrath, which as a member of the church I find beneath my notice or desire to respond to at this moment. In the near future I trust there will be a time of calm reflection on his part, when he will ponder upon what he has said. He will, I sincerely hope, have cause to regret his hasty words. I came to your home with the best of intentions. I leave with my prayers for my host's recovery from this fit of insanity."

He paused to close his eyes and draw a deep breath. Then, recollecting that he was still within arm's length of Mr. Bennet's study, moved swiftly along the hall, while glancing nervously over his shoulder. Mrs. Bennet hovered before him near the front door, so he was forced to bow to her. She made a gesture to stay him saying "I pray you sir, be not so hasty, there may yet be time to,-"

But he walked on past her in silence, head held high and opened the door. There was a chill in the air. He put his hand to his head, paused in confusion, then turned back. Behind him, Mrs. Bennet had been joined by Hill who held out his broad, black, clerical hat. He took it with ill grace and placed it firmly on his head. He crossed the threshold and sought to leave them all immediately. However, there was an awkward delay as no preparations had been made for his conveyance. He glanced around the empty drive aware that several pairs of eyes were gazing at his discomposure from the shadowed windows.

It was cold in the bitter wind that had suddenly arisen so he pulled on his cape and wondered if he should return to the house. The humiliation, not to mention the possibility of physical assault, made him hesitate. As he wavered, the front door slowly opened. Mary clad in her grey shawl emerged, looking nervous. She shyly ran to him and pushed a piece of paper into his hands. Holding her glasses on to her blushing face, she ducked around the side of the house to be lost in the shrubbery.

Wednesday 11th April

That child must surely have been born to be the vexation of my life! To think a second chance of a Bennet girl marrying a clergyman has been thrown away! Such pride and such stupidity! Worse, the fury of her temper was enraged against me, her mother, who has worked so hard to secure her marriage! Was ever a woman so abused?

Foolish, foolish Kitty. But I shall not give up, despite her stubborn refusal.

Mr. Bennet is no support. The whole matter appears to cause him the utmost amusement. If it were not for the kindness of my sister, I know not what I should do. Though her affection comes at a price - the home-brewed reviver looks most unappetising and tastes even worse. It is fortunate that I had some fortified wine in my bedroom store cupboard to follow the reviver.

Chapter III

In Mrs. Bennet's room Hill was administering the reviver, Mary was sniffing into her handkerchief and Kitty looked mutinous.

"I cannot believe that you rejected Mr. Collins, Kitty. My palpitations are so terrible, with my heart knocking against my ribs. I am sure I shall have a seizure. Such ingratitude. I don't know what will become of us if your father dies. Do you think your married sisters will keep you?"

"I'm Lydia's favourite sister, mama. She will look after me," Kitty boldly replied.

"Lydia squanders every penny she gets," said her mother tartly.

"Well, Jane and Lizzy are so rich they'll have money to spare," Kitty pouted.

"Jane might be affable to the visitor who comes for a month, but a permanent relative is altogether a different matter. As for Lizzy, she would do what she could but there would be severe limits placed by her husband," she said firmly. Mrs. Bennet retained an ambivalent attitude to Mr. Darcy; while admiring his income, she was mortally afraid of his intellect.

"I shall do as Jane, Lydia and Lizzy all did—marry for love or not at all."

Her mother's face registered astonishment at Kitty's defiance, but as a parent, there was to be no surrender. With a flushed face and raising all her will to assert her authority she shouted, "You will do as you are bid, child!"

At this, Kitty stamped her foot, furiously replying "I shall never, never, never marry Mr. Collins, mama. I would rather enter a convent!" With a sudden movement Kitty left the room, slamming the door behind her.

"Oh the ungrateful child to treat her mother so. My poor head. My poor nerves. Does nobody pity me?"

To vent her feelings she rounded on her other daughter.

"And what are you crying about Mary? I am sure I don't know. Did Mr. Collins do anything untoward? Tell me girl. Did he?"

It would seem that the clergyman was highly acceptable for one daughter but completely beyond wholesome society for the other.

Mary's distressed face rose wetly from her handkerchief.

"Mama, I need to go to my room". She could not meet her mother's eyes as she left. Mrs. Bennet fussed about with her own handkerchief, dabbing at her eyes and her forehead.

"Oh dear. Such palpitations. And the ache in my head. Fetch me some tea, Hill, please. No, some cold water from the pitcher on the table. I fear I am running a fever."

Mrs. Bennet laid herself down on the *chaise longue* and all was quiet in the house for a full half hour. But the lack of direct and voluble confrontation with her daughters did not mean she had gained a degree of tranquillity. Mrs. Bennet could find no interval of ease and forgetfulness. She felt wretched. Her pulse raced, her brow was damp, her skin felt over-heated and her mind was in turmoil. Would she ever be free of these torments?

Kitty had spent this time in her room and after banging her fist on the pillow, gradually calmed herself. She felt strongly about marrying Mr. Collins but knew from Lizzy's experience that if it came to a confrontation, she could appeal to her father and from this memory she drew some comfort. Perhaps all would be well.

Hearing no sound from Mrs. Bennet's apartment, Kitty surmised her mother's temper was now cooled and she ventured along the corridor, intending to apologise for her behaviour. On opening the door she saw her mother lying white faced on the sofa, looking most ill.

"Oh mama, I am so sorry. You appear quite spent."

"Kitty? Is that you? "

"May I fetch you anything?"

"Yes, Kitty. I fear I am not myself. My head burns so and throbs with pain. Could you give me a glass of water?"

"Yes, mama" said Kitty who despite her mother's scolding, held a real affection for her. She was sorry to see her so brought down. While Mrs. Bennet sipped the water, Kitty cooled her brow. The temperature was indeed no fabrication; her mother's forehead was like a furnace. Kitty tried not to show her alarm.

"Mama, I shall just fetch some lavender water and a fresh muslin neckerchief. This one is now so warm it must feel most unpleasant to wear."

She ran downstairs to her father's study and tapped respectfully before entering. He was reading and looked irritated at being disturbed.

"Papa. I am anxious about mama. She is most unwell. I am sure she is running a fever. Should we send for Mr. Jones?" she said rapidly.

"Kitty calm yourself. I am sure that Mr. Jones will not be necessary. I have just been looking over the accounts and we must be aware of our limited means. A call to the doctor would make a sizeable depletion in our resources. Your mother is suffering again from her nerves. It will be the upset with Mr. Collins that has done it."

"But papa, I am really concerned. Could you not come to her room to see for yourself?" Kitty asked.

"All in good time, my dear. All in good time." Mr. Bennet turned back to his book. This feminine ailment he reflected, was no worse than he had heard a thousand times before. It would die down like every other, of that he was certain.

On Kitty's way along the corridor she passed through the hall and heard a sobbing above. It emanated from her sister's room. Before seeking a fresh neckerchief she turned away from the linen cupboard and ran upstairs. Her timid knock on Mary's door brought no response. Neither did a second. She tiptoed in and saw Mary stooped over her dressing table holding a piece of paper. Kitty approached her sister and gently took her hand.

"Mary dear, why are you crying?"

A muffled sob was the reply.

"This is so unlike you, Mary. Is it something serious? Has someone upset you?"

Mary lifted her head and gazed mistily through her glasses.

"Oh Kitty, I have never been so happy and unhappy in my entire life." She broke into tears again.

Kitty stroked her sister's forehead.

"If it helps, tell me what has happened Mary."

"It is an affair of the heart that can never be resolved," cried Mary.

Intrigue now overshadowed Kitty's concern. She continued to hold her sister's hand, while Mary slowly raised her head, wiped her eyes and replaced her spectacles. In a trembling, quiet monotone she began to tell her story.

"It is Mr. Collins. You recall that this morning when you and mama went to Meryton I stayed at home?"

"To practice your piano pieces, wasn't it? "

"To some extent that was the case. But I had a secondary reason. I wished to consult with our visitor on a sermon I had read." Here Mary blushed.

"Well" she went on "even that is not the whole picture, if I am to be honest with you. I wanted to spend a little time with him alone."

Kitty was astonished at this admission in her reserved sister.

"But did you not consider how this would appear Mary? What if papa had found the two of you together?"

"I know, I know" cried Mary, looking very agitated, "but I felt it to be a matter of some compulsion. He had been so meaningful in his looks and hints towards a possible union with one of us, that I felt I must speak as I knew you had no objections."

(Indeed not, thought Kitty.)

"So I waited in the drawing room with the door ajar, to see him coming down the stairs. Just as I was beginning to believe he was not coming at all, he walked down into the hall. I called out to him and he entered at once. Oh such a handsome figure!"

(Not the first word I'd call to mind in describing Mr. Collins, thought Kitty.)

"He agreed to look at the sermon and we began discussing the content. While talking to him, I felt a degree of admiration for him. He had so much wisdom, such knowledge of theology. As the time passed, I began to realise there was mutual understanding in our religious views. He spoke with a calm authority tempered by patience. His sincerity towards me aroused feelings of gratitude for his kindness; so much so, I was emboldened to show my feelings, for I hoped that our sentiments coincided in every particular. Little knowing what I was doing, as his hand rested on the page, I touched it."

Kitty had her eyes wide open—such daring!

"I believe I can now understand how Lydia came to elope with Captain Wickham. How maidenly modesty is thrown to the winds when emotions are inflamed. I had to confess that my former admonition whereby 'females cannot be too much guarded in their behaviour towards the opposite sex' and in believing that 'one false step may bring endless ruin,' were completely brushed aside. If Mr. Collins had urged me to run away with him at that moment, I am sure I would have done so." Mary paused, her eyes bright and looking into the distance. To say that Kitty was surprised in this sudden and unprecedented alteration in her sister is to belie her degree of astonishment.

"But what happened next, Mary?"

"Alas, Mr. Collins seemed unaware and stood up, saying politely that he had to leave me as he was going to ask for *your* hand, Kitty, and had been on the way to papa's study to ask his permission, when I had called out to him."

"Oh Mary, dear Mary" said Kitty.

"I thought my heart would break. It falls to the female to suffer pain with dignity and so I said nothing more. It was clear that I was not at the forefront of his mind, but you. Do not believe that I was jealous, Kitty, for I know I have no beauty and you have such pretty looks. I could understand his preference. Nevertheless, our mutual interest in theology led me to hope that perhaps he might change his mind. Before I could make it clear how I felt, the house was disturbed by your return, so Mr. Collins fled and I was left alone with only Fordyce's sermons for comfort."

"I am so sorry Mary to have unwittingly been the means of such hurt," said Kitty.

"Then came the moment of hope in my despair when I learned you had rejected Mr. Collins' proposal, but my hopes dwindled again when papa ordered him out. Once Mr. Collins had left the house, I wrote him a brief note, now that you had turned down the proposal, and pushed it into his hand before the carriage came."

"And did you have a response?"

"This came today." She spread out a letter and gave it to her sister to read.

'Brompton Park, Rochester, Kent.
April 25th.

Miss Mary Bennet,

It is with some abhorrence that I find myself writing to you since leaving the portals of your family residence. I had resolved that all communication between our two families was at an end. It is only in the spirit of Christian charity that I am responding to your letter.

It would seem that my visitation to your home was troubled by misunderstandings. I travelled to your abode in humility and hope, feeling reasonably assured of a welcome due to both my person as a cousin and as a clergyman. But the treatment I received left me feeling an object of humiliation. However, on some consideration, my religious vocation has made me put aside personal feelings of hurt and rejection. One must be wary of judging too hastily. I feel it is incumbent on me to clarify the matter of my visit and proposal.

When first hearing of my brother William's hopes of marrying one of Mr. Bennet's daughters, I confess I felt a certain curiosity myself concerning you all. It would not be understating the fact that over the next three months I spent much time in prayer regarding my own single situation and any future nuptials. On learning that Miss Jane, Miss Elizabeth and Miss Lydia had each assumed the married state, I was eager to make the acquaintance of your family myself, as soon as could be arranged. Of course you will have acknowledged already that I had to overcome the social stigma attached to Miss Lydia's elopement. This will of course blight your family forever, but as she is now married and residing in the North of England it would appear an obstacle that need not stand in my way. To err is human, to forgive divine, as we are often told.

Thus my letter to your parents was conceived and eventually written. The visit to Longbourn swiftly followed and I was able to meet your family for myself. It was with an appraising eye that I regarded the two Bennet girls. I was immediately enchanted by your sister, Miss Kitty Bennet, and despite the diffidence (which I took to be maidenly modesty) that fell as a slight shadow across our relationship, I was convinced that she was secretly

*cherishing my every word. She
appeared to have all the qualities that
would be useful to a man in my
position. The value of a docile, dutiful
wife would be an asset to me in my
parish work.'*

(Kitty's face was a picture at this).

*'It was my Christian duty to make a
proposal to Miss Kitty while I was in
your home. It came therefore, as a
bitter blow to find she rejected my
suit. Then your father came upon us
with such suddenness that I had no
time to collect myself. He had made
the unfounded and wild assumption
that I had trifled with the affections of
both his daughters. This was entirely
beyond credulity, as I am a man both
of complete honour and as a
representative of the church. It
horrified me that such an allegation
might at some time find its way to the
ears of my parishioners. I have been
dutiful in my time here in Rochester
and been assiduous in my conduct.
Once a reputation is lost, it is lost
forever. Your father, for all his
admirable qualities, may be judged to
be over-zealous in protecting the
virtue of his daughters. He gave me
no opportunity to point out his error
and drove me from your home like*

*our Holy Master once drove the herd
of swine over the cliff in the parable.*

*Your note was one of sisterly comfort
(had I but had a sister) that came
unexpectedly and at a time when I
was resolved never to communicate
with any of your household ever
again. For this I thank you.*

*This letter however is one of final
correspondence with your family. I
have no wish to offer myself to
ridicule a second time. Thus have I
shaken the dust of Longbourn from
my feet for ever.*

Yours respectfully

Charles Collins (Reverend).'

"All is lost" ended Mary.

"No. No. There is hope. We can devise a plan to
win his affections and papa's approval, I am sure of
it".

Kitty spoke so convincingly that Mary's spirits
rallied a little.

"But first what was in the note you wrote to
Mister Collins?"

"Oh that I had never given it to him! I should
have held back at such a turbulent time for him. He
was so angry with us all. Had he seen my note at a
time of quiet, perhaps he would have felt more
kindly disposed to one who had caused him no
hurt." Mary cried afresh at the memory.

"Perhaps he looked again at it later."

"No, no. From the window I saw him crush it in his hand and throw it to the floor, before the carriage called. I retrieved it when he had departed."

"May I see it Mary? Perhaps your intentions were unclear."

"I fear not, Kitty. I should never have made my feelings so plain." She looked into her work-basket and found the paper, then handed it to her sister.

> *'Longbourn.*
>
> *April 10th.*
>
> *Dear Mr. Collins,*
>
> *It is with some degree of trepidation that I write to you and in such a hasty manner. I wish to communicate my personal sadness that a visitor to Longbourn has curtailed his stay so abruptly. It is to my family's regret that such an event has occurred. It is to be hoped that in time a cordial relationship will be resumed.*
>
> *I would urge you as a member of the church and as a cousin, to forgive any slights and look kindly once more upon my family.*
>
> *Yours sincerely,*
>
> *Miss Mary Bennet.'*

"Why Mary this can only be well received," said Kitty. "There is no reason to feel embarrassed. In fact you have made no declaration of your feelings, only an expression of family regret. If you are sincerely interested in securing him, then there is much to be done."

Mary felt some reassurance in Kitty's practical manner and under her sister's instructions, took up her pen to write.

'Longbourn.

April 28th.

Dear Mr. Collins,

In reply to your recent letter it would seem that there has been much to forgive on both sides. May the Bennet family begin by offering the olive branch and hope that our ties of kinship may resume on a more cordial note.

It is good to remember that, "a soft answer turneth away wrath".

I remain yours sincerely,

Miss Mary Bennet.'

To Mary's delight, a letter in Mr. Collins' flourishing hand arrived some weeks later addressed to her. She was desirous of not arousing any suspicions from her parents and told Mrs. Hill to bring any letters from Mr. Collins directly to herself. Should there be any enquiry, Mary would tell them that the letters contained theological matters, which she believed would ensure no further investigation. This was after all no more than the truth. Thus assuaging any doubts in her conscience, she hurried to her room to read the letter's contents.

'BromptonPark, Rochester, Kent.

May 10th.

Dear Miss Bennet,

Thank you for the recent letter in which you express such honourable feelings on behalf of your family. They do you credit. On reflection, I am disposed to agree with you and forgive all previous misunderstandings and hurtful conduct. I admit that as a cousin and a clergyman my pride was injured by the presumptuous, specious and completely erroneous allegations made against me whilst under the Bennet family roof; I had come only in the spirit of noble generosity with a plan of making amends and atonement, seeking to act by that grace which Newton's hymn so bountifully displays.

The days following my visit have been those of contemplation. Your letter of apology spurred me to forgiveness.

I should like to direct you and your family to The Beatitudes when seeking further guidance for human behaviour. They have always been of supreme importance. Fordyce has much useful commentary upon the subject.

I remain respectfully,

Charles Collins.'

And so the correspondence between Miss Mary Bennet and the Reverend Charles Collins began.

*

May 12th

Kitty is still determined to refuse Mr. Collins. She must be the greatest simpleton on earth. Impudent madam! As for Mary, she seems as though she is hiding some secret, she says so little. If it weren't such a foolish notion, one might almost believe she's in love.

How I miss all my married daughters; Jane's quiet ways were so calming, while Lydia's antics kept me in fits of laughter. True, Lizzy was one to provoke and argue, but she would have quelled Kitty's obstinate nature. When I mentioned this to Mr. Bennet, he merely smiled and said—I am sure that Lizzy would take Kitty's part. She would tell Kitty "Your mother will not see you again if you don't marry Mr. Collins and I will never see you again if you do."

Insufferable!

Chapter IV

Mrs. Bennet had spent another restless night. She had come to the end of her limited resources in moderating the sweats, flushes, lassitude and general debility. Her dressing table bore witness to the number of remedies she had tried; a jug of water was leaning precariously upon a pile of medical books, while small bottles of lemon, rose and lavender water rubbed elbows with dampened napkins, china bowls, her sister's restorative vials and a variety of cups and glasses.

She gazed in the dawn light at her surroundings and sobbed. Her turbulent mind tossed from self-pity to anger. How could she present a confident presence in society by day, when her nights gave her no rest? Surely things would get better soon? It was clear that all these remedies had effected little improvement so far. In looking ahead, she felt a dull dread at the prospect of warm summer nights, where her symptoms would grow more wearisome. She felt too weak to take action and longed for some end to her distress. Mr. Bennet was unsympathetic and the girls, though well intentioned, were of little practical comfort. She slept fitfully for some time then awoke to the sound of somebody knocking at her front door.

Mrs. Bennet poked her night-capped head out of the window. It was her sister, Mrs. Philips. Within a few minutes, the women were together. Mrs. Philips' customary amiability was rather lessened when she beheld her hostess.

"My dear sister!" exclaimed Mrs. Philips. "You look most unwell."

"Alas, my troubles are still with me. I am cruelly used. All remedies have been tried. Even your reviver. Am I to suffer forever?" She spoke with much bitterness of spirit and some exaggeration. There was melancholy in her voice as she lamented, "Those who do not complain are never pitied."

Mrs. Philips was inwardly alarmed at her sister's condition. The pale cheeks, sweating forehead and general listlessness were evidence that, in her opinion, a medical professional should be consulted. She broached the subject.

"No, no, sister. Mr. Bennet will not hear of it."

"Mr. Bennet need not know of it. I shall go myself to Mr. Jones, appraise him of your condition and then arrange a visit when Mr. Bennet is busy elsewhere."

"Setting that aside, I fear that a doctor will dismiss my maladies as nothing more than nerves. This is the term that Mr. Bennet uses. And there is the very awkward situation too of speaking about my symptoms to a man. I have not revealed the extent of my true suffering to Mr. Bennet, nor its causes. I cannot begin to imagine telling our family doctor, Mr. Jones. It would be mortifying and humiliating in the extreme."

"But my dear, something must and shall be done. I cannot sit by and see you suffer so. My intention is only to seek intelligence of a person who may well have remedies other than ours at his disposal. It can do no harm, surely."

Despite further protests, rendered by a mild flutter of Mrs. Bennet's pale hand, Mrs. Philips prevailed. In a small notebook she set down every symptom and every remedy that her sister had tried. Mrs. Bennet's constant repinings at the dullness of her lot as she related her maladies, cast a gloom on the domestic scene.

As she was finishing, Mary entered. She kissed her aunt who said, "Ah Mary dear, I see your mother is most unwell. She has suffered too long with these debilitating disorders. I am taking action. My purpose is to consult the doctor. But this must be kept from Mr. Bennet's knowledge, since he will not sanction such a course of action. I trust you and Kitty approve of this plan?"

Mary's face grew stern. She peered at her mother and drew closer. Her voice took on a sanctimonious tone.

"Mama, one must bear one's misfortunes with womanly fortitude. It is the mark of patience to be admired in the weaker sex when our inferior bodies are so often prey to ill health. The opportunity to exhibit such stoicism is one to welcome, rather than to rail against. Such suffering here on earth will surely gain an honoured place in heaven."

This admonition caused Mrs. Bennet to pause in her handkerchief fluttering and regard her middle daughter with something like disbelief, followed immediately by parental affront. Rallying her not inconsiderable forces, she once more dabbed her temples, sat herself up a little higher in her bed and said "Nonsense child, how can you speak so? Is there no charity in you? I am in a most pitiable state. How can you see your mother suffering every day and not wish to help?"

"But mama, if my father should hear of this, it will bring more trouble upon the family. He is, after all, the head of the house and as such, his will is paramount. It is wrong to seek to deceive. Your sufferings will pass away eventually mama, and the fees saved will provide our ledgers with a balance long overdue. Indeed Papa will cherish you all the more for your parsimony." Mary believed her mother had little turn for economy and it was the caution exhibited by Mr. Bennet that generally prevented the family exceeding their income.

Her pedantic air grated with her mother. Mrs. Bennet's formerly pale face now reddened with anger, but before she could give vent to her feelings, Mrs. Philips intervened. With a look towards her sister, which betokened some secret intelligence, she smiled and sat upright.

"My dear Mary, that view is not the one I had hoped for, but your feelings are noted. Well, well, here is dear Kitty, just as I am about to share some good news with you all. Have you heard that there is to be an assembly next month?"

Kitty clapped her hands in delight. " That is such an agreeable prospect, aunt. I am filled with excitement." She looked at her sister and was saddened to observe no similarity of spirit.

"Those evenings hold small pleasure for me," said Mary, "since I have no great interest in dancing."

"How little you know as yet," said her aunt," for it is an occasion which is not confined to dancing.

There will be opportunities for young people to exhibit their pianoforte and singing skills during the evening."

On seeing Kitty's disappointment and receiving this new information, Mary reconsidered. "Well, while I can have my mornings to myself, it is enough. I think it no sacrifice to join occasionally in evening engagements. I acknowledge society has claims on us all; intervals of recreation and amusement are desirable for everybody, if not repeated too frequently."

Kitty smiled while her mother rolled her eyes. Aunt Philips continued, "I also am given to believe there will be two families present who are new to the neighbourhood. One is deemed to have a serious, scholarly background and the other to have connections with the navy."

Mary allowed herself to be interested, while Kitty was eager with anticipation to learn more. Mrs. Bennet ceased to frown at Mary and immediately made a mental plan to look afresh at her wardrobe. She smiled saying " This will be an occasion to wear our best attire." Kitty was pleased to see her mother in better spirits. Her ill humour and ill health seemed lifted. She gave her mother a kiss.

"Oh aunt, that is good tidings. Will there be officers at the assembly?"

"No, Kitty. There is a military exercise that week and the regiment are all away, but the assembly will be none the less entertaining for the officers' absence."

This topic of conversation led to some lively contributions from Kitty and Mrs. Philips, which distracted Mrs. Bennet sufficiently to rouse her from her bed and tell Mary to bring out the best of her evening gowns from her closet. Mary went silently from the room returning first with her mother's gowns, then with her own and her sister's.

"These will need to be altered again," said Mrs. Bennet "so as to ring the changes."

"Perhaps a flounce on your green gown, Mary, for you have grown somewhat taller since the last assembly."

"We shall then need to ask Miss Boulding to call," said Mrs. Bennet.

Aunt Philips looked closely at the white muslin dress that Kitty was holding. "Some white embroidery at neck and hem would look very fetching and I believe this could be done without calling on the services of a seamstress. We may economise there. Kitty is quite able to undertake such a task with my help. And your flounce, Mary, could be simply done. We can embroider the gathers with some pretty silks in a chain stitch."

"I believe there are several colours in my work-basket," said Mary.

"What do you think of this peach gown, sister? Is it not most becoming? I vow I never saw anything made so pretty this season," said Mrs. Bennet.

"It is a little dated but I think the use of some netting as an over-layer would disguise its age."

"Why, yes" nodded Mrs. Bennet, "I have a netting bow with all the materials. We could place the netting over the sleeves and trim the bodice with knotting."

Aunt Philips glanced at her sister's face and was quietly pleased to see this change in her spirits.

Kitty added excitedly "Mama, what if we added some knotting to the shawls? Fringing looks so elegant."

"There is so much to do," said Mrs. Bennet anxiously."Shall we have time?''

Her sister gave them all a look of reassurance. "I'm sure it will all be achieved, my dears. I shall call at the draper's today to look at the silks, calicos and muslins when I visit Mr. Jones in Meryton and we shall commence tomorrow."

"May I come with you?" asked Kitty.

"Certainly, my dear."

"And I shall stay here with mama," said Mary. "She can rest while I sort through the garments and put them in order. Not that I care too much for frills and furbelows, for we should always bear in mind to pay little heed to our raiment, but cultivate the inner man." (No need to heed that, since we are all females, thought Kitty). "However, it is important on occasions of social interaction that the family does not appear to disadvantage," Mary ended.

Mrs. Bennet forebore to comment and placed her gowns carefully back in the closet.

*

It was on their walk to Meryton that Mrs. Philips questioned her niece about Mrs. Bennet.

"Poor mama! She is a creature much to be pitied, but she is very difficult to live with, being so unpredictable. She is fierce and spiteful so often that Mary and I are afraid to go near her." Kitty's slight flush as she uttered these symptoms showed her self-doubt as to sharing such private information with another, albeit her mother's sister and long-time friend. She wished she had more of Jane's generosity in speaking of others' flaws.

Mrs. Philips was eager to learn more. Her natural disposition for news and gossip was not always a matter for inquisitive or presumptuous enquiry, since she was truly concerned for her sister. It would mean some close questioning to ascertain the degree of Mrs. Bennet's sickness and its effect on her family. She pressed on with her questions.

"I have observed her lassitude and pale looks for myself but to hear she is also ill-tempered is another matter. Is this a temporary malady, Kitty?"

Kitty struggled between truth and loyalty. She bit her lip then reluctantly decided that the facts would speak for themselves.

"Mama's health is uncertain, Aunt Philips. On occasion she is able to rally her spirits and become something of her normal self, as you saw today when we discussed the assembly and our gowns. But within the family, the moments of ill-temper have become more frequent of late. These invectives are directed at whosoever is nearest. The slightest provocation sets her off. A few days ago it was over the matter of her compliance in Mr. Charles Collins' proposal and her fury at my refusal. She vented her anger so cruelly on me that I am afraid I was less than polite. On such occasions mama turns into a creature I do not recognise."

"But her anger was probably because she feels her business in life is to see all her daughters married, Kitty. Surely that is very understandable?"

Kitty felt a little nettled, judging that the conversation was taking a turn where she, rather than her mother, could now become the focus of her aunt's interest. She continued, "Yes of course, aunt. But it was the manner of her anger. Her rage was extremely violent, being so loud in her speech and her face so changed I scarcely recognised her."

"But if this is the only incident…" said Mrs. Philips, with a view to gaining a balanced view.

"Oh no, aunt. These tantrums are not uncommon. My mother shouts at the servants too. I would say this is every day over some little matter or other. Nobody dares to disagree with her comments or instructions. And when discussing other people she veers between violent dislike and violent approval. Though once Lady Lucas was her best friend, she now abjures her company since Charlotte married Mr. Collins, and that was so long ago as you know. Mama's resentment at the match is as strong as ever. Yet she can change in a moment and talk with great passion about someone new in Meryton whom she's scarcely seen, extolling their virtues to the skies. Her effusions and exaggerations leave the family breathless!"

"She has always been a woman of strong emotions, Kitty. Though I can begin to see that these changes of mood are unsettling."

Kitty was not to be deterred from giving her aunt a full picture. She continued, "And when she feels crossed, if she is not condemning or praising somebody, she bursts into storms of weeping. She seems inconsolable. No amount of comforting from Mary, myself or even dear old Mrs. Hill can lift her spirits."

"This is sad, Kitty," said Mrs. Philips and would perhaps have stayed her niece from going on since she observed how agitated Kitty was becoming. However this proved impossible as Kitty was determined to pour out her concerns. Besides, Mrs. Philips wished most keenly to learn as much about her sister's condition as she could.

"Just one more matter, aunt, I have to share with you. It is such a relief to speak. Another feature of her condition is her indecision; she makes one statement then swiftly contradicts herself and if we point this out she tells us *we* are provoking *her*. The servants are so often in confusion that Mary and I have to privately give them the housekeeping directions." Kitty ceased talking. She felt quite spent.

Mrs. Philips pursued another line of enquiry and perhaps with more perseverance than politeness asked, "And does Mr. Bennet never intervene?"

"Papa prefers the leisure and tranquillity of his library" she replied quietly, not wishing to have her aunt condemn her father. She kept to herself his recent words on the subject of her mother's illness. "Well, well, Kitty. I will sit in my library, in my nightcap and powdering gown and give as much trouble as I can."

"Oh, I am sorry to hear that, Kitty." So much for Mr. Bennet and any help from him! Aunt Philips paused and looked at her niece. This was a young woman who herself seemed to be undergoing a change; she was emerging from the former weak-spirited, selfish girl who had been completely under Lydia's guidance only last year, to a person who was opening her eyes to others' misfortunes.

"Thank you for your candour, Kitty. It seems your mother cannot help herself. I shall do what I can to aid her, poor woman."

"Any help would be welcome, aunt. But look, here are the shops coming into view."

With these words the conversation was terminated, but their separate thoughts were not.

*

That evening at dinner, Mr. Bennet announced, "I shall be travelling to London tomorrow. My intention is to visit your brother Gardiner and his family. I shall be gone about a week."

"May we know the purpose of your journey, Mr. Bennet?" asked his wife.

"Well my dear, there are several pressing reasons, most of which appertain to business. You need trouble yourself no further in studying my itinerary. There will be time enough for that on my return. While I am away I urge you to be careful with the house keeping. As for the girls"—looking with some meaning at Kitty and then Mary—"support your mother and do as you are bid."

"Yes, papa," they said together.

Mrs. Bennet did not think any further as to the reason for his going, only that she would be free to see the doctor and make several purchases at the draper's store.

The minute Mr. Bennet's conveyance turned the corner of the lane and was out of sight Mrs. Bennet went to the library to write a list of the needlework items from Meryton she would require. She longed to go herself but felt this would be a wearisome expedition, so she called her daughters.

"Kitty, you must walk with Mary to Meryton to make our necessary purchases. You may tell Mr. Brown to put it on Mr. Bennet's account. It will be settled by the end of the month."

*

A few days later, Mr. Jones' brougham drew up at the Longbourn home. It contained not only the cheerful, elderly doctor, but also his middle-aged wife and Aunt Philips. They were all ushered into the vestibule by Hill, who asked them to wait while she went to her mistress in her bedroom.

"Sorry to disturb you. ma'am, but there are three visitors to see you."

Mrs. Bennet looked up wearily, "Who are they, Hill?"

"Mr. Jones, Mrs. Jones and Mrs. Philips, ma'am."

"Oh dear me, no. I cannot come down. You must send them away. I am in no state to receive visitors."

Hill curtsied and left the room.

Mrs. Bennet felt a cold wave of dread run over her. The colour left her face. To think she must speak to a man about her condition and moreover to one who only had visited when the children or servants were ill, sent her heart quickening with fear. Almost a complete stranger! No, it was impossible for her. He would not understand. There would be no sympathy. Her symptoms, if she could explain at all without breaking down into tears, would sound so foolish. And the ultimate humiliation would be to hear the doctor dismiss all her suffering as 'nerves'. Why, he might even think her insane. At this thought she caught her breath. She was stricken with fear. Such diagnoses of ladies with their flushes, indecision, sleeplessness and sudden changes of temper were not unknown. As a girl, she had heard whispered tales of a distant great aunt who had suffered fits of 'insanity' so often that she had been taken to a place of retreat, far from her family and never came home. Had this poor woman been really been mad? Or had she exhibited the symptoms of the mature woman whose body, no longer able to bear children, turned treacherous and bewildering? Was she driven to a seeming madness to those who surrounded her? Was she in desperation and despair at being unable to share her problems? Was she merely misunderstood? And if she resisted the people who came to take her away, as she probably did, would this make her family, even more convinced of her insanity? How terrible if this should happen to herself.

What if Mr. Jones aided by his wife and her own sister had come to take her to an undisclosed location? Away from her family and all whom she knew and loved?

Her anxiety made her heart race and she felt her forehead perspire. Perhaps a small glass of wine would calm her. She unlocked the cupboard and swiftly drank two glasses. Then, lest her breath should smell, she chewed on a handful of candied fennel seeds wiped her mouth with a handkerchief and hid bottle, glasses and seed box in the cupboard.

A soft tap at the door made Mrs. Bennet start. She clenched her hands in fear. The door opened to admit her sister, alone. Her kindly face made Mrs. Bennet relax for a moment. Then she again grew tense. What if this were a ploy to gain her confidence?

"My dearest sister," Aunt Philips began and sat down on the end of the *chaise longue*. "Do not look so fearful. I have brought Mr. Jones here to see you. I have talked to him a little, saying that you are unwell and that I am concerned. He arranged a time to call by on an unofficial basis, since he and Mrs. Jones have business in the next village. But if you do not wish to see him, there is no need today. I share your apprehension that doctors may dismiss such symptoms as yours, but you may wish to see his wife."

"And why should I do that?" asked Mrs. Bennet guardedly.

"Mrs. Jones is a woman of some wisdom. She was an assistant to her father, who ran an apothecary's shop, before she married. In helping him, she developed a substantial knowledge of herbs and other natural remedies. She may well be able to help you."

Aunt Philips took her hand and smiled encouragingly. Mrs. Bennet dropped her head and whispered, "But what if they think me mad?"

"Is that what is worrying you, my dear?"

Mrs. Bennet could not raise her eyes lest she should see confirmation in her face. There was a short silence. Then Mrs. Philips said very gently, "Sister, look at me."

Mrs. Bennet slowly looked up. There was no confirmation of madness. Instead, she saw amusement. Her sister laughed out loud.

"You mad? Have no fear. You are as sane as any person I know. And should anyone think otherwise I shall knock them down with my parasol!"

Mrs. Bennet found tears coursing down her cheeks. They were no longer tears of self-pity, but shared laughter.

"Now, would you like me to ask them to come up? I shall allow no one to intimidate you, I promise."

"No, I shall come down. Please help me tidy my hair and I shall wash my face."

Aunt Philips rang the bell for Hill and asked her to tell the doctor and his wife to wait in the drawing room until Mrs. Bennet came down to join them.

A few minutes later, and arm in arm, the sisters came downstairs. They entered the room to find Mr Jones with his wife seated on a sofa. They smiled at Mrs. Bennet then stood up to bow and curtsey. Mary and Kitty were nearby, nodding encouragingly to their mother.

"Now, Mrs. Bennet, please sit here. This is an informal visit so please allow yourself to tell us calmly of your symptoms."

"Has my sister apprised you of what I am suffering?"

"She has, Mrs. Bennet. She observed that you are incapable of exertion and require constant attention. She added that you are undergoing other unpleasant maladies at this time. These symptoms render you nervous and indecisive."

"Yes sir." She was glad her sister had not divulged more personal details.

"Your symptoms, as related by your sister, are indicative of a climacteric. Recent medical theory suggests our bodies undergo a change every seven years. These changes can be a dangerous time for women of your age. There has been some study by physicians in France who believe one of theses change is linked to the cessation of the menses. This is still uncharted territory and may or may not have a bearing on women who suffer from nervous disorders. They also hold that the symptoms once gone leave the sufferer with a renewed sense of vigour. Let us hope this theory turns out to hold some truth. But I have to be honest and say that I'm afraid I have little comfort to give you in the present, since there are no cures. The best I can offer is that it is a complaint that will gradually fade over time. What you are undergoing is a natural occurrence and must be accepted."

Mrs. Bennet felt only despair at these words. She visibly drooped, then raised her head and asked fearfully "How long might I be likely to endure these weakening strictures, Mr. Jones?"

"Oh, that is uncertain, Mrs. Bennet. The symptoms may be with you for years. Indeed, I have a patient who still suffers from the heats and she is in her seventies," he said.

Mrs. Bennet felt immensely despondent. Was there nothing to be done? As she was gathering her courage to ask, Mrs. Jones spoke.

"Now do not believe all is lost, Mrs. Bennet. Although I am unable to practise myself I have taken a keen interest in the condition for many years. There are many women who endure unhappy symptoms at this time in their lives. Since working as an apothecary's assistant with my father and helping my husband, there are many tried and trusted remedies that may bring relief."

"How kind you are, dear Mrs. Jones. It gladdens my heart to hear this," said Mrs. Bennet.

"You see, I suffered myself for several years and the medical world was unable to advise me. But Mr. Jones was so full of compassion at my state of health that he left no stone unturned in searching out a remedy." Mrs. Jones looked fondly at her husband. By her calm manner alone, the apothecary's wife was sufficient in restoring the patient's nerves a little, but when she brought out a small volume from her bag, Mrs. Bennet's spirits rose. It contained remedies for ladies' maladies and from it Mrs. Jones read aloud suggestions for managing symptoms and recipes for draughts.

"There should be no need for alarming drastic action Mrs. Bennet, in change of habit or consumption of remedies. Everything here is in moderation. It is by these means the symptoms may be alleviated, come under control and eventually subside."

"Oh, Mrs. Jones, if only my sufferings were made a little less irksome, I would be indebted to you for life," said the patient.

"I cannot offer you a guaranteed cure, Mrs. Bennet, but my experience tells me that these suggestions should relieve your symptoms and render them more bearable."

"Oh thank you, thank you," she replied.

Mrs. Jones held up her hand. "No thanks yet. All patients differ. What may work for one may not suit another. But we can try a range of them and see what relief may be useful for your particular condition."

Mrs. Bennet smiled and then was cut short by another hot flush that rapidly reddened her face and neck. Her flesh felt as if it were burning up. Perspiration broke out on her forehead. Mrs. Jones sympathetically reached for a cotton napkin, dipped it in a basin of water and offered it.

"How often are these occurring?"

"About five or six times an hour. They last about two minutes and when the flush has passed, I feel as drained as this wrung out napkin."

"We must begin at once, Mrs. Bennet. My husband will be leaving to visit another patient in the neighbourhood and while he is gone we shall advance our understanding of what is happening and how we may best deal with it."

Mr. Jones took up his hat and bag, gave Mrs. Bennet an encouraging smile and withdrew.

"Firstly, Mrs. Bennet, we shall discuss clothing, sleeping patterns, then what you eat and drink, move on to daytime management and discuss what medicines are at our disposal. You will need to be assiduous in keeping records and reports, so that when I make my regular visits, we are able to see what progress has been made. Here your daughters will be of much help; for I surmise that 'The Change' affects both the ability to think logically and the female memory. Have you found this to be so?"

Mrs. Bennet did not readily admit to making mistakes and kept quiet. Kitty cut through the silence.

"Oh yes, Mrs. Jones, there have been several errors in the housekeeping."

"That is a little disloyal, Kitty!" said her mother sharply.

"But only on Tuesday you ordered a leg of mutton and when I looked in the pantry, you already had *two* there!" said Kitty.

"Yes, mama," Mary added. "You sometimes put things in wrong places. This morning I found a pair of your shoes in my glove drawer."

"Nonsense! I'm sure that wasn't my doing. It could well have been Hill. She is getting forgetful, you know," said her mother.

"No mama, I had just been to the drawer. I left the bedroom to go to the top of the servants' stairs and turned to see you go into my room carrying the shoes. You came out a few minutes later without them."

"What a thing it is to be accused by one's own children!" said Mrs. Bennet angrily, "You sound as if I am going mad!"

"My dear Mrs. Bennet," said Mrs. Jones, "do not distress yourself. These are all common signs of the menopause. Most mental problems are due to interrupted sleep. They do not indicate a personal fault, nor in any way cast a slur on your sanity. It is always amazing to me that women at this phase in their lives are able to function at all. Here I see a well-ordered household and a contented family. This is a testament to your fortitude, Mrs. Bennet. Your daughters, by describing your behaviour, are giving me much useful information."

Somewhat mollified, Mrs. Bennet cast an admonishing glance at her daughters, then subsided. She observed the proceedings in hopeful silence. Mrs. Jones looked at her medical journal, fingered through the yellowed pages and after making notes, said, "I think we shall initially try you out with some drops of valerian with hops to help you sleep. I shall ask the apothecary in Meryton for some pills containing iron for your anaemia, camomile for calming your nerves, sage and red clover for the hot flushes. These are to be taken after breakfast and again after dinner. Just four small tablets."

"For how long?"

"For the first three months."

Mary was wondering what these tablets would cost. Kitty wondered if her mother would be able to remember to take them.

"Is there anything else I should do?"

"We must pay attention to your clothing and general habits," Mrs. Jones went on.

"Wear only garments of cotton. Change them frequently. Keep cool at all times. Do not sit too near the fires and kitchen stoves. Avoid hot drinks, hot food and alcohol." Mrs. Bennet thought she would find it hard to forgo her daily glasses of orange wine at meals, her sherry in the early evening and the hot toddies she enjoyed on cold winter days, not to mention the fortified wine store in her room.

"Drink plenty of water and do not neglect to take a glass with you to sip at night. Finally, wash in tepid water Mrs. Bennet. Oh, and remember to keep a strict record of all foods, drinks and medication. You may find a little cooled lavender water eases the flushes if rubbed on the temples. You may also take up new interests and keep yourself busy. Such distractions will avoid the temptation to brood."

"That is a lot to digest, Mrs. Jones, but it is all useful advice. I shall endeavour to do as you prescribe," said Mrs. Bennet.

"I must leave you now. Ensure Kitty or Mary write down all my instructions then keep these by you for reference. Should you require further assistance, send for me. A bill for the treatments will be sent to you in due course."

Mrs. Jones collected her gloves and hat, replacing the little book in her capacious leather bag.

"I shall call again on the first of next month, Mrs. Bennet. Meanwhile I shall instruct our manservant to order the ingredients from the apothecary. They should be ready by next week. If Mr. Bennet could be prevailed upon to take you to Brighton or one of the summer sea-bathing places, you might find that a change of scene could ease your condition considerably."

This latter idea appealed to the patient as she recalled her daughter Lydia's stories of Brighton, but realised it would mean taking Mr. Bennet into her confidence.

"I cannot see that Mr. Bennet would approve such a journey. I shall have to be content with the treatments you recommend, Mrs. Jones."

"Well, perhaps the visit will come later in the year when we see the effects of these first remedies. One step at a time, Mrs. Bennet, yes?'

With this last utterance and a kindly glance, she left the family to discuss her visit and all that it implied.

May 25th

I cannot count the number of neckerchiefs I have used today. The linen basket was full to overflowing.

I would venture that many women of my standing would be surprised to learn that I assisted my housekeeper this morning. Hill and I stood together in the scullery up to the elbows in soapsuds, washing the personal clothing. Indeed in a moment of confidence we remarked on the increase on washing since the five girls entered womanhood and I started The Change. To while away our time, we sang favourite songs from our youth. We marvelled at our memories, never once lost for the words. I thoroughly enjoyed myself. It will be kept a secret from general society, but I shall happily repeat the experiment.

The impending assembly has lifted all our spirits. Well, all the females, that is. Excitement has been tempered with diligence in preparation. It was good to share this time with the girls. Felt close to Kitty and Mary as we discussed our dresses. This did not last long. Each rounded on me in front of their aunt and Mrs. Jones, concerning my apparent odd behaviour of late. I must confess to great fears the doctor's wife will declare me insane. The advice she gave me seems useful in general, but giving up wine and other alcoholic beverages is not so welcome. As it is, I do not think I over indulge. It calms my anxiety and gives me confidence. No, Mrs. Jones, your other remedies may work but I shall not so easily be persuaded of the virtues of abstinence. It shall be my little secret.

Chapter V

Mr. Bennet returned from London in good spirits. It was with no little pleasure that he enjoyed the company of his brother-in-law, Mr. Gardiner. Respite from feminine company and feminine maladies, was always welcome. It also renewed his daughters' affection after such an absence.

"Papa, papa!" they called as they ran to the carriage and they hardly allowed him to divest himself of his great coat before plying him with questions.

"How are our uncle and aunt?" said Kitty.

"Are all the children well? " asked Mary. "We hear that London air is not as wholesome as here."

"How are the fashions, Papa? Are all the ladies wearing turbans? Are there double frills of lace on their gowns? Did you attend any concerts?" Kitty asked breathlessly.

"Now, now, girls. First let me attend to your mother. How is she?"

"She keeps to her room, Papa. Her nerves are unimproved, but we are hopeful that—"

Mary's speech was cut short by a sudden kick on her ankle. Kitty broke in,

"Papa, we have all missed you. Would you like us to fetch you some tea or wine to refresh you after your journey?"

"Indeed Kitty that would be most welcome. Please bring a glass of claret to me in my study. Also let your mother know of my return and ask her to prepare for visitors tomorrow morning. I shall see her shortly."

This was news indeed. Kitty ran upstairs to their mother while Mary went to seek the wine.

"What nonsense!" exclaimed Mrs. Bennet at the news of early visitors. "What can your father be thinking? There's so little in the house. And who can these people be? I'm sure I've no wish to see anyone new and we have so much to do before the assembly, I can afford no time to make conversation with strangers. Kitty, ask your father to come up to my room immediately."

Mrs. Bennet felt quite exhausted by the news of more faces, probably unknown to her. She had all her windows open and the early spring sunshine fell across the room. The sound of birdsong came flooding through, though the occupant paid little heed. She rang the bell for Hill and wrung out a napkin to spread across her heated face, then lay down.

Hill entered and screamed, " Lord, help us! A ghost!"

"Nonsense, woman" said Mrs. Bennet, pulling the cloth from her face.

"Oh ma'am, I was so affrighted. Beg pardon."

"That will do, Hill. I need your assistance in changing my pelisse. Fetch me the blue muslin." Her voice was sharp. She felt warm, wet and weary. After a change of clothes she might feel a little restored. Hill helped her mistress with the dress, smoothed her hair and plumped up the cushions behind her as she lay on the *chaise longue*. A few moments of quiet after Hill had left, gave Mrs. Bennet some degree of calm. She was beginning to believe she could gain some measure of control over herself when there was a brisk rap on the door. Mr. Bennet entered and bid his wife a curt salutation. In his hand he held a bill.

He asked, "Can you explain this, Mrs. Bennet?"

His wife raised her head and saw with some dismay that they were the bills from the doctor, his wife and the apothecary.

"What is the meaning of this? I instructed you expressly to spend our little income prudently during my absence and here are requests for no small amounts appertaining to wine, medical fees, tablets and other tinctures that are beyond my comprehension."

Mrs. Bennet's demeanour changed from one of suffering debilitation to that of mutiny. She was in an agony of ill humour. His lack of courtesy in not coming immediately to see her on his return stirred up in her a temporary resentment that made her sit up and face him sternly. Her reply sounded more violent than she intended, but the words were supported by the anger she felt at a husband who had afforded her no sympathy through the long months of suffering she had undergone.

"Yes! I have taken matters into my own hands, Mr. Bennet. I have been in a state of distress for many months and my mild requests for seeking medical assistance have fallen on deaf ears. This bill is for some treatment to alleviate my suffering."

"Suffering? Suffering? You need but to gain control over your nerves and you would soon recover. Much of your so-called suffering is imagined. If you would stir yourself to think of others or get involved in some useful activity, you would find these symptoms disappearing overnight. You suffer from nothing other than the sin of self-pity."

"Oh Mr. Bennet! How can you be so cruel? I am sure I do not deserve such censure. Have I not brought up five daughters and seen three married? Such nurture and success did not come by accident. All was down to my care and worry."

"Your three eldest must bless themselves that they are no longer forced daily to dance attendance on a falsely ailing mother. Jane and Elizabeth are tolerably sensible I grant, but as for Lydia, it was principally your over-indulgence that encouraged the reprehensible behaviour, which brought such shame on our family. As for Kitty and Mary, they show as little sense as Lydia. This is unsurprising, since in having the feeble figure of their mother daily before them who succumbs to imaginary ailments at every opportunity, they have a lamentable example of womanhood as their guide."

Mrs. Bennet was momentarily stunned. She started, coloured, doubted herself and was silent. Then her mind quickly turned the subject matter from herself, to a consideration of her husband's role as parent, for the first time in their marriage. With raised voice she said "And what do you think you as a father have offered them, Mr. Bennet? You have left the care and discipline of them entirely to me. I thought you had resolved to take more interest in their affairs after Lydia's elopement. Fortunately, she now is married, though with no thanks to yourself."

She continued, "Have you no conscience, sir? Your attitude to fatherhood is to lock yourself away in your study among your books, giving no consideration to your children's fortunes."

"Ah, my dear, that is where you are wrong. Tomorrow I am interviewing several applicants as possible tutors to the girls."

Mrs. Bennet's surprised silence was noted by her husband with some satisfaction. He continued, "They are in need of further education if they are to acquire more status in the marriage market. They must have regular tuition."

Here Mrs. Bennet gasped. Her admiration for his paternal foresight was tempered by anger at the high-handed way of dealing with a matter of such importance in terms of the girls' education, without consulting her. Her thoughts completely negated his good deed and dwelt instead on her personal grievance.

"Well sir, you quite astonish me! As their mother I would have thought I should be the first to be consulted. This is an impertinence not to be borne!"

"Mrs. Bennet, I should have thought you would be the first to congratulate me on such an enterprise. I have learned something from the foolishness of our youngest. Lydia always was ignorant, idle and vain. I have little doubt, given her present circumstances and natural disposition, she will remain so. Her inadequacies have not been improved by the faulty degree of indulgence her mother has exhibited. It is with this in mind that I entered alone on the notion of tutoring our two younger daughters. They are each in need of gaining greater accomplishment; Mary has musical ability but her voice is weak and her manner affected. Kitty has even less to recommend her at the moment. Both are foolish young women. Despite the extra expense, I am undertaking the forwarding of their education. I have taken it upon myself to organise the interviews since this business would falter if left to yourself, madam. Your 'nerves' would soon have given way under the pressure of arranging such a venture."

To say Mrs. Bennet felt insulted would be to understate her resentment at this conduct. She was about to reply when there was a knock at the door and Hill entered carrying a small parcel marked, 'Brown, Drapers of Meryton.'

"Good morning, sir" said Hill. "This has come for Mrs. Bennet. The carrier said as there is a bill enclosed."

Mr. Bennet relieved Hill of the box and tore it open. He found the paper that listed all the items and turned to his wife with a fury only held back from oral expression until the servant left.

"What can you mean by this, Mrs. Bennet?" he remonstrated. "There are over a dozen articles listed here. Fabrics, trimmings, and I know not what. How could you be so profligate? They must all be returned at once."

To his surprise, his wife did not acquiesce. She raised herself from the cushions and with unusual determination faced him.

"Mr. Bennet, in your paternal capacity you have just told me that you are hiring tutors for our girls, in order to educate them to grace society. I have not been indolent myself for I have done the same in my own way; our daughters will need to impress any future suitors and their families by their appearance, as well as their education. By paying attention to their outward aspect I am merely playing the same game as yourself. Are they to suffer disadvantage when in society because their dress is unfashionable? What use are their skills and arts if they present so poor a picture?"

"But the cost…" he interrupted, "the cost!"

"An investment, Mr. Bennet, an investment. If you are not content at my working on their behalf, then you may send away *my* drapers' products and *your* tutors."

Her husband found himself at a loss in defying his wife's logic.

"Well," he said guardedly, "there is perhaps some merit in your argument, Mrs. Bennet. Your views are noted. But the finances required to achieve these projects may be too high."

"As to that, we may haggle over the fees and costs with both parties. I have only ordered the fabrics on approval. There has been no payment yet. And I take it that you have not yet engaged a tutor?"

"Indeed not."

"In that case, may I suggest I am invited to attend the interviews? I should like to think my presence might assist the situation." Mr. Bennet laughed but she held up her hand, forbidding interruption. She went on "While you may dismiss my expenditure for medical and drapery as extravagance, in the matter of managing the housekeeping you must concede that I have demonstrated reasonable carefulness. You may well find my support a useful implement when negotiating the terms of contract."

Here Mr. Bennet nodded despite himself; he had long since allowed his wife to manage the household negotiations with the local suppliers. Indeed, he had been favourably impressed when learning of other households' arrangements, that Longbourn's compared well. He preferred to leave the domestic organisation to her while he managed the farm. He had never formerly acknowledged his wife's competency in this area, but had paid the bills as they occurred. However, this new and positive stance on the girls' education and the household economy came as a surprise. For his wife to express her views in such a logical manner left him momentarily without speech.

"And now, Mr. Bennet, I believe we have visitors. Please ring for Hill. I shall dress then join you in the library."

Shaking his head at this new turn in his wife's temperament, Mr. Bennet left her.

Although still weary, the exchange had given her new motivation. Calling for Hill's assistance, she immediately began her preparations to adhere to Mrs. Jones' advice. She washed her face, put on a patterned pelisse and fresh cap, wrapped a light cotton shawl around her shoulders then looked closely at her reflection in the tall mirror. Hill combed her hair into a neater style saying, "Well ma'am, you look brighter today, if I may say so."

"Thank you Hill. I shall try to overcome these afflictions and put the welfare of my daughters before my own considerations."

She swallowed one of the potions that had been prescribed, drank two glasses of wine and gathered up her fan, before descending the stairs.

On entering the library, she found there were two men standing beside her husband.

"Mrs. Bennet, may I introduce Mr. Chawton from Canterbury, who tutors in Music and Dancing, and Mr. Lockhart from Worcester, who offers French and Drawing."

Both gentlemen bowed, said "Good morning, madam" and stood back to let Mrs. Bennet pass between them to the chairs. They were each of medium height, but whereas Mr. Chawton smiled with an open face, his companion appeared more solemn.

Mr. Chawton was an attractive young man, not above thirty who was dressed in a modest fashion. His curly dark hair fell engagingly over his collar at the nape and his broad shoulders were emphasised by the cut of his dark coat. His athletic figure displayed his fitness for the dancing aspect of his tutorage. Mr. Lockhart with his parted light brown hair and closed features was more reserved in demeanour, with an air of grave propriety. His figure was slighter than his companion's, but his gaze no less confident.

"Well," said Mr. Bennet, "may we start with you, Mr. Chawton? Perhaps Hill would be so good as to show Mr. Lockhart to the library?"

Mrs. Bennet allowed her husband to question the young man as to his previous experiences, his references and the knowledge of his subjects. Mr. Chawton replied in a pleasant, southern counties accent with good diction and with an earnestness beneath the good-humoured countenance that impressed his listeners.

"And now," said Mrs. Bennet, "are you able to offer a variety of the masters' works when teaching music; pieces that will enchant when played or sung in society? The girls will be called on to display their skills at small and large social gatherings. There will be other young women eager to show their prowess and our daughters must shine at these events."

"Really my dear," began Mr. Bennet, feeling his wife was parading her offspring as prize heifers at a cattle market who must show the glossiest coat and finer points, to outflank the opposition.

"I understand your concerns, Mrs. Bennet," said Mr. Chawton. "I believe I have the qualities to draw out the best in my pupils and enable them to perform to their potential in singing, pianoforte or violin and dancing, when in the public eye." Here he handed over some copies of certificates to his hosts. They showed prizes awarded to young people under his tutelage. Mrs. Bennet read them carefully then rattled off a string of questions, each more direct than the last to her husband's embarrassed ears.

To all these Mr. Chawton answered good-humouredly. There was an easiness of temper, which rendered him unperturbed by such informal queries, even though Mr. Bennet feared that such impropriety might frighten him away.

"Now sir, I assume you have brought your references with you?"

The young man searched his bag and brought out several sheets of paper. She read each with great concentration and was moved to say, "I see, sir, you are well-regarded by former employers and it would appear you have some elegant connections in the city of Canterbury?"

"That is happily the case, madam. My family have lived there for several generations."

"And what, pray, made you choose your vocation?"

Mr. Bennet was wondering where these questions were tending. He hoped rather than expected his wife would not intrude much further into Mr. Chawton's personal affairs.

"My father is a judge and both my brothers are studying the law, but after seeing the value of a good education in my own family, I wished to make my contribution to society in the same field. It was with this in mind and the strong support of my mother that I was able to go to Cambridge, obtain my degree, then practise the profession near home. It is with a view to obtaining further experience in teaching that I applied for this position."

"May one ask why your mother felt so desirous to encourage you in your chosen career?"

If Mr. Chawton felt this question was straying a little too far in the direction of his personal life, he did not show it, but answered honestly, "I believe she felt herself the privilege of an excellent education, being a member of the Clifford family, and would have loved nothing better than to have become a governess herself. But her family strongly disapproved. However, she determined once she married, she would give her children the benefit of her education. Thus we three sons were able to receive that advantage and I have followed in her footsteps."

Mrs. Bennet at last looked satisfied and, ignoring any further questions form her husband, said, "Everything seems to be in order, Mr. Chawton. We offer you the position of music and dancing tutor to our two daughters providing you agree terms and conditions. We should like you to start on Monday. Will that suit you?"

Mr. Bennet looked alarmed at this proposal since he had planned to communicate privately with his wife before offering the tutor the position. He could merely echo his wife's words, asking "Yes sir, would that suit you?"

"Indeed, sir, it would," said the tutor. "I have already made enquiries in Meryton as to accommodation should the position be offered to me. I look forward to beginning my work with your daughters. Thank you for the interview." He stood up, shook Mr. and Mrs. Bennet's hands and agreeing to settle the details of contract and payment after the second tutor's interview, departed.

"Well!" exclaimed Mr. Bennet. "That quite took my breath away Mrs. Bennet. Perhaps we were a little hasty?"

"No time like the present. And these tutors may be snapped up by other parents, if we do not move swiftly."

Mrs. Bennet called for Hill to usher in Mr. Lockhart. His quieter manner was rather a relief for

Mr. Bennet, who tersely whispered to his wife, "Allow *me* to conduct the interview…"

Questions of a similar nature followed and the Art tutor's responses were those of a considered nature. His speech was precise. His voice revealed a cultured upbringing and he answered all Mr. Bennet's enquiries well. To Mrs. Bennet's sharper questions he was able to respond sufficiently intelligently to satisfy even her. His references were looked over and were impeccable. Mr. and Mrs. Bennet exchanged glances. They were in accord. He anticipated his wife by quickly asking Mr. Lockhart if there were any reason why he could not take up the position if offered. The young man said, "Indeed not, sir. At least, there is only one slight impediment."

Mrs. Bennet looked worried. She wanted no delay in starting.

"It is only that I would wish to meet my future charges before agreeing to the position."

The Bennets smiled and Hill was rung for.

"Hill, we should be obliged if you would bring Mr. Chawton here, then fetch Miss Mary and Miss Kitty." Hill bobbed a curtsey then withdrew.

"I should say that Mr. Chawton is a little more trusting than yourself, Mr. Lockhart, since he agreed to the post before meeting the young ladies."

"Ah, that is not fully the case, Mr. Bennet, since he happened to catch sight of them on his approach to the house as they were gathering flowers in the front garden. He probably formed a positive opinion then and confided as much to me while we were awaiting interview."

At this information, Mr. Bennet looked thoughtful but his wife smiled. Mr. Chawton returned and the atmosphere lightened a little when the earlier meeting was disclosed, as he said, "Well it did help to make up my mind, sir."

Further conversation was halted as the girls knocked, then entered the room in a slightly nervous manner. Mary in blue and Kitty in lavender made an attractive picture. They each glanced down modestly on seeing the young men, though inwardly eager to see their new tutors at closer quarters.

"Well, girls' said their father, "we have appointed Mr. Chawton and Mr. Lockhart to teach you Music, Dancing, Drawing and French. They will be commencing their duties next Monday, once terms are agreed. They will expect punctuality, diligence and persistence in your studies. The appointments are initially for six months. The lessons will take place one morning each week. There will be regular progress reports." Kitty suppressed her natural inclination to giggle when she caught her father's stern eye.

Mrs. Bennet added "You will do well to remember girls, that this education is at your parents' expense. We expect to see your prospects advanced by this investment." At this, everyone except the hostess looked uncomfortable.

"And now," she said, picking up her fan to flutter at her flushed countenance, "I really must leave you all. Kitty, Mary, please ensure you understand what will be necessary to prepare you for the first lesson. We look forward to your education and therefore your prospects being much advanced by this tutoring." With this Mrs. Bennet left the room, much to everyone's relief.

Mr. Bennet asked his daughters to quit the room then sat down to discuss the financial side of the tutoring arrangements, which he was rather dreading. The idea of committing his far-from-grand income to yet another outlay, and for the next six months, was worrying. While seeing the logic of his wife's view, though the fact that he could acknowledge such a virtue in his wife was difficult, he feared the possible embarrassment of having to cease the contract before official termination. Usually a man to procrastinate where his daughters were concerned, he was in a position where negotiation was imperative and the most favourable terms he could secure were of the utmost importance.

May 27th

Another violent quarrel with Mr. Bennet. Over finances. Again. I find such wrangling exhausting, but I will stand up for myself. Yet despite the clashing of views, there is an element of some amusement to be had in our differences. An altercation can be invigorating, especially when I have the upper hand as I did today.

The appointment of two young tutors for the girls will certainly shake up the household. They appear to be intelligent and well-educated young men. Indeed I am a little in awe of them; I am glad they were not interviewing me!

I note that the entries in this journal have become more frequent; three this month! Does this imply I have more energy now? Perhaps the combination of Mrs. Jones' potions and my secret restoratives may take the credit for this renewal of good spirits.

Chapter VI

"Well, my dears" said Mrs. Bennet calmly to her daughters after breakfast, "you may spend the morning with your tutors while your Aunt Philips calls and then the afternoon with us at needlework, preparing for the assembly. All the fabrics and trimmings are now come from the draper's and there is less than a fortnight to prepare."

"Yes, mama. Am I to have the pale blue muslin?" Kitty asked. "I already have a pair of Jane's shoes which will match the dress."

"But mama," interrupted Mary plaintively, "I am sure I chose that muslin when we were in the drapery store. It was the lovat green cotton lawn that Kitty wanted then."

"Ah, but that was before Jane sent the shoes. Besides, Mary, you know blue is my colour," said Kitty looking firm.

"Girls, girls!" their mother cried, "consider my nerves! I cannot bear this quarrelling. We shall look again at the fabrics and discuss it all this afternoon."

Mary cast a hard but suffering look at her mother while Kitty bounced from the room, convinced she would get her way. Hill ushered in Aunt Philips, who greeted her sister with affectionate solicitude.

"And how are you my dear? Are the girls being good? I thought I heard a door slam as I came into the house and shouting on the landing. Is all well?"

"Ah sister, daughters are a trial. But nevertheless, I feel a little better in myself, since my sleep is improving. It is, of course, early days yet, but the remedies from the apothecary seem to be having a positive effect."

"I am glad of it. Now tell me all your news," said Mrs. Philips. "How are the lessons progressing?"

The lessons in question had now been in session for three weeks. The girls were without much outdoor amusement with the onset of Spring rains, hence the regular practice on piano and violin and learning of French vocabulary. And though sketching in the garden was not possible, Mr. Lockhart set up a series of still life objects in the drawing room for his charges.

While he assisted Kitty with her French, Mr. Chawton tutored Mary on the pianoforte.

"Well Mary, it is clear that you have a genuine talent for the instrument. Your diligent daily practice is paying dividends. Here are some scherzos that you may like to look through when you next have time."

Mary blushed with pleasure, for she was rarely given a compliment. Although she was a little uncomfortable with her tutor's informality and would have preferred to be accorded the title "Miss Bennet", she thanked him and resolved to write something of her musical progress in her next letter to Mr. Collins.

In the library, Kitty had spent an hour reading French poems aloud with Mr. Lockhart and was eager to change with her sister for the livelier tutor. She found Mr. Lockhart's solemn voice and demeanour lacked a certain passion which would have enlivened the *poesie d'amour*

"Your accent is reasonable, Miss Bennet, but you rush the words. This causes you to stumble over even the simplest phrase. The pace is all wrong for such serious work." Kitty found his formal manner irksome and longed for the lesson to end.

"You may prepare for our next lesson by translating the first two poems in this anthology," he concluded. Kitty was less than delighted since she felt the learning of French was of little value.

"After all," she privately reasoned, "unless Boney invades, I shall have no need of such a devilish language. And even then, I shall tell him in English, that Wellington will soon defeat him."

She smiled at the thought of Napoleon doffing his Emperor's hat to the British military commander, then begging for his mercy. "And if I were Wellington, I should insist he attend English lessons while in captivity." The notion of the great French leader sitting at a school desk, being subjected to the plays of Shakespeare and being instructed to translate them into French made her laugh out loud. She still had the smile on her face when she walked into the drawing room, where Mary was just finishing her piece.

"That sounds very pretty, Mary," said Kitty.

"Mary, you may play that lively gavotte if you please, while I teach Kitty the new steps," said Mr. Chawton, smiling. He held out his hand in an elegant way and Kitty took it, curtseying as she did so. The music immediately lifted the atmosphere and the couple danced in time. Their reflection was caught in the long mirror and Mary, glancing up from her active fingers, saw how well they suited each other; their relaxed movements were perfectly in tune and their eyes met often. Whether this was by accident or design is uncertain.

As they bowed, Mr. Chawton said, "Thank you Kitty. I fear you will be late for your Art class, Mary, if you do not go now. Thank you for your lively rendition."

Mary placed her piano pieces tidily on the side table and withdrew. Kitty, with flushed cheeks from the exercise, sat at the piano. Mr. Chawton laid a selection of sheet music before her. Kitty looked at them with some trepidation; her technical ability was not as great as her sister's.

In the library, Mary seated herself in front of the still life, while Mr. Lockhart busied himself with pens, pencils and paper. With pens trimmed, pencils sharpened and paper set straight, the master and pupil were ready.

"Observe before drawing, Miss Bennet. Look at shape, texture, light. See the solidity of the objects. Notice their outline against the background. Only draw the shapes of each at first. I shall draw also and we shall work in silence for a while."

After a half hour of the tutor and his pupil silently engaged in drawing, Mr. Lockhart left his work and stood near Mary.

"Miss Bennet, that is a fair beginning. You show some understanding of line and form. You need now to consider the shading. A light in a light is always lighter than a light in a dark," he added.

"How do I do that, Mr. Lockhart? I seem to make it look so flat."

The tutor sat down next to Mary and, taking the pencil gently from her, expertly shaded a little of the vase that stood to the forefront of the still life, while explaining clearly the theory he was putting into practice. Mary listened attentively and when he had sketched a little, he let her resume. She continued more confidently, daring to ask advice, and this was given seriously. She found this quiet, purposeful approach much more to her liking than the light-hearted manner of the lively music tutor.

Meanwhile, Kitty was undergoing the piano tuition with Mr. Chawton. He handed her a portfolio of French songs. Kitty's heart sank. Two encounters with that alien language in one day was unbearable. Had there been some collusion between the tutors?

"Mr. Chawton, I fear my competence in French is not high. Mr. Lockhart tells me that my reading of the French poems we studied this morning was too rapid."

"Kitty, I can see your hesitation. But be assured, there is nothing to fear. I will go as far as to say that by the end of this lesson you will not only surprise yourself at your progress, but you may have cause to admit you even found them enjoyable."

Despite his winning smile, Kitty felt most ill at ease. If the poems had caused so much trouble, the songs would surely display her lack of skill even more. At least with the poems she had only to hold the book and read the words (however poorly), but the songs would require reading music, comprehending the libretto, playing the piano and singing.

"Here," said her tutor cheerfully, "we'll start with a simple, traditional air that will soon have you smiling."

To Kitty's surprise, instead of waiting in silence for his pupil to begin, Mr. Chawton made a gracious bow before her and asked, "Will you do me the honour of dancing with me again, Miss Bennet?" She hesitated, unsure of what would follow. The tutor then burst into singing "Au pres de ma blonde" while he swept his partner nimbly across the room. By the second verse, Kitty felt able to join him in the chorus and they danced until Kitty was smiling.

"You see, Kitty, French can be fun. Do not become mired in the pronunciation, just enjoy the flow of the music and you will find the words will come naturally."

He continued, "Now we shall take the rhythms of 'Au pres de ma blonde' and use the piano. Here is the music. I shall sit beside you while we play the basic tune together. We'll sing the chorus as if our lives depended on it, yes?"

Kitty began with vigour and though there were several halts and mistakes in the tune, the music began to flow, improving at every renewal. Whenever it broke down, Kitty laughed at herself while her tutor patiently smiled and began the music again.

At twelve o' clock the tutors ended for the day and left until next week. Kitty and Mary, while collecting their music, papers and pencils, found it necessary to discuss their separate experiences of the young men.

Kitty began by complaining, "Mr. Lockhart is well named, with his straight face and joyless nature; sombre as a judge. There was no encouragement in my struggle with that abominable language. He constantly picked holes in my accent. How could I get the poems to flow when he continually stopped me?"

"Contrary to you, Kitty, I found Mr. Lockhart to be a man of quiet judgement and integrity. The French poetry reading led to a philosophical discourse on Voltaire. Most illuminating. He is much travelled in France and undertook a period of study at The Sorbonne, before the wars started."

Kitty laughed. "So he returns to England spreading that devil Boney's language here in the hopes of converting us! And my sketching efforts fared no better; the still life was too hard, so we tried portraits. He sketched my face and then I asked to draw his. It was such fun, after the French gloom. But I elongated his nose and chin and exaggerated his stiff hair so that when his eye fell upon my finished drawing he said sharply, 'I think in future, we shall adhere to botanical specimens, Miss Bennet'."

"On the contrary, Kitty, I enjoyed the quiet atmosphere of the studio while we were sketching. There is much to be said for silence."

Mrs. Bennet's querulous voice arose from the hall; "Mary! Kitty! You are needed now for lunch. It will be a swift affair, as we shall be clearing the room for our sewing. Make haste!"

The lunch was a small repast of eggs, ham, bread and fruit pudding. Mr. Bennet attended. His kindly overtures asking his daughters about their morning lessons were brushed aside by his wife.

"I am certain the girls are doing well under such admirable guidance, Mr. Bennet. It is of greater importance to discuss the work of the afternoon. Mrs. Philips and I will be joined by Hill to look over our wardrobes for the assembly. Such a deal to be accomplished in so very short a time; there will be the muslin to lay out, cut and make up. Then there's the embroidery on the hems. And of course, the shawls must be trimmed. The lace—"

Mr. Bennet held up his hands in horror. "No more, Mrs. Bennet, no more! I would be obliged if you would spare me the details. I wish to have as little trouble in the business as possible. I believe I have made my contribution in paying the draper's bill. To sit here and listen to talk of trimmings, lace, stitches and I know not what, would be insupportable." With the last words falling from his lips he reached the door, and whisked through it, disappearing into his study.

And so began the first of many sessions with the womenfolk of Longbourn and Aunt Philips sewing, trimming, embroidering, fitting and discarding, then taking up again. The mirror was both their enemy and their friend. While they worked small confidences and gossip were exchanged. Mrs. Bennet's moods were noticeable in their uncertainty. It appeared they were often influenced by the person or subject under discussion. Where she felt herself safe, she was generous, but when at odds with her daughters, she felt under attack and was peevish and harsh by turns. In either circumstance, she was violent in believing she was always in the right.

The first subject was the inclusion of the tutors at the assembly. She halted in her sewing to stab the air with her needle. Irritation was shown in face and voice.

"They should not have been invited," said Mrs. Bennet. "They are not immediate neighbours, are in neither the militia or navy, appear of small means and they have few connections." By which comment she inferred that they had no potential as suitors.

"But mama," said Kitty, "they are respectable young men and know our family at least."

Mrs. Bennet was feeling warm, as the weight of the fabrics had been draped across her lap for some time. Wave after wave of perspiration drenched her. She turned her flushed face towards her younger daughter and said brusquely, "Kitty, you know nothing about such matters. Your judgment on what is socially correct is immature and poorly perceived."

"Anyone who can afford the appropriate mode of dress may attend an assembly, mama," said Kitty with some asperity.

"Hold your tongue, girl, and refrain from speaking to your mother in such a fashion," Mrs. Bennet cried sharply.

"Though Kitty may be couching her statement in an unacceptable tone, mama" said Mary thoughtfully, "she is quite correct in her facts."

"What, two of you now, contradicting me? This will not be borne. Continue your sewing in silence at once, the pair of you." The girls looked at each other in mute resignation, feeling this was yet another of their mother's moods and must be endured though privately resented.

Aunt Philips saw her sister's discomfiture and smoothed the situation by saying, "I believe there may be the naval captain and his son at the ball. They have not yet been seen by the inhabitants of Longbourn, but have recently taken lodgings at my neighbour's in Meryton."

"Oh!" said Mrs. Bennet, surprised. "And who are they, I pray?"

"Captain James Wainwright and his son Lieutenant James Wainwright."

"How old are they, aunt?" said Kitty.

"Are they respectable gentlemen?" asked Mary.

"Well, I have heard that the father is a widower and is around the age of five and forty, while his son is declared a handsome young man of twenty who is well-mannered and personable."

Kitty and Mary exchanged glances. Mrs. Bennet took an immediate interest,

"Are they on a lengthy shore leave? Or planning to settle in the district?" She was not going to waste her time making conversation at the assembly if the gentlemen would soon be departing, perhaps to go abroad again. There again, she silently mused, if they were in two minds, between shore and ship, a pair of desirable, accomplished young ladies might secure their permanent establishment in the locality.....

*

Over the course of the week the dresses were fitted, sewn, refitted, hemmed and hung. Kitty and Mary took it in turns to stand on the little wooden stool while their mother, Aunt Philips and Hill attended. Mrs. Bennet's manner had lightened; she had slept better of late and her renewed energy gave a lift to her spirits.

"Kitty, your figure looks well in that blue muslin. And Mary, the lovat green suits your brown hair beautifully. I have ordered some shoe-roses which will complement the cream shawls you will be wearing." Here she smiled indulgently.

Aunt Philips finished the little head ribbons and, while Hill with a mouthful of pins turned up Kitty's hem as she stood on the stool, her aunt tucked the cream braid into Mary's hair as she sat at the dressing table.

"Yes, Kitty, the pleated bodice fits you well; a very becoming style. As to presentation, deportment is all in showing off your figures. Just remember to sit upright with your shoulders back, hands folded in your lap during the entire evening."

"All evening, mama? A little difficult to dance the quadrille in that pose, aunt, " laughed Kitty. Mary surprised them all by turning round on the chair at the dressing table and giving an impeccable performance of the quadrille steps while still seated with her hands together. Her face wore such an overly serious expression, looking over the top of her glasses, that they all burst into laughter.

"Like this, Aunt Philips?"

"Such a good joke, Mary!" laughed her mother. Then to everyone's surprise Mrs. Bennet stood up and danced across the drawing room, humming a tune and using a dress as her dancing partner. The elegant swirl she achieved as she reached the corner, held her audience's admiration. Despite the added weight and years, she moved lightly on her toes and there was real poise in her movements. Her observers were enchanted. Their gaze followed Mrs. Bennet's graceful steps around the furniture, willing her on. She seemed lost in a trance of youthful memories until, passing the *chaise longue* for the fourth time, she sank exhausted into the soft upholstery. Her sides were heaving, the breath coming in short gasps, but her eyes were as bright as her daughters'. When she could draw breath, she laughed out loud.

"Oh mama!" exclaimed Kitty, " I never knew you could dance so well."

Mrs. Philips added, "My dear sister. That was wonderful! How that took me back to those days when we were your age, girls. We danced every dance at the assemblies and were never short of partners. Happy times."

This drew forth several questions from the daughters regarding fashions, music, refreshments and so much else that the older women begged them to cease. While Mrs. Bennet regained her breath Aunt Philips said, "Of course, the main object of young people dressing in their best and attending balls and assemblies was, and always has been, to take an opportunity to become acquainted with members of the opposite sex. The importance of such gatherings cannot be underestimated, particularly for females. As my husband never fails to point out, 'engagements and marriages are events that determine the entire future of the female half of the race, for they have no other destiny if they wish to make their fortunes'. Your mother and I are in complete accord on this matter."

Kitty and Mary were caught between giggling and frowning at this open reasoning.

Their aunt continued, "He also quotes a handsome but impoverished lady of his acquaintance who rebuked a wealthy gentleman on his advice that she take up horse riding lessons in order to ingratiate herself with the local gentry. She said, 'Female economy will do a great deal my lord, but it cannot turn a small income into a large one.' So you see my dear nieces, the necessity of presenting yourselves as favourably as possible at this assembly."

"Yes, Aunt Philips," said the girls in unison. They were hoping that the enjoyment of the evening would outweigh the serious obligations they felt to find a partner for life in such a short evening.

"A final word on the subject of assemblies, my dears," said Mrs. Bennet, who had now recovered. "They were not as they are now, sophisticated social gatherings. Oh dear no. In our youth, England was 'a nation of country bumpkins', but it was Mr. 'Beau' Nash who did so much to regulate polite behaviour. We had our fun of course, but we learned, as did everyone, the new dances which demonstrated polish, elegance and decorum."

"Oh yes" agreed her sister "the style of dancing originated in the French court and here in England we adapted and developed it. We learned the skills of perfectly executing the steps of the English country-dance. These were hard enough, but add to that the virtues of being still when required, move when required and make polite conversation while remaining alert to the demands of the dance, needed real skill."

"And did you converse with many young gentlemen or even fall in love, while dancing?" asked Kitty smiling at her aunt.

"Well my dears, the exchange of a few words, and a glance over the shoulder was highly conducive to engaging the interest of the opposite sex," said Mrs. Bennet.

"And this," finished her sister, "is still the reason for single young people to attend assemblies. So if you wish to shine, you both must heed your dancing master well in the coming fortnight!"

> *June 1ˢᵗ*
>
> *Judging by the music coming from the piano room, Mr. Bennet must agree that our money has been well invested. Kitty always emerges from her dancing lessons flushed with enthusiasm and Mary pronounces every evening on her newly acquired knowledge.*
>
> *Kitty shared with me her sketch of Mr. Lockhart; it made me laugh despite its irreverence for she had captured his stiff hair and long features to perfection. We did not expose the portrait to her father.*

The girls' quarrels over their dresses annoyed me but after my hasty and I confess, harsh, admonitions I felt some shame. Their silence upbraided me more than sharp rejoinders. I am sorry now that I was so quick-tempered. They will look very pretty in their blue and lovat.

News of some naval men in the neighbourhood. A captain and his son, both single. Marriage material?

There was a moment today when all my cares fell away. Upon a whim I danced before the girls and their aunt. No heats or melancholy prevented me. I felt the return of my youthful spirits. Albeit temporary respite, the elation was most welcome.

Chapter VII

"The figured silk or the muslin?" Mrs. Bennet stood before her mirror, putting first one dress and then the other against her. She then threw them both on the bed and walking quickly to her closet, pulled out several other robes that she regarded critically. She fidgeted with alarm and vexation.

Aunt Philips looked at the clock.

"I am in such confusion, sister. I do not know which to choose. If I select my silk it is sure to be warm and if the muslin, the rooms will be cold and I shall catch my death."

Aunt Philips glanced again at the clock; they had but thirty minutes before the carriage came. The girls still needed attention, her sister was dithering and she herself was only half-dressed. A firm hand was needed, with a large helping of reassurance.

"My dear sister, the muslin always suits you. It compliments your complexion and is of medium weight. Should you feel cool, you may wear the silk shawl over your shoulders. If the rooms grow heated, or you are enduring one of the flushes, you may easily take off the shawl. Now come, let me help you into the dress while I call Hill or the maid to finish the girls' hair and attend to us."

Mrs. Bennet looked relieved. Kitty and Mary came running into the room, their faces alight with expectation of the evening. Kitty's hair was prettily braided with cream ribbons and flowers making the most of her dark tresses. Mary had allowed the maid to pull a few curling tendrils of hair about her square face and the effect was to soften her features.

Though she often spoke against 'adornment', Mary was secretly pleased when she saw her reflection. She even allowed her aunt to pull a few more tendrils at the nape of her neck. Mrs. Bennet, now fully dressed, beamed at her two daughters.

"How elegant you look! I am so proud of you. On this special occasion, I shall lend my silver brooch to you Mary, as the elder. And for you Kitty, here is my sapphire ring. It will go beautifully with that dress."

"Thank you mama," said Kitty and Mary together.

"Now sister, pray sit here at your ease while Hill adjusts your pelisse—it is wrinkled at the back where you have caught it. Robson will then attend to your hair and I shall find our shawls, bags and shoes," said Mrs. Bennet. Her felicity at the prospect of the assembly had temporarily removed her languor. She was restored to her former querulous serenity.

Mr. Bennet knocked and entered the room. His presence halted the voices.

"The carriage has come. Time to be on our way. But let me first look at my girls: Mary, Kitty you are a credit to the family. And Mrs. Bennet, you are as handsome as either of them." His wife blushed at this unusual praise. He continued, "Sister Philips, you look lovely as always. I know full well how you have helped the family this past fortnight. Hill and Robson, your efforts are appreciated; you may have the evening free of duties."

"Thank you, sir."

"Most grateful, sir."

Mrs. Bennet gathered her own shawl, adjusted the girls' and Hill helped Aunt Philips into her cloak. Mr. Bennet held out his arm to his wife and she, with a girlish laugh, took it, her eyes sparkling. He felt, thus far, he had done his duty. A moderate amount of feminine company was acceptable if within the house, whence he might escape to his library; a full half hour inside a cramped coach with four excited females was not. He silently made his decision; he would ride next to the driver. James helped his master up to the seat beside himself, then handed each lady into the carriage. Even before she was seated, Mrs. Bennet was giving advice to the girls as to etiquette, deportment and modes of conduct for the evening.

The daughters did their best to deflect the instructions by asking a stream of questions, none of which the older women could answer with any certainty.

"Shall we be given dance cards as we enter?"

"Will there be hot and cold dishes?"

"Are the musicians familiar with all the dances we have learned?"

As they drew up outside the Assembly Rooms, they could hear the musicians striking up and see lights in all the windows. Couples and families were being set down from their modes of conveyance and walking in animated conversation towards the steps, while the queues of horses stamped impatiently or moved on. It was a fine night, as the Bennets descended from their carriage. They were lit to the front doors of the building by lads bearing torches and joined the chattering throng mounting the steps.

Once inside, Mary and Kitty looked around them with delight. The scent of flowers, candle wax, warm air and polished wooden floors greeted them. All was bustle and colour. They saw the Lucas party just ahead and the rector's, but there were many new faces whose identities they longed to discover. Divested of cloaks, the Bennet party entered the main room; a long hall where already there were twenty pairs dancing, Their glowing faces told of the energy and happiness in such a situation. Aunt Philips excused herself from the group as she had seen a former neighbour in the throng and wished to renew her acquaintance.

"I shall return soon, once I have exchanged news with Mrs. Thomas. It has been a full twelvemonth since we last met."

A pause in the musical pieces enabled couples to sit down, take refreshment or seek fresh partners. Mrs. Bennet was careful to ensure her family were seated in a place where they could view the gathering and where the gathering could view them. They were therefore able to note the arrival of the naval captain and his son. While inwardly mourning the absence of red-coated officers, Mrs. Bennet and Kitty were soon diverted by the newcomers. These gentlemen looked to be men of fine figure and had a geniality that allowed them to converse with ease to everyone near them.

It was not long before Sir William Lucas walked the pair over to the Bennets to introduce them.

"Allow me, ma'am, to introduce an old friend of mine, Captain Wainwright and his son James."

"Good evening, gentlemen," said Mr. Bennet bowing.

"A pleasure to make your acquaintance gentlemen" added Mr. Bennet, "May I introduce my wife?" Mrs. Bennet curtsied. The Wainwrights bowed. "And my two daughters, Miss Mary and Miss Kitty Bennet?"

Both girls gracefully curtsied. The music struck up, bringing couples to their feet.

"May we have the honour of securing your daughters for the first dance?" asked the captain. The girls were delighted. Captain Wainwright led Mary to the floor and James escorted Kitty. The Bennet girls' light figures and graceful movement were an elegant addition to the scene. Mrs. Bennet looked on with a smile, though her husband appeared less pleased.

"I hope the captain finds other partners nearer his age this evening," he whispered to his wife.

"And why should he do that? Mary is old beyond her years while he has made a good career from his naval exploits. They make a fine couple. Ah, there is Lady Lucas!" She called out her name and as soon as Lady Lucas was in earshot, Mrs. Bennet said, "Do you know what a captain's income might be?"

"Hush, Mrs. Bennet!" said her husband. "Would you have Captain Wainwright hear you? I beg you to desist."

"Nonsense, nonsense. I shall do no such thing." Lest he hear more to further embarrass him, Mr. Bennet shrugged his shoulders and retired to a quieter corner away from the gossip of women. He had brought a favourite novel in his pocket and, seating himself behind the pots of plants which stood massed in a corner, was able to while away the evening.

Mrs. Bennet was unabashed. Her curiosity about the naval gentleman rose above her long-held resentment over her companion's daughter's marriage. She had it confirmed by Lady Lucas that the captain was a man of some substance, widowed eight years ago and now come to reside in the neighbourhood.

The quadrille ended, Kitty appeared with a flushed face. Her partner begged her for the next two dances before turning away. Mary's partner elegantly handed her into her chair and turned to Mrs. Bennet.

"May I have the honour of your hand for the next dance, ma'am?"

"Oh Captain Wainwright, am I not a little old for such activities?" she asked.

"Indeed not, ma'am. From the way you were tapping your fan to the music I believe it would bring back your youth if you were to join me. If your husband has no objection, and I do not see him here to say no, then please honour me with you presence."

Mrs. Bennet, feeling a mixture of surprise and pleasure towards the captain and no small annoyance at being left alone by her husband so early in the evening, decided one dance could be embarked upon without obligation. She would take the opportunity to speak of Mary to the captain as they moved to the reel. Kitty and her sister were uneasy, but looked in vain for their father as the couple moved off, joining other couples to make up a set.

"Should we find papa?" said Mary in some consternation.

Kitty was about to agree, when to their surprise, Mr. Chawton and Mr. Lockhart appeared.

"May I have the pleasure of this dance, Miss Bennet?" asked the dancing tutor, bowing to Kitty. He took her hand with poise and looked steadily into her eyes.

"And may I ask to lead you, Miss Bennet, in the next dance?" asked Mr. Lockhart.

"Indeed you may, sir," answered Mary, following her sister's example. Both girls felt flattered and, with no parent here to forbid them, they were easily persuaded to accept. After all, the tutors were respectable young men and had their father's approval at Longbourn.

"Mrs. Bennet," said Captain Wainwright as they threaded their way up the dance, "I am so glad you attended this evening."

"You are, sir?" said Mrs. Bennet,

"Indeed, ma'am. I have learned something of your daughters' beauty and have much interest in becoming better acquainted with the whole family." This beginning was exceedingly intriguing to his partner.

The captain was obliged to move closer to Mrs. Bennet as the dance progressed and the various sets were become numerous, quite filling the room.

"There must be forty couples at least, here this evening," she said. She was beginning to feel the heat and sensed that her face was growing red. Her bodice felt too tight and she knew her skin was damp with perspiration. The embarrassment of suffering a hot flush while close to a gentleman was foremost in her mind. The captain danced with some skill and, while desiring the music would come to an end, Mrs Bennet aimed at distracting his attention from her growing discomfort, by chattering brightly about Mary.

"An accomplished girl, with a steady nature, Captain Wainwright."

Among the guests that evening was Mrs. Long, a woman of some importance in Meryton and who was careful to ensure she and her family were in attendance at all the major public functions. She prevailed upon her ailing husband to accompany her in each dance whether he wished or no, in order to maintain her prominent position in society and acquaint herself with everybody's business. The situation gave her every opportunity to observe and judge her neighbours.

Mrs. Long was nearby waiting for her turn to move up the set and while thus engaged, was exchanging conversation with her neighbour, Mrs. Johnson. The former had been an acquaintance of the Bennets and Mrs. Philips for many years but one to whom the term "friend" had never applied. Her dislike of one sister much exceeded her affection for the other. The main cause of her animosity was the sole fact that she too had daughters of marriageable age. Her own eldest had failed to attract a husband when Jane and Elizabeth Bennet were courted by Mr. Bingley and Mr. Darcy. Mrs. Long had watched the progress of those relationships, and noted how Mrs. Bennet's contrivance had been instrumental in the successful forwarding of Jane and Bingley's marriage, while her own daughters were ignored. In short, Mrs. Long was jealous. She now had the acute dissatisfaction of seeing Mrs. Bennet's younger daughters asked to dance while her own sat idly by. It was widely believed that the people of Meryton imputed this to the fact that their mother stood guard like a stern sentinel and the young men were too nervous to draw close.

Mrs. Long looked with ill-disguised contempt at the Bennet girls as they danced. She turned to the lady standing next to her. In so doing she was unaware of how near to herself Mrs. Bennet was now moving. By the perverseness of mischance, the two women were now with their backs to each other. Speaking in a voice loud enough for her immediate neighbour Mrs. Johnson to hear above the music she said, "It is clear that the Bennet girls are out to catch husbands tonight. One would think that the disgrace of Lydia Bennet's elopement would have made them less ambitious in polite society." Her listener was a quiet, placid soul whose response was to utter soothing replies to Mrs. Long's remarks in the hope that Mrs. Long would desist, but her politeness only seemed to fan the flames of the speaker's disdain. Her peevish words were coloured by a bitterness of spirit and no little exaggeration.

"How ill they all look; the mother in particular. She has grown broader of late and so unpredictable in her tempers, they say. The servants have it on good authority that she shouts at her children, muddles the household accounts, and her husband hardly speaks to her. I fear she is slowly losing her mind." Her ill-natured tone was accompanied by a complacent smile.

Mrs. Johnson mouthed to her to cease and indicated by a nod of her head that Mrs. Bennet, who was immediately behind them, could hear every word. This, however, had no restraining effect on the speaker, who continued, "Have you seen her this evening? Dressed in a fashion far too youthful for one of her age. Moreover she accepted Captain Wainwright's invitation to dance while her husband was elsewhere. A married woman bent on using her arts and allurements in licentious behaviour. What a spectacle she makes of herself!" In turning to look for the subject of her censure, she found herself staring straight into the eyes of that very person.

Usually able to manage or even dominate a social situation, Mrs. Bennet found herself feeling overcome with doubt. The flush that had assailed her in the dance was giving way to the customary sense of chill that drained her strength, energy and confidence. She was close to tears for she felt herself to be a figure of fun; an unattractive, red-faced woman dressed in a fashion more suited to her daughters and whose mind was unbalanced. She experienced a momentary confusion and her spirits were further discomposed as she regarded the hard stare of Mrs. Long moving from her to her partner. It was not difficult to guess that lady's thoughts and her vexatious conclusions, nor how these notions would soon spread from the observer to her social circle, with suitable embellishment. The captain perceived Mrs. Bennet's distress and sought to remove her from immediate embarrassment.

"Allow me to escort you to a quieter place, away from the crowded dancing space, Mrs. Bennet." This placed her in no small dilemma; if she stayed where she was and bade the captain leave, this would seem impolite. It might also diminish the chance of Mary becoming better acquainted with him. She surmised how eagerly Mrs. Long would prevail upon the wealthy widower to dance with her own daughters, all of whom stood nearby, still awaiting partners. To accompany him to a 'quieter place,' however, might give rise to more conjecture and social condemnation. The predicament was resolved by her deciding to walk away with him, since she would at least be out of the sight and hearing of Mrs. Long, thus providing some respite whatever the consequences.

A scarce-concealed whisper behind the gloved hand of that keenly observant lady as the couple withdrew, had Mrs. Johnson raise her genteel eyebrows and follow their movement with a mixture of surprise and disbelief. Greater indiscretion was curtailed by the cessation of the music. With an encouraging smile, Sir William Lucas stepped up to the platform in order to invite pianists and singers to exhibit their musical talents.

"Good evening one and all. It is a pleasure to see such a good attendance. You will agree with me I am sure how well we have been served with music so far this evening. While they take a well-earned respite, it is time to turn from our professional musicians to those younger members of our little assembly who may have aspirations in this direction. It is their opportunity to exhibit and entertain."

His words caused a stir among the onlookers, some parents turning their heads to forcibly whisper instructions or requests to their offspring. Some were urging their sons, but mainly their daughters, to the fore. Kitty and Mary, being with no parent nearby and not being the most forward of young ladies where their musical prowess was concerned, held back a little. "If only mama or papa were with us," whispered Kitty, "it would be easy. But as it is I feel perhaps it would be presumptuous of us to assume our abilities are ready for the ears of Meryton society. What are your thoughts, Mary? Please do not remain silent. I am sure mama would expect us to exhibit."

Mary pulled her gaze from the platform and looked around her. Lady Lucas was gently accompanying Maria through the throng. The latter appeared apprehensive but she was smiling bravely and, seeing her father's kindly gaze ahead, drew herself up with a little more confidence and walked on. Just as Mary was about to give a reply to her sister, she felt a hard push in the small of her back. She turned and found the formidable figures of Mrs. Long and her three daughters crowding upon her. Their purposeful movement caused Mary to drop her fan and in bending to retrieve it, was almost knocked down.

"Step away Miss Bennet! We wish to come through." The eyes of Mrs. Long were willing Mary to succumb to her authority. The Long daughters were following hard on their mother's heels and, with little attention to civility, were using their elbows to ease their path. Kitty, who though a few moments before had been overcome by anxiety, now regained her self-possession. To push herself forward and perform in public was one thing, but to witness her sister's discomfiture and likely exclusion from the exhibition by the rudeness of the Long family, was quite another.

"Mary dear, take my arm. After all those hours of practice, I am sure mama would wish us to take up this invitation." Kitty slid her arm into Mary's and moved across the Long family's path. This untoward action caused Mrs. Long to set her face in anger and her voice in condescension.

"Your mama?" queried Mrs. Long. "I do not seem to see her here. One can only speculate as to where she might be. As for your father, it is clear he takes no interest at all in his daughters' welfare. Kindly allow our party to proceed while I suggest that you, meanwhile, seek your absent parents. Let us pass at once!"

While normally respectful of her elders, Kitty felt the insult to her parents keenly and opened her mouth to reply. But Mary, sensing that open argument would do the Bennet girls no favours among the familiar faces about them, tugged Kitty's arm. Her sudden movement startled Kitty and it is to her credit that she recognised her sister's silent wisdom. Her features changed in an instant and smiling broadly, she gripped Mary's hand in her own.

"Come, Mary, let us honour our dear parents by showing what skills the Bennet girls possess. Under the tutelage of Mr. Chawton, we have learned some lively pieces that may entertain this assembly tonight."

The sisters walked forward together, watched by Mrs. Long and her daughters. She turned to them and spoke in a voice of civil disdain that carried far beyond, saying, "No matter, girls, *your* prowess will eclipse theirs utterly."

Her sharp response caused those near her to regard the Long family with some dislike. The notion of younger musical scholars entertaining the older members of Meryton society at the assemblies was viewed as one of mutual, enjoyable support and was not generally regarded as an occasion for competition or self-aggrandizement.

Mrs. Long's daughters looked less than convinced of their mother's belief and hesitated for a moment, their faces registering their uncertainty. But she pushed them onward with a firm hand, following fast on the heels of the Bennet girls, muttering in the eldest's ear, "dirt before the broom, my dears, dirt before the broom."

Sir William helped the young musicians up on to the platform and gave a specially warm glance to Kitty and Mary. Despite their mother's bitterness over his daughter Charlotte marrying Mr. Collins, he bore no ill will. The Bennets were neighbours and friends and had been so for many years. He turned to the onlookers and asked, "Will anyone kindly offer to accompany the singers?"

"Sir, I am at your service," said Mr. Chawton, raising his hand. Kitty looked up with a smile and Mary some relief. While each felt fairly confident in their skills at the piano, they were less optimistic in singing to their own playing. The presence of their music tutor would be a welcome and assuring addition.

Maria Lucas was the first to play and her piece, a solemn largo, was executed with appropriate dignity and precision. Sir William led the applause and urged her to sing. Maria shook her head and after she nodded and curtsied to acknowledge the audience, she allowed her father to guide her down the platform steps. Three more young people were the next to perform. They all chose to play the piano. The pieces were again of a serious nature and their executors were of varying expertise.

"What a pleasure it is to see the young people prepared to entertain in society," said Aunt Philips to her friend, Mrs. Thompson.

"It is so good for their confidence," she acknowledged. "I am looking forward to seeing your nieces."

"You have no need to wait any longer, Mrs. Thompson. There is Kitty now. Judging by her countenance, she appears to be readying herself for one of those lively pieces she promised earlier."

Mary and Kitty stepped up together. Sir William introduced the Bennet girls to the audience who smiled in encouragement. Before Kitty announced her piece the elder sister ensured she was comfortable on the piano stool. Her gaze was directed at the whole assembly but James

Wainwright, watching with absorption at the back of the room, believed the smile lingered a little on himself. Kitty flexed her fingers, sat upright, then touched the keys. The pretty air was executed in a light, rhythmic fashion that soon had the listeners tapping their feet in time. The enjoyment was infectious and though not technically perfect, was received with far more delight than the more serious works that were played earlier. On finishing, Kitty lifted her hand, paused, then turned her head to smile at the audience. She rose and bobbed a curtsey, then was about to leave the platform when Mr. Chawton stepped forward.

"Now, Miss Bennet, I beg you not to depart before giving us a song. See, I have the music here, so there will be no fear of forgetting the words."

On further prompting from Sir William, Kitty stepped back to the piano. Mr. Chawton flicked back his coat tails, pushed up the cuffs of his jacket and began to play the introduction. He gave Kitty an encouraging glance, which was not lost on James Wainwright. The latter allowed himself some moments of regret that he had not continued his own piano studies. How pleasant to accompany such a sweet and unaffected voice, then to receive her thanks at the end.

Kitty's sincerity while performing the gentle air was evident and was appreciated by most of those who listened; there only remained the Long family who did not look on with enjoyment. As the song drew to a close Mrs. Johnson made a complimentary remark to Mrs. Long, which that lady grudgingly acknowledged by replying, "Well perhaps Miss Bennet is not entirely without ability," but felt impelled to continue, "though it begs the question as to where she inherited her voice." Feeling that any further intercourse would do little to change her neighbour's views, Mrs. Johnson made her excuses and moved to another part of the room, preferring the company of others with more charitable thoughts. Left alone, Mrs. Long's jealousy gave no-one any pain but herself.

Mr. Chawton waved away the applause of the audience, who were long in acknowledging his proficiency, and instead he applauded Kitty, who laughed. Sir William led Kitty from the piano and introduced Mary. She was less nervous than her sister for she acted in the knowledge that double the amount of practice had preceded this evening and she wished to display evidence of that endeavour. Her piece was rather sombre in tone, but was executed with such careful precision that it was technically perfect.

"A most worthy performance," whispered Mrs. Johnson to Aunt Philips, who stored up the compliment to pass on to her niece. Mary's usually pale face glowed with quiet pleasure when she finished. However, though both Sir William and Mr. Chawton pressed her to sing, they could not persuade her. She claimed a slight soreness of the throat, but nonetheless looked gratified at the exhortation.

The three Long daughters ascended the platform with their mother close behind, urging them forward. She appeared a little affronted at Sir

William's gentle suggestion that just the girls should proceed.

"But I wish to introduce them and their pieces myself. They are far too modest to do it and besides, they would make such a muddle of it, there would be complete confusion."

The three girls looked at each other in some dismay.

"As you think best, madam," murmured Sir William, stepping backwards to avoid the large, bustling figure and the sweep of her silk shawl.

*

The captain had led Mrs. Bennet to the small room set aside for refreshments. "My dear lady, allow me to fetch you a glass of cool wine. It will lift your spirits."

Mrs. Bennet nodded her assent and drew her fan from her waist to flutter at her steaming face. She felt most unwell. Her earlier exuberance had now deserted her. She recognised the symptoms of The Change overwhelming her again and wanted to weep. But she had to nerve herself for the girls' sakes. When Captain Wainwright returned with her drink, she sipped from the glass and began afresh on the merits of Mary. He drew his chair close, explaining,

"I have grown hard of hearing since taking to the life at sea. The cannon-fire, you know ma'am."

Mrs. Bennet looked directly into his face and continued her conversation.

"As I say, my daughter Mary is a very accomplished young woman."

Captain Wainwright was now paying full attention. He saw her glass was empty and reached to take it from her hand. In so doing his fingers closed on hers.

"Mrs. Bennet, I am sure Miss Mary Bennet is a young lady to whom any man would feel honoured in paying court."

Mrs. Bennet smiled and left her hand where it was for she had no wish to distract the captain from his speech. He continued, "Since moving to Meryton, I have made the acquaintance of your sister, Mrs. Philips, and her conversation has often been of the Bennet family. I confess I felt I knew you all as friends, long before I ever saw you. This evening's enjoyment has been much enhanced by seeing your lovely daughters and dancing with you, Mrs. Bennet. It is not easy for a newcomer to feel welcomed in a strange neighbourhood, but your sister and your family have made us feel part of society here already."

As Mrs. Bennet's temperature subsided so did her anxiety. She felt perhaps she had been foolish to be so affected by Mrs. Long's vindictive remarks. As to her own dress, she now began to feel that she looked quite elegant and hadn't this handsome captain singled her out? She treasured up the compliments he uttered and grew calmer.

Her spirits brightened and she said "Captain Wainwright, I should hope you would always feel welcome in our home. Perhaps you and your son would like to dine with us next week? I am sure our table would be to your taste and liking. Our family would enjoy the visit exceedingly."

"How kind of you, Mrs. Bennet. James and I shall be glad to accept. If your dinner is as well dressed as the Bennet ladies here this evening, the feast will be excellent indeed."

Mrs. Bennet laughed at the captain's gallantry.

Mr. Bennet, having finished his novel, went in search of his wife and daughters. He found the latter first. Both were seated near the musicians. Mary was engaged in reading a letter, which she hastily concealed in her bag as she saw her father approaching. Kitty and Maria Lucas were talking with animation about their dance partners so far that evening. They all turned at Mr. Bennet's sudden approach.

"My dear Kitty, could you let me know where to find your mother? She does not seem to be in the place where I left her."

"I am unsure, papa. She cannot be far away," answered Kitty carefully.

All was chatter and noise now, as the music ceased and refreshments were announced. Beneath the twinkling chandeliers, faces glowed and the scene merged into a *melange* of colour from bright gowns, flowers and red velvet curtains. The warm scent of candles and perfumed shoulders rose with the voices. The group of revellers made their good-natured way to the refreshment room, via double doors that slowed the flood of people to a floral stream. Increased restriction heightened the level of conversation and bunching of the guests. Mr. Bennet was unable to make his way through and had to wait patiently, trying to see his wife. He found Mrs. Long at his elbow.

"Are you seeking your wife, Mr. Bennet? I saw her last on the arm of Captain Wainwright, disappearing away from the dance to a place of some seclusion. It may also interest you to know that your daughters were dancing with their tutors while you were absent. It distresses me as a friend, to say it, but perhaps you should pay more attention to the ladies of your household, Mr. Bennet. The whole of Meryton was tainted with the elopement of your youngest. It would be a matter of some consequence if history were to repeat itself."

With that, the formidable figure in grey swept past him and was gone. On finally arriving in the room set aside for refreshments, Mr. Bennet was in time to see Captain Wainwright kissing his wife's hand and making a low bow, before joining his son on the other side of the room. Mrs. Bennet looked flushed, but whether this was due to the captain's farewell, the heat of the room or her nerves it was impossible for her husband to ascertain.

June 15th

Oh, to be a woman of decision! Found myself in turmoil on three occasions—each more awkward than the last. All were connected with tonight's assembly.

Getting myself ready proved a turbulent affair; which dress? Which shawl? Which shoes? Three glasses of wine were insufficient to calm my nerves. Sister P. came to my rescue;

her benign wisdom conquering my bewilderment.

The behaviour of Mr. Bennet at this time was baffling in the extreme; first there was his compliment on my appearance (as unexpected as it was acceptable), to be followed by complete abandonment of us all once we reached the Assembly Rooms. Strange! It was this avoidance that was partly to blame for the worst parts of the evening.

It all began so well; the girls' excitement in the carriage was infectious and upon our arrival the assembly rooms sparkled with colour and light.

The introduction of Captain Wainwright and his son James proved profitable for they immediately asked my girls to dance (several envious glances from other girls seated nearby). The tutors came up next and whisked the girls away, there being no father near to refuse them. To my delight the captain next asked me to partner him. He was an entertaining companion and I did my best to speak of Mary. He seemed impressed by my description.

This was the last pleasant memory of the evening. Mrs. Long ruined it all.

She stood close by in the set and made several personal and wounding remarks about the Bennet girls. Before I could collect myself to intervene, she railed against me, commenting on my figure, temper and mental health. All her invective flowed so cruelly that my usual fortitude deserted me. The barbs made me catch my breath with surprise and horror. Uncertainty overwhelmed me. Should I try to reply? Should I go or stay?

The captain gallantly offered to escort me to a quieter place. But I was again unsure; should I refuse and offend him? Or accept his kind offer and feel the censure of Mrs. Long and other onlookers?

In hindsight perhaps I should have left alone, but undeserved rudeness to him was a stronger motivation than my neighbours' eyes. I allowed him to escort me to the refreshments room. Did I do wrong?

Perhaps I did, since the final awkwardness of the day was in the form of Mr. Bennet's disapprobation. He entered the room and saw the captain and myself in communication. I was speaking of Mary and because he was hard of hearing since his time in the navy, our chairs were close of necessity. Mr. Bennet spoke not a word in greeting. His heavy silence and hard staring betokened deep hostility. I tried to explain but he turned away. His cold indifference to my plight froze out any feelings of domestic intimacy on my part. A sorry end to an eventful evening.

Chapter VIII

When next Mrs. Philips found herself alone, an unusual occurrence, she made it her business to write a letter. It contained a matter of some delicacy since its main concern was a request for financial assistance. The recipient was her niece, Elizabeth Darcy. It says much for Mrs. Philips's beneficence that she was asking for a donation on behalf of her sister, Mrs. Bennet. She was well aware that the Bennets had little money to spare and that Mr. Bennet would be mortified if the request was disclosed, but she could not stand by and watch her sister suffer. She estimated that if the finance was offered by his favourite daughter, he might not sanction its refusal. Mrs. Philips aimed to suggest some practical use of the funds to aid her sister's return to health. She thought that a change of scene perhaps would benefit Mrs. Bennet. Since starting the course of treatment, Mrs. Bennet had begun to partially recover her former high spirits. It was necessary to ensure that the recovery was complete, so Mrs. Philips wrote to Elizabeth outlining the circumstances and hoped she would receive a favourable reply.

The notion had occurred to her last week when Mrs. Bennet related her quarrel with her husband over a wish to go to Brighton.

"Brighton? Brighton? Have you no recollection of the trouble that ensued from that infamous resort last year when we allowed Lydia to go?"

"But a little sea-bathing would set me up for the winter, I am sure. It is a very fashionable resort and I should be diverted from my present troubles."

The mention of 'fashion' and his wife's 'troubles' were the two least likely ways to persuade her husband of the benefits of Brighton.

"Madam, the society of that town has turned one head in our family, it shall not claim another."

"Nonsense, nonsense. Lydia would have eloped with Mr. Wickham if she had gone to any place of recreation. And since she is now a married woman, where was the harm, after all?" In this matter she and her husband were unlikely ever to agree, for Mrs. Bennet was untroubled by any sentiment of shame in remembrance of their youngest daughter's misconduct.

"Let your love of fashion be confined to window gazing in the locality and your change of scene to a ramble in the local countryside, Mrs. Bennet."

"So I am to be tied forever to Meryton?"

"Financial constraints and a sense of propriety dictate that this shall be so. Let that be the end of the matter."

Neither Mrs. Bennet's tears or her arguments could persuade her husband to change his mind. There was no reasoning with her, so Mr. Bennet left her to her own devices.

It was hearing of such distressing scenes that prompted Mrs. Philips to look beyond Longbourn for support. She trusted that Elizabeth would not think her too forward in such a request, but, from the knowledge she had of her niece's nature, hoped that the letter would not be received with indifference.

*

Mary had continued her private correspondence with Mr. Collins. The ever-lengthening letters were not disclosed to her family. She would meet the letter-bearer in the lane before he reached the house, then take any post for herself to her bedroom to read over privately. At each new epistle, Mary's demeanour grew happier. Over the course of his communications, the tone of his expression was changing; from cold civility to warm interest. She studied his recommended texts and wrote diligent replies, revealing the solidity of her reflections. Mr. Collins, for his part, found himself impressed by Miss Bennet's depth of understanding and had to admit to himself that he looked forward to the deliveries that were now becoming a weekly occurrence. In fact, he sometimes used her commentaries in his sermons.

*

It was in early summer when the parish were apprised of the intelligence that there was to be a church fete, raising funds for the wounded sailors of Longbourn who had fought in the great sea battles of the Napoleonic War. The fete was to be held in the grounds of the vicarage. There would be stalls and sideshows, food and drinks, flower and garden produce and children's races. The local gentry supplied prizes for the various competitions. The best of these was a large pig, which was to be awarded to the winner of the ninepins contest. Other attractions, such as wrestling and bare-knuckle fighting, had been considered then rejected on the grounds of its being a church fete and the feeling of those with influence was such that semi-clothed men contending in open competition would be improper. It was further recognised that such a spectacle would attract the rougher elements of the village and, worse, lead to gaming; an activity not to be encouraged.

The idea of the fete gathered strength. A date was arranged for the first day of July. Interest grew from surrounding villages and beyond. In many kitchens there was an increase in the baking cakes and pies. Store cupboards were looked into and those preserves that could be spared from the previous autumn's jam and pickle making were donated for the produce stall. Drawers of needlework were sorted and embroidered tablecloths, crochet mats and knitted shawls, which were surplus to requirements, were given. Soft fruits and summer vegetables from orchard or kitchen garden were loaded into barrows and carts, then trundled down the lanes to the vicarage.

The day dawned warm and with the sort of cloud that would burn off later.

Captain Wainwright and Sir William readily supported the scheme, travelling to various parts of the parish to collect bunting, awning and tables, just after dawn. James made it his business to set up the stalls with his father's able assistance. The tutors came early on the day to organise and swell the ranks of village men who were erecting a large marquee. Mrs. Bennet, Mrs. Philips and Mrs. Hill joined the crowd of women here to watch. Then as soon as the large white tent was erect, they entered and set up their tables for the sale of refreshments.

In a side meadow the elderly rector, Reverend Johnson, was supervising the flattening of the ground for the afternoon children's races. It was hot work for the roller was heavy. This monstrous piece of equipment was normally used for work on the cricket square and could only be operated by four men. The early morning dew had made the grass slippery and on turning the roller round, to flatten the course from the opposite direction, it had slithered sideways down a slight slope.

"Hold it lads!" shouted one of them, and the sweating men strained their utmost, their muscles taut with the effort. The rector moved as swiftly as his aged limbs would allow, in order to get out of the way. In so doing, his hat fell off and without thinking he turned and stooped to retrieve it, just as the roller started its second slide. His hand snatched at his hat, grabbed it and, looking up, the rector saw the roller thumping slowly in his direction.

"Hold it!" yelled the man again. The four men pulled back with all their might. The roller swayed back a little, veered to the right and, gathering speed, slid away from the men's control.

"Look out, rector!" they shouted. Reverend Johnson fell on his side and, with surprising agility, managed to roll away from the oncoming machine. All would have been well, but his frock coat-tails lay in the roller's path. They were caught fast. He frenziedly tugged at his coat-tails while the machine rolled over them. The men could hold the roller back no longer; its lumbering gait dragged the coat down the slope pulling it from its owner, over his head, trapping his face in the grass. The metal rollers were but a few inches from his head. Then the machine seemed to come to a halt. Slow seconds slipped by. Eventually the roller careered on its way, crushing the coat into the ground and leaving the rector lying gasping for breath in its wake.

One of the first to notice this incident was Captain Wainwright. He ran over to the gentleman and knelt down beside him. He felt for his pulse and was relieved to observe a trace of life. Gently he turned the rector face upwards and saw the old man's eyes open.

"My dear sir, are you able to speak?"

"Scarce—able—to—draw—breath, sir," wheezed the rector.

His face was pale and his chest heaved with the effort.

"Let me help you to sit up sir." However, this proved to be an impossibility, since he was too stunned.

Mrs. Bennet arrived at that moment and dropped to her knees beside the rector.

"Sir, I have a little balm here which may restore you." She dabbed some on to a handkerchief and wiped his brow, uttering soothing words, while the Captain ordered a hurdle to be sent for.

"A bad business, ma'am," whispered the captain to her. "I think the rector may be some time before he recovers, so another must take over his duties."

Led by Mr. Bennet, who had seen the accident from afar, two churchwardens and the rector's servant appeared, conveying water, blankets and a hurdle from a nearby field. The venerable gentleman was gently lifted on to it and carried to the house.

There was some consternation among the group who gathered round the captain and Mrs. Bennet. Some questioned whether the event should still go ahead. Others insisted it must. Captain Wainwright stepped on to a dais and surveyed the scene. The stalls were now erected, well stocked, with many goods on display. The early arrivals were streaming into the park, dressed in their best and admiring the fluttering flags and flowers Children ran excitedly through the throng, darting from one attraction to another. The church choir were looking agitated, as were the musicians. Would all their weeks of rehearsal have been for nothing? Those who had brought produce to sell were equally concerned. The children lost their exuberance and grew hushed as they saw the worried faces around them.

"Good morning to you all," began the captain. "You will have either witnessed or heard that an accident has befallen our dear rector. Mr. Jones has been called to his bedside and we hope to have intelligence of his condition before long. There is now a decision whether to proceed. I put it to you all. My own opinion is that we should seize the day. So much preparation has preceded this event."

Heads nodded.

He went on "After all, the cause is such a worthy one and I feel that Reverend Johnson would be mortified if the day was cancelled on his account."

More heads nodded.

"May I have a show of hands to show how you feel? Should we go ahead with the raising of funds for our naval heroes who lie wounded in our hospital at Greenwich? Shall we be the means of sending them some cheer?"

"Aye!" shouted the crowd.

"Well then," the captain declared. "Let the day commence. Choir master and musicians are you ready?"

"Ready and willing, sir," they severally replied.

"Strike up then, lads," he called out.

The band struck up "Hearts of Oak". The choir led the song and were joined, and nearly outsung, by the good people of Longbourn.

As the strains died away and the crowds thinned out to attend stalls, contests and refreshments, the Captain turned to Mrs. Bennet.

"Your prompt attention did much to relieve the rector's fears, Mrs. Bennet".

"Oh sir, you are too kind. A little lavender oil is all I provided."

"Nevertheless, dear lady, I have seen many a man on my ship in the heat of battle who, once struck down, and frightened of his wounds, loses his spirit of survival. And I have seen those same men revive and hope kindle in their faces when a kind hand touches them and a voice offers words of comfort."

He moved closer to her.

"A woman's gentle touch often restores a lost man in this lonely world."

Taking Mrs. Bennet's hand, the captain raised it to his lips in a gallant but tender gesture, then looked directly at her. Mrs. Bennet felt her breath cease and could not think clearly at all. Was the captain merely being a gentleman? Or was there another intention?

She turned away to avoid his gaze and to cover her confusion. In looking towards the rector's house, she discerned a familiar, if unwelcome figure, making his way purposely towards them. The captain loosed her hand.

"Good morning!" hailed the newcomer.

"Why, Mr. Collins!" exclaimed Mrs. Bennet. She wondered if he had seen what had just passed. Mr. Collins bowed to them both.

"Indeed ma'am," replied that gentleman. "Fear not that I am come to disobey your husband's last instruction to me, though I think it still a misjudgement. However, the Lord urges us to forgive. I came to visit the rector, who invited me to preach this coming Sunday. I arrive here to find he is indisposed. This surely is fortuitous. For happily I am free of duties in my own parish for a month, the bishop advising me to take a vacation, so I may take up the living here, till the dear rector is restored to health again."

Mrs. Bennet, hiding her irritation at Mr. Collins' unwelcome intrusion, with as much civility as she could command said "Indeed sir, I see that the coincidence may prove to be most useful to the church here at Longbourn."

She wondered how little social intercourse she might politely offer him during his sojourn in the district, without feeling the censure of the parish.

Mr. Collins smiled, then bowed to the captain,

"I am wondering, Mrs. Bennet, if the rest of your family is nearby?"

"They are all severally employed in useful or recreational activities within the house or gardens, sir," she replied. Mr. Collins bowed deeply to them both and made his way quickly across the vicarage lawns.

"It seems, ma'am, we are destined to be interrupted," Captain Wainwright said. He could see Mr. Bennet approaching and at some pace. Mrs. Bennet hastily smoothed her hair and dress and walked towards her husband.

"Ah, Mrs. Bennet. May I crave a few minutes of your time to discuss our daughters? Or am I calling selfishly upon your situation?" asked her husband. Here he glanced in the captain's direction.

The naval gentleman gave a graceful bow to Mr. Bennet, kissed his wife's hand elegantly and said, "Sir, I would in no way suspend any pleasure of yours." While this remark was directed at both, his eyes remained fixed on her. "Till we meet again then, ma'am. May that not be too long in occurring."

He was scarcely out of earshot when Mr. Bennet furiously began, "Well madam, there seems to be a noticeable lack of maternal duty this afternoon; first I find your daughter Kitty engaged in conversation, without a chaperone, in the shrubbery with Lieutenant James Wainwright. Then Mary is discovered with a tutor in the library, again, without a chaperone. I believe that we agreed our daughters were at all times to be supervised in others' company, did we not?"

"Which one, sir?"

"Which one? What on earth do you mean?'

"You did not specify which tutor."

"Does it matter, which tutor?"

"Indeed it does sir, for if Mary were with Mr. Lockhart then there would be little to concern you. But Mr. Chawton seems a more forward gentleman, altogether."

"That is neither here nor there" expostulated her husband. "The fact remains that neither should be alone in the company of young men."

Mrs. Bennet felt the urge to laugh on the tautology of her husband's remarks, for were the girls not receiving unchaperoned, individual tuition on a weekly basis? But he was not to be laughed out of his present mood.

"And where were you to be found, madam?"

"As you see sir, here."

"Yes, dallying with that upstart. It was Mrs. Long who alerted me to the situation and showed me, from the drawing room window, the pair of you together."

Mrs. Bennet made no reply. It was a moment of some tension, for she felt her complexion was reddened and she knew not whether to ascribe this to the presence of the Captain, her affront at her husband's unnecessarily officious attitude, or a heated flush caused by his comment. Was there some danger in spending time with Captain

Wainwright? Surely a secure married woman was in no danger when merely exchanging conversation with a widower? She recognised her own enjoyment of his company and admitted to herself that Mr. Bennet's lack of attention was not a positive factor. Should she avoid the captain's company in the future? There again, preserving the civilities with Captain Wainwright would seem an essential ingredient if she were to help Mary in the gaining of a husband. She could hardly turn him away. Besides, she had invited him and his son to dine next week. There was no escaping the meeting now. She would have to speak with Mr. Bennet and appeal to his better nature. Mrs. Bennet cut short her distant surmises and thought it prudent to reply by deflecting the argument from the captain to Mrs. Long.

"Mr. Bennet, it is a well-known fact that the lady you mention is a spiteful, hypocritical woman who is out to make mischief. Surely a man of your judgement will put no store by her remarks?"

This response caused him to consider its truth and while he was searching for a rejoinder, Sir William Lucas came across the lawns, smiling and calling out to him in his customary genial fashion.

"Why, Mr. Bennet, you have yet to roll up your sleeves and bowl for the pig, sir."

"I am occupied at present, Sir William, and would be obliged if you would take your request elsewhere," was his taciturn reply. Sir William's genial expression was tempered with discomfiture and glancing towards Mrs. Bennet he noted her serious countenance.

"My sincere apologies to you both. I am obliged to you for your attention. I leave you with my compliments. Madam. Sir," he nodded in farewell. Mrs. Bennet felt a genuine sympathy for their old friend as she watched his retreating back.

"Mr. Bennet, that was very remiss of you, to speak to Sir William in such a way. He is a neighbour and a friend. His invitation was kindly meant," said his wife.

"Insufferable fool! Now Mrs. Bennet, you will explain fully to me just what.." His angry admonition was curtailed by grating sounds from violins and cello, which set his teeth on edge.

The band was striking up again and couples were being invited to dance, the air being cooler now. Kitty and Mary joined them. They were wiping cake crumbs from their mouths and trying to regain composure as they looked eagerly at the scene.

"May I ask for your daughter's hand for the first dance, sir?" asked Mr. Lockhart, appearing at their side. Mr. Bennet was about to refuse, having seen enough men in pursuit of his women for one day. But recognising that this was not Mr. Chawton and seeing James Wainwright approaching (the greater of two evils) he felt he could at least keep an eye on all his ladies if they were on the lawn by the musicians in front of him.

"You may, Mr. Lockhart, you may."

Mr. Bennet wondered which daughter would be asked to dance and was annoyed to see it was Mary, since this left Kitty likely to be at the mercy of the young lieutenant.

"Well, I shall just refuse him permission," he whispered to Mrs. Bennet as Mary and her partner moved away.

"You will do no such thing," whispered his wife. "Kitty needs to smooth the way for Mary with James' father. Have you no wish to see your girls settled?"

It was difficult not to agree, so he brusquely acquiesced when James approached him. He turned to the smiling young man, saying "But one dance young man and one dance only, then return her to me."

"Indeed sir, you have my assurance on that."

"Oh papa, no need to alarm yourself, " exclaimed Kitty with a smile. "I shall be in good hands."

The following dances saw several changes of partner within the throng and Mr. Bennet grew quite giddy trying to keep an eye on both his daughters. Captain Wainwright, James, Mr. Chawton and Mr. Collins were among the revellers. Mr. Bennet made it his duty to be aware at all times as to their situations and note the expressions on their faces. Mrs. Bennet's feet were tapping as she watched. She begged her husband to dance at least once with her, but he was immovable. However, when Sir William appeared with Lady Lucas, he was unable to stand by any longer and was forced to pay her the courtesy of dancing at least once; so while his wife stepped out with Sir William, he took to the lawn with Sir William's wife. Despite himself, Mr. Bennet was compelled to make polite conversation, until the music ceased and he could bow, then retire to the side.

The band struck up once more and Sir William announced that this was to be "a cotillion". The dancers laughed and clapped, but what caused anger to rise in Mr. Bennet's breast created pleasure in Mrs. Bennet's when she found the captain in front of her. She felt herself in the liveliest of spirits at this coincidence. When the strains of the new set began they discovered to their delight that their steps matched well. It seemed that other couples turned their heads to look in admiration at such a competent performance. It was Mrs. Bennet's joy to feel such a rise in self-esteem and to be on the arm of the gallant captain. Her attempts to introduce the topic of Mary were met with smiles but no further exchange on his part. There was an open pleasantry between them and she resolved to enjoy the moment for what it was and face the consequences from her husband later. To the onlookers there was a brilliancy about Mrs. Bennet's countenance which exercise had given to her complexion. Her lively, sportive manner and his gallantry drew others' attention. It seemed to those who observed it that there was an affinity between the couple, which could not be denied.

Mrs. Long, on perceiving Mr. Bennet standing alone, passed behind him to whisper, "There is a saying, sir, which is universally acknowledged to be true; that to be fond of dancing is a certain step towards falling in love." Here she nodded towards his wife. Mr. Bennet's face expressed the vehemence of his disapprobation at the dancing couple but he directed his comments at Mrs. Long.

"Madam, there is an over-scrupulous attention and ill-judged officiousness in the affairs of my family that I must protest against. I would wish you to cease such circumspection."

"I speak only that which I observe, sir."

"Your ingenious suppositions are most unwelcome. I can assure you madam that there is nothing untoward in what you see," he retorted forcibly.

"Pray excuse my interference, sir. My observations are kindly meant. I leave you to your own conclusions." With these words Mrs. Long turned away with a sneer and departed.

It was a tight-lipped Mr. Bennet who seized the earliest opportunity to call for their carriage and accompany his family home. He admitted no protests from his daughters and made his hurried farewells.

While Mr. Bennet remained silent throughout the journey, his wife and daughters left no space for quiet reflection, but talked incessantly. Their united volubility put Mr. Bennet in an agony of ill humour. He allowed himself no comment on the day but sat silently in the corner of the carriage, resolving to utter his violent thoughts when he and his wife were alone.

"Well, my dears," began Mrs. Bennet. "What an agreeable time we have had! I am sure that no small amount was raised today for the wounded seamen. You both looked so lovely today. I overheard several compliments about the Bennet girls. Did you enjoy the fete?"

"Oh yes," smiled Kitty. "It was delightful to dance with James Wainwright and Mr. Chawton, though Mr. Lockhart said so little, I cannot think why he asked me. I may as well have been one of his still life arrangements rather than a living human being."

It was not until that evening when the girls had gone to their rooms that Mr. Bennet spoke to his wife. "Now we are alone, I may speak openly, Mrs. Bennet. After seeing the events of today, I have to broach a subject, which is causing me some unease. To be short, it is the attention that Captain Wainwright is paying you."

Mrs. Bennet coloured at this unexpected remark, then replied, "How can you talk so? Your concerns are without foundation, I can assure you, Mr. Bennet. You may depend upon it. Do not alarm yourself. It is only on Mary's behalf that I converse with him at all. He cares nothing for me, or only in respect perhaps of my position as a future mother-in-law."

"Be that as it may, madam, I shall remain alert to the situation. There will be no more occasions where you are at risk. You will shun society, at least for the present."

This instruction was sufficiently unprecedented and provoking to prompt his wife to an indignant response. "Now that I cannot allow, sir. Aunt Philips has invited us all tomorrow evening for cards. As for the captain, I have no intelligence of his plans. That is a matter between my sister and Captain Wainwright. The girls and I shall certainly attend. It will look ill and a subject for speculation if our family are not there. Even if you choose not to accompany us, then we shall be present and you may stay at home."

Mr. Bennet's customary tranquillity was lost at this repulse. His face and voice displayed a firmness that surprised her. "No, madam, I have had sufficient worries today; you will send your excuses."

She was incredulous at his obstinacy. "Am I to be kept as a prisoner in my own home?" cried Mrs. Bennet. This was shameful! The promised evening was a regular monthly engagement. "Am I not allowed to visit my own sister?"

"Madam, I have seldom played the heavy-handed husband, but after the worries our family have suffered over the wretched business concerning the elopement of our youngest daughter Lydia and the eagerness that the Captain displays in your company, I must be on my guard."

As Mrs. Bennet started to protest, he interrupted her by saying, "Moreover, madam, I have weightier matters to discuss with you."

"And what may they be, sir?" she asked, wondering what new rebukes were about to unfold.

"The account from the drapers and other creditors in Meryton came today. It would seem you have taken leave of your senses! How can these bills remain unpaid? When I agreed to a small sum for the clothing of our daughters and yourself, I did in no way imagine that it would amount to a month's income from the farm." He pulled some pieces of paper from his writing desk and spread them out on the table before her.

"You have been profligate, secretive and entirely without sense in this matter. Such irrational behaviour which your nerves have wrought upon you will render us a family of paupers in time, and all caused by your foolish expenditure." The usually mild tones of her husband had turned sharp and his austere countenance seemed to her to be one of a total stranger. Former indifference had turned to active contempt.

Mrs. Bennet, tired now from the exertions of this altercation, found tears spilling over and sweats of heat, then cold, flushing her body. She had never felt more wretched. The joy of the day had been stolen and she had certainly never felt so alone.

July 3rd

It is some time since I made the last journal entry—a full month or more. My fortunes have soared and dipped leaving me in the lowest of spirits. Events originated at the church fete. A morning of sunshine after a week of rain raised everyone's mood. This country festival involved the whole village; tents and bunting decked the green. It was sheer joy to fetch out summer bonnets and parasols. Mine had a small tear, but by turning it to the side I believe it went unobserved.

During the early preparations of the day an accident occurred. Our aged and rather deaf rector was almost bowled over by the heavy roller. Poor fellow! Captain W. was first to help and I supplied some small relief. Mr. Bennet organised the servants and a makeshift litter to assist the old gentleman into the house. The captain was touchingly appreciative of my assistance. His taking command of the situation was admirable. He made an heroic figure on the dais asking the villagers for their support. Such a handsome gentleman!

The dancing that followed proved the high point of the day, watching Kitty and Mary secure partners and the captain honouring me. I loved moving among the throng, my feet keeping time to the lively music. Excellent!

Alas, an altercation with Mr. Bennet ruined the day. He ridiculously accused me of becoming too close with Captain W. and tried to forbid me from society; in particular, our monthly engagement at sister Philips' card evening. How dare he!

However, I shall pay him no heed. The girls and I shall attend, despite his unreasonable orders.

There is now a deep divide between us. I am both furious and deeply saddened. Such feelings inflame the hot sweats, particularly at night when I toss and turn, unable to sleep. I thump my pillows in the greatest of despair. This journal is written at 3 am. I have not yet slept. My only dependable solace is wine, which I now find a nightly necessity.

Chapter IX

The following morning produced no abatement in Mrs. Bennet's condition; she had slept very ill and, though up, was feverish and not well enough to leave her room. Her head ached acutely. The energy of yesterday seemed to have belonged to another woman altogether; *she* had been a creature of confidence. Today she was in a misery of shame. On looking into the mirror, the face of a female twenty years older rebuked her. Had she been so very profligate of finances and modesty? She must surely be a person of some iniquity to have merited her husband's ire. Her mind raced over the events of the past few weeks and yesterday in particular. Was she totally at fault? Had she really encouraged a flirtation with Captain Wainwright? As to that, wasn't Mr. Bennet seeing more than was the truth? Oh, that wretched Mrs. Long with her sharp eyes and mischievous tongue!

She had imagined that yesterday she had looked better than of late, but was she deluded? Perhaps her choice of clothes in recent times was misguided and instead of appearing as an elegant, respectable matron, she increasingly looked a foolish old woman dressed in an inappropriately youthful style that had the ladies of the county laughing at her behind their false smiles. How unbearable!

And what if they shared her husband's thoughts on her behaviour? Did they regard her now as a wanton, trying to compete with her own daughters for the attention of the handsome widower captain? Was she, this very morning, the subject of wagging tongues throughout Longbourn and Meryton? Such humiliation! She felt she could never leave her house again.

There was a knock on the door. It was Hill.

"Pardon me for interrupting you, ma'am, but there's a letter come from Derbyshire. The rider wishes a reply by return. Mr. Bennet is away in one of the big fields on the farm, so I thought I'd do best to ask you, ma'am."

"Oh very well, Hill. Thank you. Bring the letter to me. It may be of some urgency."

Hill disappeared and soon after could be heard treading the stairs on her return.

The letter was in Jane's neat handwriting.

> *'Hanscombe House, Little Bolton, Derbyshire.*
>
> *June 26th.*
>
> *Dearest Mama and Papa,*
>
> *Forgive the brevity of this letter, but Mr. Bingley and I shall be shortly passing through the area on some business and we should very much like to visit. Would this be an inconvenience? We shall be travelling on the 20th July to Longbourn and would arrive around four o' clock. Our stay cannot be for more than four days, as further engagements in Derbyshire will necessitate our leaving you on the morning of the 25th. It would bring us both such joy*

> *to see you, Mary and Kitty
> again.Please could you reply by the
> messenger?*
>
> *Your affectionate daughter,*
>
> *Jane.'*

If anything could rouse Mrs. Bennet's spirits, it would be a visit from her eldest daughter. She stood only slightly lower than dear Lydia in her mother's favour.

"Oh, yes, yes," she said and looked up from the letter. "Hill. Quick! Please bring me my pelisse, then pen and parchment to reply. Make haste."

Upon being wrapped in her blue gown and seated at the little bureau, Mrs. Bennet penned the following reply.

> *'Longbourn, Hertfordshire.*
>
> *July 2nd.*
>
> *My dear Jane ,*
>
> *Thank you for your letter. It will give
> us the greatest pleasure to receive
> you and Mr. Bingley here.We shall
> look forward to seeing you as soon as
> the carriage may bring you!*
>
> *Yours in anticipation,affectionately,
> Mama.'*

The letter was despatched and Mrs. Bennet felt she could now bear a little breakfast. Hill was delighted to see her mistress improve in spirits. It was while she was carrying the tray to the bedroom that there was a further arrival at the house. Mrs. Bennet looked out of the window. It was a carriage holding her brother Gardiner, his wife and family. This was indeed a pleasure. They had been so supportive in the recent matter of Lydia and Wickham's marriage and had always regarded the Bennet daughters as if they were their own. When the carriage stopped, the two eldest children alighted and ran to the porch where, Kitty and Mary waited to greet them.

"Why, Tom and Celia, how much you have grown!" laughed Kitty as she embraced her cousins.

"How wonderful to see you again, my dear nieces," called their uncle fondly as he stepped out. His honest smile beamed upon everyone, then he turned to help down the rest of the family. "See, I have also brought Aunt Gardiner, Anne and William. We had the pleasure of our business being settled earlier than we expected and have taken advantage of the fair weather to travel," he said.

Warm greetings were exchanged on the sunlit path, then they all moved into the vestibule where Mr. and Mrs. Bennet (who had dressed with some haste) were waiting to greet them.

"My dear brother!" exclaimed the host, shaking his hand. "How very good to see you."

Both Mr. and Mrs. Bennet showed eager faces at this unexpected arrival. The house now rang with laughter as the younger members distributed themselves in all the rooms with impatient activity, soon playing with rediscovered toys and games. It was not long before they asked permission of their older relatives to play quoits in the sunny garden, leaving the others to sip elderflower cordial and talk.

"My dear brother," began Mr. Bennet, "it would give me the greatest pleasure to show you over the farm, if that would suit you?" Uncle Gardiner, a man of easy and pleasant manners, needed no second invitation to accompany him.

They left the house, with Mr. Bennet saying, "By the look of the young wheat, we entertain the hope that this year will be better than last."

Watching them go, Aunt Gardiner turned to her sister-in-law. She looked thoughtfully at her and began, "Dear sister, I have heard from Mr. Bennet that you are still troubled by your nerves."

"My nerves? Mr. Bennet has no right—" She shook her head and stopped. Aunt Gardiner sat patiently, waiting for Mrs. Bennet to continue.

At length she went on. "It is sadly the case that since last seeing you I have suffered much with The Change; the heats and chills, lack of sleep and incessant debilitation have rendered me a creature of low spirits. Where my former self has always been a social person of lively disposition, I am now an altered woman. 'The Change' is aptly named; I do not recognise my self at all."

Aunt Gardiner looked concerned. A lady of genuine kindness herself, she felt for her husband's sister. This stage in her life was not dissimilar from the one a friend had experienced only a short time ago. She knew how isolating the condition could be and the loss of self-esteem that accompanied it.

"Are you receiving any advice? How does Mr. Bennet show his concern? Are the girls sympathetic?"

Mrs. Bennet's face altered with every question. To the first she disclosed the aid the doctor's wife had given her and how grateful she felt.

"Sister Philips has seen my distress and alerted our doctor. I am now in possession of medication that may slowly be having a beneficial effect," she smiled bravely. "But Mr. Bennet shows no understanding at all!" Her face grew stiff with apprehension. "He ignores me by day, visiting his farm or retiring to his library, and has long adopted the custom of sleeping in another room. He persists in calling my distress 'your nerves' and has grown very short-tempered with me of late. Every day he finds fault. Only recently he accused me of being careless with our finances. He upbraids me for wasting money on treatments for myself."

"My dear sister, this is a sad state of affairs," said Aunt Gardiner. She went on to ask, "And what of your daughters?"

"Ah, there I have some comfort," Mrs. Bennet admitted, looking less perturbed. "Mary and Kitty are kind as far as they are able, but they are not Jane with her quiet ways and I confess sometimes their help is more of a hindrance. I fear that even their attentions may soon decline, since Mary is increasingly absorbed in her room, I presume with reading, and Kitty is succumbing to the charms of the outside world." Here she sighed, looking utterly lost.

"And does this heavy mood beset you every day?"

Mrs. Bennet glanced up and round the room. She paused to consider. In general she felt so altered and brought down by her symptoms that her secret fear was to remain thus for the rest of her life. The very notion filled her with dread. Furthermore, she was gripped by a deep anxiety that she might be declared insane. Her despair was evident in her lowered eyes and drooping shoulders. She had withdrawn into herself. Mrs. Gardiner gently reached for her sister-in-law's hand and held it.

It says much for Mrs. Bennet that she slowly responded to this affectionate gesture by returning the pressure and, looking round the room, said quietly, "I look for comfort where I can. Since starting the medication I have noticed a slight appeasement of my torments; although my moods are often dark and render me sharp-tongued, there have been times of brighter temper recently."

"And these are when, my dear?"

"They seem to happen mostly when I am away from the house. I attended the Assembly Ball in Meryton and the Parish Fete, where I found people who made me feel welcome and happy. In fact, there was one who …"

Here Mrs. Bennet's eyes grew bright and her cheek reddened. She paused and ceased from talking.

"Well, it would seem that being in society is one solution that would ease some of the problems," commented Aunt Gardiner. "By venturing outside the home, and mixing with others, you would view your situation from a distance and feel better about your troubles. All the family would benefit. People who approve of you would help you to regain your confidence. Such activities undertaken on a regular basis would raise your spirits. I shall speak to my husband about it and he will speak to Mr. Bennet. It would be to your advantage if he encouraged you to go out more."

Mrs. Bennet looked both relieved and thoughtful. The hope of a bridge being constructed between her and her husband was appealing, but she was uncertain as to how he would react to the proposal that his wife be seen more often in society. Would he not censure such exposure?

Kitty, Mary and the two young Gardiners appeared at the door declaring, in a variety of tones, that they were hungry, that Mr. Bennet was now in the house and that there were two gentlemen tutors at the door who were asking for the Miss Bennets.

"Goodness girls! Your lessons!" exclaimed Mrs. Bennet hastily. All was youthful movement and voices, as the elder girls were dispatched to the rooms for study, the Gardiner children to the kitchen to ask for small cakes from Hill, while the women took themselves to meet the host and his brother for a stroll in the grounds.

With the change of air and her kind relations present, Mrs. Bennet felt matters were looking less bleak. She carried a parasol to shade her and had changed into a cool muslin dress. In her pocket was a handkerchief soaked with lavender water that she might dab at her face if a hot flush should ensue. After some whispered discourse with her husband,

Mrs. Gardiner took Mrs. Bennet's arm in hers and led her into the shady walk, while her husband moved off in a different direction with Mr. Bennet.

It was a less openly hostile husband that greeted his wife next day. His words to her were more of a factual nature, than heretofore. He spoke to her in private.

"Mrs. Bennet, we have had our differences. For the sake of our visitors we should endeavour to keep the peace at least until their departure. Are we agreed?"

However, the passivity of his words was not supported by the speaker's tone or manner. His voice was cold and his face a stern mask. His wife nodded and silently assented. She felt physically unable to respond with the remotest degree of exertion. Mr. Bennet left the room, stating firmly, "We shall address each other with civility while under others' eyes, but in private, there need be no communication. Meanwhile, I shall oversee the education of our daughters, for their mama feels no other duty but wilful neglect."

Mrs. Bennet felt her eyes sting with tears. She was too well aware of her shortcomings to think her husband's remarks were untrue. She had hoped the Gardiners' intervention would bring reconciliation, encourage his understanding and generate some tenderness towards her. She fell asleep again in a stupor of sadness.

*

The tutors had spent their morning session with Kitty and Mary in useful study, while Mr. Bennet stood looking on.

"How are the girls progressing?" he asked.

Mr. Chawton drew forth the musical compositions each student had written and Mr. Lockhart showed their drawings and French exercise books. The young men stood anxiously by as their employer scrutinised the work. He made no comment on it but pursed his lips and said, "I should like to hear them play now."

First Mary, then Kitty sat down at the pianoforte. Their anxiety at having to impress their father was evident in tense faces and fixed stares at the music. But after breathing slowly to compose themselves, they each began performing with accuracy. The pieces were played with growing confidence and with no small level of fluency. Technical skill was evident and their fingers sped briskly over the keys. It was with modest smiles of pleasure that they concluded their work, before glancing at their father in enquiry.

"Well, you have not entirely wasted your time, gentlemen. You may continue with the lessons and I look forward to another recital next month."

Both tutors looked relieved and smiled at their charges. The girls glanced at their tutors and their father. All had gone well. Mr. Bennet departed and the studies were resumed.

After two more hours, the lessons were over. Mary left the room to find Aunt Gardiner, while Kitty took her books to the garden. Jane would be coming tomorrow and she had promised to return her sister's novel. Mary was glad to find her aunt alone, in the drawing room. She approached her aunt with a high degree of anxiety. There was much on her young mind and she needed to place her confidence in someone she could trust. After some initial faltering, she finally managed to say, "Dear aunt I am in need of your advice."

Mary stopped and blushed. She glanced at her aunt's face, and seeing an encouraging smile, said, "I trust you will not be startled by what I have to tell you, nor censure me until at least I have told you all." Here she paused, then gathering her courage she continued, "I have been secretly corresponding with a young man. I have told nobody except Kitty. She has been forbidden to tell anyone else. I am aware that this is not an honest state of affairs and am unhappy about the duplicitous nature of the situation. It places me in an uncomfortable predicament. I am torn between telling them what has occurred, as a dutiful daughter should, and keeping my secret; for I fear they may disapprove and then forbid any further correspondence. Oh aunt, please tell me what to do."

Alerted to this unorthodox situation, Aunt Gardiner refrained from comment, sensing that any judgement at this stage of the conversation might impede further revelations and perhaps prevent advice being taken. Instead she decided to try to elicit more information by asking her niece gently, "Have your parents met this young man?"

"Oh yes, but the circumstances were awkward. It all turned out so badly."

"Why was that, Mary?"

Here Mary explained the unfortunate visit by Mr. Collins. When she spoke his name for the first time she blushed. As her niece related those events, it was evident that she entertained a genuine interest in this young man, which was a cause of concern for Aunt Gardiner. To carry on a correspondence without parental knowledge or consent was a matter of some risk.

"May I ask how often you correspond and the nature of that correspondence? I do not wish to pry but I would be in a better position to advise you if I knew more."

Mary looked apprehensive at uttering details of a correspondence which had until this moment, been private. She twisted her hands in her lap then summoned up all her resolve to ask, "You will not let this be known to my parents if I tell you, aunt?"

"Mary, you know you may trust me. I am here to listen if you wish to share your thoughts, but shall fully understand if you cannot. I shall not speak of it to your parents unless you give permission," she said kindly.

"Well, we began by writing about theological matters. There was an exchange of biblical references and interpretations. His knowledge was illuminating and he was kind enough to say that my commentaries were interesting."

"That sounds very laudable, Mary."

"We started exchanging letters every few weeks at first, but, in recent times, have become more frequent correspondents. The theological discourse has deepened but, in addition, the letters are of a more personal nature now." She stopped speaking and looked out of the window.

Mrs. Gardiner was thoughtful at this silence. She was aware of her niece's change of countenance and conjectured that this might well be an indication of some commitment, at least on her side. She wondered how far Mary might have revealed her feelings to this young man. She waited until Mary looked again at her before she asked her next question.

"And how does this young man feel about you, Mary?"

"This is one of the complications. He tells me that he admires my thinking on theological subjects and has been kind enough to say he has not met any other woman so able to write such logical interpretations and commentaries."

"This seems to be a flattering observation. Has he made any more remarks of a similar nature?"

"Yes, aunt. He has stated that he finds most young women to be frivolous in nature, but is pleased to have found a sensible correspondent with serious views."

"And do such personal remarks please you, Mary?"

" I have to admit that they do. I find myself looking forward to his letters more and more."

"Do you think it might be prudent to confide in your parents about this correspondence, at this juncture?" Aunt Gardiner understood Mary's reticence, but was concerned as to the growing intimacy between their daughter and a relatively unknown stranger. Her niece looked apprehensive.

Perhaps asking Mary to reveal her correspondence to Mr. and Mrs. Bennet was a step too far. To urge her further was to invite rejection and perhaps turn Mary away from communicating with her aunt altogether. Yet she needed to know the extent of Mary's feelings for this man and if possible, his for her. Mrs. Gardiner tried another avenue.

"Are you hoping that the relationship will become more than merely one of acquaintance?"

Mary bit her lower lip in uncertainty. Was this indicative of her fear of revelation or her uncertainty over Mr. Collins?

"I believe I am, though I cannot be certain of the degree of my regard, nor of its own reasonableness, since our communication has been solely by correspondence. It is difficult to forward the relationship since he is forbidden from our house and lives in another county. We have not met face to face since his unfortunate visit to Longbourn. At least, that *had* been the situation until last month. It was then he came to be in Meryton, visiting Reverend Johnson. As you will have heard, due to the rector's accident at the fete, Mr. Collins was asked to stay on in the parish to take up church duties until he recovered. So I have seen him conducting the services when we attend on Sunday mornings. However, no situation has arisen to converse with him in private, so the exact nature of our relationship is still far from resolved."

Aunt Gardiner spent the next half an hour gently eliciting information as to suitability, respectability, occupation, intentions and background of this possible suitor. She was more than a little relieved to learn that Mr. Collins appeared to be a respectable clergyman and had a living in Chatham, though apart from the ability to write letters on a regular basis, his intentions towards Mary were by no means clear.

The auguries for their relationship had not been the most promising. Its beginning had been arrested from a smooth start by the preference of the gentleman for Mary's younger sister. Added to this, Reverend Collins' hurt feelings and resentment at the unexpected rejection of his marriage proposal to Kitty, the abrupt curtailment of his stay (when Mary might have reasonably hoped for a development of their relationship) and her own natural shyness, all contributed to the difficulties of progressing their intimacy. Aunt Gardiner was curious to learn the details of Mr. Collin's departure. She perceived that it was essential to regain Mr. Bennet's approval if Mary were to entertain any hope of a lifelong connection with the clergyman. On learning of the manner of his dismissal from Longbourn, Aunt Gardiner could readily see how the misunderstanding arose. Its effect upon any future acceptance of Mr. Collins by Mr. Bennet, was a barrier to be surmounted with no little degree of difficulty.

Mary tearfully continued, "In addition to the hostility with which my father regards Mr. Collins, I fear my parents may have another person in mind for my future. A naval widower has recently moved to Meryton. It would seem that my mother, at least, is eager to forward that acquaintance. The very notion of marriage to a man over twice my age who has spent his life engaged in battles at sea is abhorrent to me."

"Oh, Mary dear, I am sure your parents would not force you to marry such a man."

"I believe it is his financial standing that makes him an attractive proposition in my mother's eyes, aunt. And my father may easily be persuaded that this attribute alone would render the captain a suitable husband. They fail to see the goodness, meekness and quiet dignity of Mr. Collins and have completely misunderstood his character." Here Mary started to cry and her aunt held her in a comforting way until the tears stopped.

"Oh, do say you will help me," she sobbed.

Inwardly, Aunt Gardiner was doubtful as to her own influence in the matter, but she felt the necessity of offering her niece some support.

"I shall consider what you have told me while I am at Longbourn, Mary, and seek a way to help you." She realised that Mary's fascination with Mr. Collins was well on the way to becoming serious, but thought the likelihood of the captain ever being accepted by Mr. Bennet as Mary's husband was small. From the comments he had made in her presence and the open contempt he felt for his wife's erstwhile dancing partner, Aunt Gardiner guessed these emotions were improbable to alter. However, she felt she might offer Mary some temporary comfort.

"Dry your eyes, Mary dear, and hope for the best. Regarding Mr. Collins and Mr. Bennet, time is a great healer, they say. By the regular meetings at church, he may yet grow in your father's graces. It is probable that your own feelings for him and his for you will be strengthened while he is in Meryton society. And I think your fears respecting the captain are very premature.

"Regarding your anxieties about the secrecy of your correspondence, it may well be judicious to apprise your parents, once Mr. Collins is more favourably regarded. Of course, it would be wise to seek a propitious time. Meanwhile it might be best to confine your letters to matters theological. In this way you are placing yourself under no obligation to your correspondent or the likelihood of parental censure."

Aunt Gardiner privately considered that to keep the subject of her letters on such an academic basis might draw Mr. Collins to commit himself if he thought there was a likelihood of losing Mary, or it might show that he was never the potential husband that Mary hoped. In either case, Mary would at least know where matters stood. On the concern of telling Mr. and Mrs. Bennet about the correspondence, she thought the best course of action was to seek a time when the couple were in better harmony. Perhaps this might be when Jane and Bingley visited.

Kitty was wondering when her mother would arrange a date for the naval officers to join them for lunch. She was eager to see James again. She asked her mother at the end of the day when she caught her alone.

"My dear Kitty, should your father ever turn into a saint, then I shall invite young James Wainwright and his father to lunch, dinner or any meal. Till then my dear, I fear it doubtful that anyone with connections with the sea would be welcome to enter this house."

Kitty frowned. She knew her father was unlikely to deviate from his strict line on young men, particularly those with military or naval links.

"It is all Lydia's fault," she muttered fretfully to herself on the way to her room, where she slammed the door and slumped resentfully into a chair.

It was only the prospect of seeing Jane and Bingley that gave any of the Bennet family cause for happiness; Mrs. Bennet looked forward to Jane's soothing manner, Mr. Bennet to some intelligent conversation, Kitty and Mary to her impartial opinion and the Gardiners to a reunion with a favourite niece.

*

The Bingleys' carriage arrived during the afternoon, and all was joyful exchanges. During the week, Jane's presence in the house drew Mr. Bennet from his study and the warm weather enabled Bingley to take up country pursuits with his father-in-law and uncle. Jane endeavoured to share her time equally with her sisters, aunt and mother. She was quietly shocked at her mother's pallor, listless manner and inconsistent conduct. It was Aunt Gardiner who informed her of the reasons and history of the condition. Once acquainted with this knowledge, Jane went straight to Mrs. Bennet.

"Now, mama, you are not without care and support," said Jane. "I am here to help in any way I can. We shall go shopping in Meryton for some cooler clothes this morning and while there, can call on Aunt Philips. The payment for the clothing will be met by myself; Mr. Bingley gives me a very generous allowance which I shall spend while I am here."

"Jane, dear, I fear I am too tired to go anywhere today. You may go without me."

Despite her protests, Mrs. Bennet found herself taken in Jane's carriage to Meryton in the balmy sunshine with Aunt Gardiner on hand to provide advice. The summer fashions were on show in the shop windows and it was not long before they were bustling through Aunt Philips' front door carrying parcels from several commercial establishments.

Over tea, Aunt Philips sought their views on her plan to invite everyone at the Bennet house for an evening of light refreshments and various card games, with a view to spending much of the time al fresco. Aunt Gardiner told them of the proximity of Mr. Collins and wondered if he could be included in the party. She made no mention of Mary's feelings for him or their correspondence. Their hostess replied, "The weather promises to remain set fair so we may entertain in the gardens. Besides our relatives I shall be inviting several other local people and this will include our parish clergy."

While Mrs. Bennet was at first uncertain of the wisdom of including Mr. Collins, she thought perhaps it might be an opportunity for Mr. Bennet to set aside their previous differences and, in meeting on neutral ground in public, begin afresh. "After all," she surmised, "perhaps Kitty will see him in a new light."

The next evening it was Jane's pleasure to assist her mother in getting ready; she could see how Mrs. Bennet's lassitude slipped away with the enjoyment of wearing new clothes, having her hair carefully dressed and being generally cherished. She looked most becoming in her new pale lavender muslin pelisse and matching flowers in her hair. Aunt Gardiner said "Your figure is flattered by the cut of that new dress, my dear. It is a shade of mauve that suits your lovely colouring."

Mrs. Bennet was delighted at these compliments and felt herself to gain in strength. An afternoon sleep had improved her usual state of fatigue and she was looking forward to an evening in the presence of her sisters and the absence of Mrs. Long. Her heightened mood spread to the rest of the house. When her daughters entered her room they brought her some fresh white roses for a corsage and amid much laughter and advice they pinned them to her bodice.

"Why, mama, you will outshine us all" smiled Kitty.

With a somewhat pedantic air Mary added, "It is incumbent upon all persons to appear in civilised society displaying their most accomplished presence. Ladies may do their part in achieving this by first preparing with care that they may not be distracted by personal self-consciousness. This relaxed state of mind allows the personage to forget self and take interest in others."

"Oh Mary," laughed Aunt Gardiner, "if you mean that it is not mere vanity that causes women to delight in looking well, no-one here would disagree".

Mrs. Bennet, Jane and Kitty joined in the laughter.

"Of course," went on Mary, "it would be wrong to become excessively concerned with one's appearance but an acceptable amount is not unwholesome. Moderation in all things."

"Indeed, Mary." said Jane, "We shall take your moral code to guide us this evening. Kitty will only smile with two of her three dimples, Mama will laugh with her sisters for two hours rather than all evening, Aunt Gardiner will play vingt-un with a view to winning but by not too much and I shall...I shall."

She stopped to think what sanction she might put upon her own behaviour. Her mother smiled broadly and said, "and you, Jane, will try to think of a single tiny flaw in one person only, for the entire evening."

*

On entering the hall, they found the gentlemen already assembled. Their gaze showed more than any words how warmly they approved the ladies' appearance. Kitty and Mary were wearing the same dresses they had for the assembly but with fresh ribbons and gloves bought by Jane. Their older sister looked beautiful in cream silk gauze and Aunt Gardiner in a light green gown of delicately sprigged satin.

"Splendid! Splendid!" cried Mr. Bingley as he kissed his wife's cheek and took her arm.

Uncle Gardiner took his wife's hand and gave a gallant bow, while Mr. Bennet, after some hesitation, nodded to his wife and waved his arm to usher her through the door. She walked forward ahead of the group with her head held high. Her husband was joined by their two younger daughters, one on either side of him. They linked arms and as they did so, nudged their father's sides and nodded towards Mrs. Bennet's back. Mr. Bennet, feeling relaxed at the prospect of an evening in the company of his brother-in law and Bingley, was surprised at this heavy and somewhat painful hint. His daughters frowned up at him, expecting some gesture of warmth towards their mother, so he felt impelled to utter a compliment. He had to concede to a difference in his wife that evening, for she looked animated and radiant.

"Mrs. Bennet, you look lovely this evening. May I escort you to the carriage?" he asked. Mrs. Bennet was a little cautious. Was this some form of her husband's wit at her expense? Was it too clever for her comprehension? Might he in fact be about to prevent her going, even at this last moment? Or give some severe instruction about her behaviour tonight? But looking into his face she perceived no hostility. She felt assured of some warmth, at least on this occasion. Bobbing a formal and slightly self-deprecating curtsey, she smiled up at him.

"Why, thank you, sir. That would be most kind."

He took her arm and led her towards the waiting carriages. If Captain Wainwright were at the evening, he would ensure that he stayed by his wife's side at the card tables. As for her wasting too much money, he felt there he was secure. He had hold of the finances this evening so that at least she would only be able to play for small sums. He tapped his pocket. "If she wants any more, she may ask Bingley," he reflected as he handed his wife into the coach.

July 16th

Am growing wary of Mr. B's conversations. Accusations of maternal negligence are mortifying. It seems our relationship is to be Public Harmony, Private Discord. What a state of affairs! The kindness of Jane and Aunt G. cannot atone for a husband's indifference.

Tonight he paid me a compliment while the family were present; sincerity or sarcasm?

Chapter X

The arrival at Aunt Philips' home was enough to promote felicity in everyone; candles blazed from every window, garlands of flowers bordered the entrance gates, lanterns winked on long poles across the lawns and the musicians were playing lively airs that set feet dancing as the purple dusk descended. There must have been upward of fifty guests spilling in and out of the house and across the gardens. It was not long before the Bennet party was absorbed among the throng, the younger ones dancing and their elders talking as they stood by.

In a large drawing room away from the ballroom, several card tables were set up for games; commerce, cribbage, speculation, vingt-un and whist. Some were already full, so Mr. Bennet hastily joined a table where three gentlemen were already seated and was soon being dealt a hand of cards. He felt his duty to his wife was over for the evening as long as she stayed within sight. Mrs. Bennet was looking to find a table playing vingt-un, which still had room, when her sister Aunt Philips approached her.

After an embrace, she said, "Why how well you are looking, my dear. The lavender is most becoming and the cream corsage sets off your complexion perfectly."

"Your kindness is always welcome, sister. This is a splendid occasion. I congratulate you and Mr. Philips most heartily." They gazed around at the bustling scene.

"Before you sit down to cards, shall we escort your girls to the ballroom?"

"Oh, yes please, aunt " said Kitty. "I would far rather be there than seated at cards."

"I think that is a hint that they would find livelier company in that room," laughed their aunt.

They found some empty chairs at the side of the dancers, beside the Lucas family. Soon Kitty, Mary and Maria were engaged in conversation, glancing intermittently at the male partners in the room as they danced by. Under cover of the music, Aunt Philips whispered to her sister that Mr. Collins was at the gathering.

"Do you mind so very much, my dear?"

"Oh no, not in the least. It was only Mr. Bennet who took against him. Perhaps this occasion will see a renewal of his attentions to Kitty. I hardly think my husband will be so obdurate in public."

"You see, I was in an awkward position when writing the invitations; it was Mrs. Long who was asking him, right after the morning service, if he would like to attend her own soiree. It fell on the same day. She is of course, desperate to marry off her eldest; approaching thirty poor dear and so very plain, you know. Well, I knew you still had hopes of him for your dear Kitty, so I smartly pressed an invitation into his hand and said, loud enough for Mrs. Long to hear, 'Well, you are so sought after, Mr. Collins! But I shall take it very hard if you do not attend my evening function since the bishop will most probably be there.' He was aware of course that the bishop is my cousin.

"I could see his face alter at the thought of putting himself in the way of a senior clergyman. I added for good measure, 'And did we not mention a future engagement when we met at the rectory last week?' This completely discomfited Mrs. Long, who had attended that occasion herself and so could not really contradict me. Suffice to say, the dear man nodded assent and apologised to her; so the triumph was mine."

"Now that was clever of you dear," said Mrs. Bennet. She gazed across the room. "I do not seem to see Mr. Collins among the dancers yet. Is he here?"

"I advised him to beware of Mr. Bennet, at least until he has made contact with Kitty and made some progress in her affections. Despite your hopes, he may take some time to overcome her initial objections. It is possible that this evening may cast him in a better light for father and daughter. We must wait and see. I do not deny that it would be a prudent match for Kitty in many ways, though children do not always do what is prudent or accede to their mother's wishes. If there is a common consent, and you also alongside, I do not see how Mr. Bennet's objections can remain," said Aunt Philips.

Mrs. Bennet shook her head. "Ah sister, what it is to have ungrateful children who do not see what their parents do for them. My daughters all hold the foolish notion that girls should marry for love or not at all. If it weren't for the lack of an inheritance and the entail I might be minded to feel the same and make allowances for their romantic ideas. But if

Kitty and Mary are not secured in financial comfort by marriage they will be turned out of their home and live in penury. I am sure if Kitty persists in her stubborn ways she will be sorry for it, and when her father dies what will become of us all?" Mrs. Bennet was close to tears.

"There, there, my dear. Put your concerns aside for this evening. Your three eldest have married for love and two of these at least are unlikely to endure poverty. This must be a great comfort to you. As for your Kitty, it may be the case that Mr. Collins, by his work in Meryton and under the bishop's eye, may gain further preferment."

"Yes, yes, sister; there is much in what you say. I shall try to calm my unease about Kitty," said Mrs. Bennet. "As for Mary, there is the widower captain to consider. Would you have any notion of a captain's income? They say he was able to gain much from the capture of a French vessel a few years ago." She looked enquiringly at her sister.

"I have heard he was in a position of favour with the Admiralty after that naval engagement and the result was a very pleasant one of a substantial figure being granted; so a 'made man' my dear."

Mrs. Bennet felt gratified, and was mentally comparing the incomes of captain and cleric, while musing how soon they might become members of her family. She moved to the table nearby that was laden with wine. Before she could take up a glass, her sister intervened whispering, "I think not, dear. Have you forgotten what Mrs. Jones said about wine?"

Mrs. Bennet was irritated at this reminder. "Surely one small glass is not forbidden?" Mrs. Philips shook her head and wagged a gloved finger. "No. my dear. Here is a glass of elderflower cordial. You must be content with that if you are to get better." She stood over her sister while she reluctantly sipped the cordial, then excusing herself, Aunt Philips moved away to attend to her other guests. Her sister used the absence to pour a glass of white wine and swiftly drink it, before taking up the cordial again. Then Mrs. Bennet stood observing the room. She saw with pleasure how Jane and Bingley were received as they renewed their acquaintance with old friends. Yes, there were certainly some aspects of her life to raise her spirits. When the music turned to a lively country tune, the couple joined others on the dance floor.

Suddenly, Captain Wainwright stood before her with his son James.

"We present ourselves before the most handsome ladies in the room" began the captain, with a bow.

"May I beg the honour of your daughter's permission for the next dance, ma'am?" asked James.

Mrs. Bennet beckoned to her girls who were not far away and adroitly manoeuvred Kitty into the widower's arms while Mary was steered into James'. All four looked most discomfited, but there was little resistance to be had as the music struck up and sets were forming.

"How fortunate to find your mother in such good health," said the captain, spending more time gazing over Kitty's shoulder than paying attention to the progress of the dance.

"Indeed, sir". Kitty wanted to keep the conversation away from herself and found the time easily passing with discussion of her mother.

"It would seem we are connected by marriage, Miss Bennet."

"And how would that be, sir?'

"Your sister Elizabeth is married to Mr. Darcy and his third cousin is my uncle. They both live in Derbyshire."

"What a happy coincidence! Do you know if they move in the same circles?"

"I believe my uncle knew the family well when old Mr. Darcy was alive, but then moved to a further part of the county. Whether there is now a close connection between them, I cannot say."

"Perhaps we shall know more when next my sister Lizzy writes to us," replied Kitty.

Near them in the next set, Kitty could see her sister silently dancing with Captain Wainwright's son. It was her partner who looked animated, but not with Mary. She found herself totally unable to converse with James Wainwright as his sole topic of interest seemed to be naming all the commanders and ships of the British navy, and all the while he was staring across Mary's head at Kitty, in his father's arms.

Jane found the evening grew tiring and after sitting out the next few dances asked Bingley to take her home.

"Are you unwell my dearest Jane?"

"I am feeling a little fatigued. Perhaps the heat of the night air, the great crowd and the music have overcome me. I am sure a rest will restore me once we return to Longbourn," she reassured her husband whose face was full of anxiety.

"We shall leave at once," said Bingley.

So the carriage was called for, farewells given and the pair left.

The dancing continued with a variety of measures. After another two hours, Aunt Philips called the assembly to order. The musicians ceased and the party turned their faces expectantly towards the podium.

"My dear guests, we are in debt to our musicians but they need to rest awhile after their labours. And as your feet will tell you, if not your stomachs, it is time for refreshments. After that we shall play charades." Everyone clapped their hands, the card tables broke up and soon the tables of food were surrounded by chattering groups.

Mr. Collins found himself next to Mary as he fastidiously selected some of the plainer food and put it on his plate.

"Ah, Miss Bennet, what a pleasure it is to see you again." He looked at her with a smile then quickly glanced all round her to ascertain if Mr. Bennet was in the vicinity. It seemed that he had no need to be anxious at present. But the recent unpleasant experience at Longbourn led him to suggest, "Are you at liberty to sit in that alcove with me, Miss Bennet?"

She nodded, quite unable to believe that Mr. Collins seemed to be singling her out. She led the way to a window seat partially obscured by long curtains and they sat down to talk, unobserved. They ate in silence for a few moments. Then Mr. Collins wiped his mouth with his napkin. He cleared his throat and said, "Miss Bennet, I am obliged to you for your illuminating correspondence."

"Thank you, sir" said Mary. She hoped the 'illumination' might be due to emotional insight as much as to religious enlightenment.

"I am in grateful receipt of your deeply thoughtful utterances and have used them as a basis for many of my sermons in Rochester. Indeed the Dean was so kind as to comment on one address when he honoured our Matins service with his presence last month."

"Am I to understand, sir, that you appreciate my letters as a theological friend?"

"Indeed I do."

Mary felt that she was at an important crossroads. If Mr. Collins viewed her solely as a fellow student of religion, then she would need to know this immediately. He would be gone in a few days and this would be the only time they would be alone. Her nature made her reticent, but if the relationship remained unqualified, there would be merely a continuation of friendship. She decided to take her courage in both hands and said, "Mr. Collins, I wish to ask you a question of a personal nature. It is one whose answer is of some interest to myself. I hope you won't think me too forward in requesting if you are still in the way of pursuing my sister or is your heart free to care for another?"

She dared not look at him. She hoped he would give her a swift reply to inflate or deflate her hopes. It was a moment of great anxiety for her. She watched Mr. Collins slowly put down his cake plate on the carpet. Then he turned his full attention to Mary.

"Miss Bennet, as you know, I was in pursuit of your sister …"

"Yes, yes, I know, Mr. Collins. Pray tell me if you still have ideas that tend in that direction." Mary was conscious of several people moving towards their alcove. One of them might be her father.

"Well, Miss Bennet, the urging of my premature exit from Longbourn by your respected father has forced me to reflect—"

"What have you decided? Do you still maintain an interest in Kitty?" asked Mary bluntly, her cheeks reddening with humiliation.

" Of course, no man would willingly admit to a failure in placing his matrimonial interest on a woman who spurns him—"

The group had moved nearer. Mary could discern her uncle's warm tones and where her uncle was, her father might also be.

"Mr. Collins," she said in a forcible whisper, "are you at all interested in any other woman as a prospective wife?"

Mary blushed to the hair roots at her own boldness. She immediately wished the words unsaid. "What a fool he will think me," she silently conjectured. She had never known such horrible embarrassment. Would he understand what the question implied?

Mr. Collins did not reply. He looked astonished. Was his sense of propriety offended? Mary was in an agony of suspense. She felt a chill of cold perspiration and a turning of her stomach. If only he would speak. Even a harsh rejection was preferable to this state. He looked at Mary as if seeing her for the first time and blinked. His face wore a thoughtful expression and he opened his mouth to speak. Getting only as far as, "Miss Bennet, I believe—" when the group rounded the velvet curtains and Mr. Bennet's was the first face that appeared. Each could not have been more surprised.

"Mr. Collins!"

"Mr. Bennet!"

"Papa!"

It was Mr. Bennet who spoke first. " Sir! What do you mean by—" but it was Mr. Collins who cut off the speech by standing quickly (albeit on the plate, which gave a dismal crack) and nearly shouting in his efforts to maintain his courage, he stuttered, "Sir, despite the ignominy that has blighted your family due to a certain young lady's reprehensible behaviour, she is now a married woman and dwells in a county far from here. As an unselfish and magnanimous act, I am at some pains to share with you my matrimonial interest in your daughter."

"What?" cried Mr. Bennet. "Which one is it this time? Or are you still hoping to commit bigamy?" Mary's face registered two emotions; disbelief at Mr. Collins' words and fear at her father's fury.

"No, sir. I wish to ask your permission for the privilege of courting Miss Bennet." He bent down in front of Mary (kneeling on the broken plate). " If she will allow me?"

He looked so piteous, that even if he were not asking for her hand, she would have still felt compassion for him and granted his request, but a glance at her father kept her rigidly silent. She felt her breathing become rapid and shallow. Could Mr. Collins really be serious in his request? And if he was, would this moment of hope end in nothing? She looked up at her father and before he could give further vent to his feelings, she gave Mr. Collins her approval.

"Oh Mr. Collins, of course I will!" Mary said. She turned to look at Mr. Bennet and pleaded, "Oh please father, please give Mr. Collins that permission."

Mr. Bennet was robbed of speech. His tumbling thoughts went from "Bounder!" to "She will get no other offers" to "He has a comfortable living" to "Which is far from Longbourn" and finally to " Thank goodness." He swallowed, as he thought how best to deal with this sudden event. Mr. Collins tried to get to his feet with as much dignity as he could manage. Pieces of cake and broken china adhered to his dark trousers. He thought that if rejected, a noble exit walking would be better than an ignominious crawl across the carpet.

There was a long silence and no movement save the slow falling of cake crumbs and shards of broken china. Mr. Bennet looked hard at each of them, read the true hope in his daughter's face and the earnest desire in Mr. Collins and thought deeply. He believed they would have as much hope of happiness as most couples, with at least the love of theological books in common. And if this evening were any harbinger, this latest Bennet son-in-law would provide him with as much amusement as the other three. He stood up straight (dwarfing Mr. Collins by several inches) and said seriously, "This has all come as a great shock to me, sir. My instinct is to allow you no access to my family ever again. However, it would seem that my daughter Mary appears to hold some feelings for you. How this has come about I should like the two of you to explain. It is a circumstance that mystifies me and will need to be fully investigated.

"As to your sincerity, I am in great doubt that you are a man who is capable of commitment, since you appear to change your mind so often. In time I may give the union my approbation Mr. Collins, but only if you keep to one woman and that woman is Mary. You must earn my trust and prove your suitability. You may have gained Mary's affection but you will have to wait a considerable time before you receive her parental consent. This is a possibility only young man, so assume nothing at present."

Despite hearing these conditions, it is difficult to overestimate the delight that Mary and Mr. Collins felt in hearing that decision. They registered their joy in similar ways; each with hands clasped together as though in supplication, eyes raised heavenward and breathing sighs of pleasure. This would have been followed by a lengthy address from the clerical gentleman and some worthy thoughts by his future wife, but Mr. Bennet held up his hand.

"No need to thank me. You may both attend my study in the morning and matters will be discussed more formally then. Until that time, breathe no word to anyone. Meanwhile, Mr. Collins, you may partner my daughter for the next two dances only and both of you will remain under my observation throughout the evening. The Bennet family will stay for the charades and then our party will retire. The hour is late and I have a round of whist that I intend to undertake before the evening ends." Mr. Bennet hurried away, leaving an open-mouthed daughter, uncle and cousin.

"Ladies! Gentlemen!" called Mrs. Philips from the ballroom. "Pray finish your refreshments and return for a game of charades."

Chairs were pushed back and crumbs wiped from clothing as the eaters turned to thespian matters. Laughter and gentle chiding filled the air.

"I'm sure I shall be no use at all," said Lady Lucas to her husband, following the throng.

"Nonsense, nonsense, my dear. All in good part, all in good part."

Mrs. Bennet turned her head to laugh, "Lady Lucas, you will recall the many charades we undertook when young women. How we confused and performed with such confidence, did we not? Let us show that we are not quite past the use of our wits yet!"

Her high spirits made Lady Lucas smile, but a more sober Mr. Bennet looked less than happy at the thought of his wife displaying her talents. Whether he was more reconciled to her low spirits or this present playful mood was uncertain. He resolved to slip away from the actors should either prevail. He had suffered sufficient embarrassment at the exploits of the female Bennets in society to last a lifetime. However, Uncle Philips had other ideas and barred his escape. "Now then brother," he laughed," I know you and I would prefer a game of cards and a glass of port, but we must humour my wife this evening. She has gone to so much trouble in preparing tonight's entertainment and as family, we men should show our support, don't you agree?" Mr. Bennet felt he was not in a position to refuse. He looked around him. Among the crowd near his sister-in-law he caught sight of Captain Wainwright. Perhaps it would be wise to take part after all. So with as much good grace as he could command, he said, "Of course, sir, it would be my pleasure on this occasion."

Aunt Philips smiled and held a large hat aloft.

"Now everyone, the actors will be chosen by lottery. Those who draw a paper with a cross on it from the hat are to perform, the rest are audience. The rules will be explained once the actors are decided." There was much excited chatter as each guest drew a paper from the hat and faces registered the outcome with smile, frown or nervous laughter.

"Those with crosses, please step forward while the rest arrange your chairs at one end of the room. The observers will be our riddle solvers and judges. Please take the papers and pencils being handed out and write your names on them. You may enjoy your conversations until the rehearsal gong sounds, signalling that the performances are starting."

Aunt Philips divided the selected guests into three groups and gave out slips of paper. She proceeded to explain the simple rules of charades and established that each group understood. This game was new to English society, but had attracted old and young in its appeal. Each group was given fifteen minutes to prepare before presenting the piece to the other guests. It would then be the task for the observers to write down their guesses. Mrs. Bennet was with Lady Lucas in a group that also contained Captain Wainwright, Mr. Chawton and Mrs. Jones.

On seeing this, Mr. Bennet, who was among another acting group, did not relish some of that combination, but endured it as a temporary evil.

"Pay attention Mr. Bennet, I beg you. We have only fifteen minutes," called Mrs. Gardiner from their corner of the room where Sir William, Kitty and Mr. Lockhart were all poring over their paper. Much whispering and some gesturing was already being undertaken.

A third group, containing Mr. Gardiner, Mary, Mr. Jones, Maria Lucas and James Wainwright were huddled in another corner. All talked rapidly, discussing scenes and strategies.

During the next quarter hour, the groups puzzled over their papers, muttering in low voices. Some were breaking into movement. There was an expectant buzz in the room.

It was not long before cries of laughter were issuing from Mrs. Bennet's group.

"Hush," said Mrs. Jones. " They must not hear our plans", as she glanced round the ballroom.

"Remember" called Aunt Philips "There is to be no mention of the actual word, or a syllable of it. There will be prizes for the best performers!" she added as an inducement.

In rehearsal, the groups discussed, disagreed, experimented, acted, improvised, sang, danced, found or created costumes, and declared, all in such a range of voices, modes, rhythms and variety, that to an impartial observer, the ballroom resembled an exuberant gala of sound and colour. All was carried out at a frantic pace; steps and scenes rehearsed, reworked, dropped, then reinstated. Sometimes everyone in the group would agree, sometimes all but one, sometimes all disagreed. When this occurred, the despair was prodigious. Then, with redoubled efforts, the actors would begin again.

Aunt Philips rang a dinner gong to signify time and beat the metal pan with some vigour.

"Cease, I pray you! Your attention please! Not one moment more! Will the audience take their seats at the end of the room? We shall observe each group perform its charade. There will be five minutes permitted to discuss the riddle with your neighbours and write down your answer. This must be handed to me, before the next group performs. Actors in the first group, please take your places on stage. Good luck to everyone!"

After a shuffling of chairs by the audience, each neck craning to ensure a better view, there was a respectful, if somewhat excited, silence.

The first group containing Mary, Mr. Gardiner, Mr. Jones the apothecary, Maria Lucas and James Wainwright stepped forward, all looking rather nervous.

Mr. Jones, in a strong thespian pose and resounding voice, read the first line aloud:
"My first is a hindrance, my second a snare".

Maria Lucas stood centre stage, looking cross. In front of her the other actors stood in a line. After this the group changed position. Maria now knelt fearfully on the floor, while the rest stood round her in a circle, entrapping her.

The second line:
"With nothing between them I boldly declare"
was enacted by the whole group in a circle, tilted towards the audience in the shape of an O.

The third line:
"My whole is a title, sometimes a reward"
showed Mr. Gardiner miming the giving of gifts from an imaginary basket to a grateful, beaming group. The final line was spoken in unison.

Mr. Gardiner then read the whole riddle again.

"My first is a hindrance, my second a snare
With nothing between them I boldly declare.
My whole is a title, sometimes a reward
Of Value and Science, but it's not a lord."

The group bowed and polite applause flickered around the ballroom. The actors looked flushed but relieved.

"Five minutes to write down your answers!" called Mrs. Philips to the audience.

Heads were bowed over their papers, while the second acting group came on to the area designated as a stage. The performers were led by Mrs. Gardiner, who was clearly enjoying the game; she was accompanied by Kitty and Sir William. The three were followed hesitantly by Mr. Bennet and Mr. Lockhart. The former wished he were home in his study and the latter his studio. But obliged to display their charade, they took up positions assigned to them by Aunt Gardiner. Her face was full of fun as she draped a piece of white muslin around Kitty's waist and wound some flowers (culled from a nearby vase) into Kitty's hair.

While this preparation was proceeding, Mrs. Philips' maidservant collected the audience's papers. Some of them were still blank as they called out, "Too soon, ma'am". But the hostess was firm and papers, written or blank, were placed in her basket.

The second group were more inventive altogether than the first; apart from the muslin-draped Kitty, there were costumed actors in the forms of Mr. Lockhart, Mr. Collins, Mr. Bennet and Sir William, who wore scarves tied over their faces, black hats pulled down low and black capes hanging from their shoulders. The garments had been temporarily purloined from the cloakroom. Mr. Bennet, at least, was pleased to be virtually incognito. The men stood stiffly with arms folded at the back of the stage. They made a menacing group.

(Mrs. Bennet wondered how rehearsals had gone between the clergyman and her husband).

Mrs. Gardiner, clad in a yellow turban and cape (that Mrs. Bennet recognised immediately as belonging to the hostess), clapped her hands loudly for attention. She stepped forward in a confident manner to face the audience, pointed her arm at Kitty and read out the first line of the riddle.

"My first is a task of a young girl of spirit".

Here Kitty stepped forward, skipping enchantingly round the stage, then sank gently down. She made an expressive mime of sewing, while seated on the floor.

In the audience James and Mr. Chawton were fascinated by the Bennets' daughter; gazing at her light figure in the movement and admiring the change of mood as she gracefully descended to the carpet. The latter gentleman thought how much she had improved since her early dancing lessons with him. He felt the danger of attraction and his imagination led him to wonder if her feelings might be similar. James' thoughts also turned to romance, envisaging Kitty as a Naval Lieutenant's wife and how pleasurable it would be to find such a lovely creature at home when he returned on shore leave. Further surmise was cut short, as Aunt Gardiner made a show of weeping as she sadly delivered the line,

"And my second confines her to finish the piece".

At this, the four dark figures moved forward and circled Kitty.

They all pointed a finger at the cowed girl, who continued to stitch her imaginary cloth. Then, a single gesture of turning a key, was performed by the men in unison.

The third half-line, *"how hard is her fate"* was delivered by them all in a sharp tone. It was well done and could have been pronounced excellent, had not one masked figure, whom we must presume to be Mr. Collins, not said 'mate', rather than 'fate' and this, half a second behind the rest. Then realising his error, he broke the dramatic tableau by stuttering, "Oh, I mean, fate. I am so very sorry. How foolish of me." He raised his hand to his face in embarrassment and turned to the narrator, expressing his sorrow further.

This drew conspicuous glances from his fellow-performers and chuckles from the audience.

Mrs. Gardiner rescued the group from total disintegration by waving her hand gracefully at Kitty, stepping in to the circle to say, *"how great is the merit"*. Then she gently raised the young girl to a standing position, while bringing forth a small vial containing red liquid. While she held this aloft, she dramatically cried:

"If by taking all, she affects her release!"

Kitty took the vial, held it in front of her, with a look of fear. She took one glance at the menacing figures behind her and resolutely drained the vial to the last drop. The audience gasped. Kitty stumbled gracefully across the stage, first one way, then more slowly the other, before falling down in the arms of Mrs. Gardiner.

The men adopted poses of extreme surprise and remained in that frozen posture, creating a stunning tableau of black, satanic figures surrounding the white-clad victim. It was spellbinding. The room was silent in admiration. After a full minute, Mrs.

Gardiner and Kitty moved and all the actors bowed. This charade was greeted with a gust of loud applause.

"Bravo!" called James Wainwright. Not to be outdone, Mr. Chawton called " Encore! Encore!'

This provoked a second bow from the men and graceful curtsies from the ladies.

"To repeat," said Aunt Gardiner, "here is the riddle:

My first is a task to a young girl of spirit,
And my second confines her to finish the piece.
How hard is her fate! But how great is the merit,
If by taking all, she affects her release!"

Once more the audience members puzzled over the word and after the permitted time, Aunt Philips collected the papers.

By now, the atmosphere was charged with excitement.

The final group stepped forward. This comprised: Lady Lucas, Mrs. Jones, Mr. Chawton, Mrs. Bennet and Captain Wainwright. Mrs. Bennet looked radiant in a gown made from swathes of scarlet silk (part of the dining cloth from the refreshments area),with a headdress of crystals and pearls (contrived from the glass table decorations and her sister's necklace) and carried a small, gold harp (taken from a Christmas box). The Captain was in his full naval uniform, with a magnificent cockade of white feathers and a sword on his hip. The pair fairly glowed, as they stood side by side.

Mr. Bennet, in the audience, watched with some unease.

The two other ladies were elegant in green fabric (the hall curtains) and Mr. Chawton, in top hat and frock coat, was all formality save for a large, white soft bow tied under the chin. He held a violin. John Chawton bowed and introduced each actor and the roles they were to play. This brought a touch of sophistication to the performance. After her introduction, Mrs. Bennet left the stage.

The group adopted a pose: the captain lay across three chairs covered in green velvet. Lady Lucas and Mrs. Jones dressed in green stood behind him with arms delicately held aloft.

The scene began with Mr. Chawton playing a familiar, romantic air. The ladies started gently to wave their arms while softly singing the line:

"You may lie on my first by the side of the stream."

The sound was enchanting, for each of them had a beautiful soprano voice. They repeated the line with volume varying between mezzo forte and pianissimo, but always in rhythm to their swaying movements. The audience were completely absorbed.

As the music died away, Mr. Chawton changed the mood with a more lively pace on the violin and sang the second line of the riddle,

"And my second compose to the nymph you adore," in a fine baritone.

As he sang, Captain Wainwright slowly rose to a sitting position. He drew a paper from his pocket and with much exaggerated action, mimed the writing of a love poem. His constant stopping for inspiration, clapping his hand to his brow and sucking his quill, brought forth gales of laughter. Each love-torn effort was read over, then furiously scored across as if unworthy of his beloved. He left the seat to stride across the performance space, back and forth, lost in mental effort. Occasionally he halted, his face alight with inspiration, which was swiftly followed by more scribbling. His scroll of paper became longer and longer, as each line was set down, till the end of it rolled out into the audience. This brought more laughter.

Just as he began to roll up the interminable ode, his eye was caught by something off stage. The audience followed his stare. He stopped suddenly, as if stunned and became transfixed as the scarlet vision of Mrs. Bennet glided from the wings. Her movement across the stage was mesmerising; her feet were on tiptoe so the effect was one of floating rather than walking.

She paused at the front of the stage upon a low pedestal and stood perfectly still, looking like a goddess, her red silk garment fitted becomingly to her full but statuesque figure. Her face gazed into the distance, a picture of serenity.

She completely held the audience's attention. This was a Mrs. Bennet who had poise, beauty and control. Her own family were astonished, barely recognising her as the same driven woman who dwelt at Longbourn.

The violin softly began again and the captain came out of his trance. He let the poem fall to the floor and approached Mrs. Bennet. She turned gracefully to look at him. He doffed his hat and made her a gallant bow. He took her hand and kissed it. She gazed into his eyes and smiled. They made an attractive couple. He lifted her down and carried her to the chairs, where they froze in an amorous embrace.

Mr. Bennet looked unmoved, but the rest of the audience was smiling and sighing in sentimental approval.

A sharp chord from the violin changed the mood. The couple broke apart. Behind them the women sang in a forte staccato:

"But if, when you've none of my whole,"

The couple gazed in surprise at each other. The singers pointed at them and sang:

"Here esteem and affection diminish."

The couple drew further apart. Their faces registered differing emotions as he looked at her with dismay and she at him with pity. Captain Wainwright stood dejected. His hands pulled out the insides of his pockets. He looked thoroughly helpless.

Mrs. Bennet sang in a wistful voice,

"—think of me no more!" She appeared to be battling with inner turmoil, her brow furrowed with care, her hands raised as if to ward off the tragedy engulfing them both. His face was turned to his 'inamorata' in mute appeal, but Mrs. Bennet turned slowly away, looking immensely regretful and gracefully left the stage.

The violin played a doleful tune as the captain sank on to the chair with his head in his hands. This pose was held as the music played out its melancholy notes and the 'willow trees' waved their arms in time. The scene finished with the sad refrain repeated as if in echo by the singers:

'no more, no more, no more,' dying to a whisper, then away into silence.

This tableau was so affecting that several watching females dabbed their eyes. There was a quiet in the room that nobody wished to break; it would be intruding on the rejected lover's grief. Even Mr. Bennet was moved. He looked exceedingly thoughtful. From his former positions of anger and indifference towards his wife, he had been overcome with another emotion; that of self-doubt. The silence was eventually broken by the audience, who loudly applauded, their white-gloved hands fluttering like so many doves.

All the actors came forward and stood together on the stage. They linked arms and bowed.

Aunt Philips called out, "Listen to the riddle again before you write your answers."

Mr. Chawton recited in a voice filled with emotion:

"You may lie on my first by the side of the stream.
And my second compose to the nymph you adore.
But if, when you've none of my whole, here esteem
And affection diminish—think of me no more!"

The whole presentation had been so polished that it was the triumph of the evening. Everyone was calling "Encore!" and "Bravo!" while their hands clapped and clapped again. For the final time, Aunt Philips collected the papers and the audience broke into chatter. Performers mingled with those who had merely observed.

"Capital! Capital!" said Sir William Lucas, beaming.

Kitty darted across the room to hug her mother.

"Mama, you were wonderful! You look so lovely!"

Mary, with a little more reserve, approached her mother saying, "An accomplished performance, mama."

Mrs. Bennet looked round for her husband, but he had disappeared. "Is he so ashamed of me?" she thought.

For a second, she felt a plunge of low esteem, but when she saw the eager faces and heard the praise for the charade, she knew she had done well.

The captain stepped smartly to her side and kissed her hand.

"A nymph worthy of adoration," he whispered, looking into her eyes. She could not help but feel happy. What a very long time it had been since she had felt so assured or received such attention. Aunt Philips and the Gardiners surrounded her, smiling their approval.

Kitty found herself dwarfed by the tall figures of James Wainwright and John Chawton. Mary looked unsurprised to see the masked man unmask as Mr. Collins.

The charade gong was sounded again and Aunt Philips announced, "Your attention please. The answers to the three riddles are as follows: the first was 'Baronet', the second 'Hemlock' and the third, 'Banknote'."

At these revelations everyone broke into either exclamations of surprise or nodded with agreement. The animated chatter went on for several minutes, until Mrs. Philips raised her voice again.

"And now to our actors. Would they kindly enter the stage again?"

The fifteen thespians, still wearing costumes, moved to the area. They again received a round of applause.

"As I am related to several of these worthy participants, I have asked a local attorney and his wife to be our judges. There will be no dispute that needs taking to court, I trust," she smiled.

The adjudicators came forward amid a tide of general agreement. Mr. and Mrs. Walton were a well-respected couple in Meryton. Their cheery countenances beamed at the crowd. Mr. Walton coughed and drew himself up, a commanding figure. He rustled his papers and waited till there was silence. In a deep, measured rumble he began.

"For best group I think there will be few voices of dissent in my choosing the third group." This utterance raised a general cheer.

"For the best performer, we had much more trouble. The choice would seem to lie between two strong contenders: Captain Wainwright and Mrs. Bennet. So I have made it a joint award."

The group rose to receive prizes of wine, then three stepped back to leave Mrs. Bennet and the captain at centre stage. They stood arm-in-arm, laughing, enjoying the moment as the whole audience rose to applaud.

Mr. Bennet was standing to the rear of the throng and found Mr. Gardiner at his shoulder. The latter gentleman whispered to his brother-in-law, "A wise man would take heed of tonight's events. Your wife has blossomed in the attention she has received. It would seem a good time to renew your own. The riddle reminds us that as husbands, we neglect our wives at our peril."

After initial rejection, Mr. Bennet felt such advice was perhaps worthy of some consideration, since it issued from a respected friend and relative. He had been wrestling with his own emotions regarding his wife, but had not realised till now there was any real danger of losing her. This was food for thought…

The musicians struck up some lively pieces to round off the evening, while people finished their conversations. There followed a vote of thanks for formal appreciation of the hostess and her household. A vast bouquet of hothouse flowers was presented to her on behalf of all. Then the drift towards cloaks and carriages proceeded. Under cover of the general motion, Aunt Philips spoke quietly to her sister.

"You look so radiant this evening, my dear. I am sure your illness is now nearly over."

"This evening played its part in restoring some of my former confidence. My thanks for your kindness."

"Well, adieu for the present, then. Your charade this evening was memorable. I would add a word of caution, though, and do not take this amiss; just be clear in your understanding of the difference between Drama and Reality. Do not confuse one with the other. Charades are merely charades, my dear." She gave her sister an affectionate embrace, put her cloak around her shoulders and waved her off into the night.

July 30th

Baronet, Hemlock and Banknote. How clever! I'm sure I should never have guessed them.

Charades have much to commend them. Playing a part is a truly transforming experience; this evening I was another creature entirely. This new Mrs. Bennet had poise and certainty. I loved our brief time together and wish she would appear more often in society. Yes, there is a great deal to be said for stepping into another's shoes.

How inventive my fellow thespians were! How foolish Mr. Collins appeared!

How gracefully Kitty moved! An absolute delight.

As for myself, 'a nymph worthy of adoration'. Elevation indeed! I was lifted into another world, entirely!

Head in the clouds!! How all my fears fled as I performed!

Why, I could even face Mrs. Long without trembling. She was in the audience, applauding the cast and looking directly at me. Her smile was as affectionate as it was insincere.

Is not life all one long charade?

Chapter XI

The Bennets' carriage was initially full of lively conversations between mother and daughters, discussing details of the evening. Only Mr. Bennet remained silent.

"And now Kitty, what of the progress of your courtship?' said Mrs. Bennet. Kitty was immediately wary.

"Why, mama, I'm sure I have no interest in advancing that subject."

"Well, Mr. Collins was there, wasn't he? Did he pay you some attention?"

Mr. Bennet started to speak, avoided looking at Mary and held his tongue. Mary looked pale. She hoped her secret would not come to light just yet, but she certainly did not want her mother to arrange another meeting between her sister and Mr. Collins. This may have been a presentiment or coincidence, since Mrs. Bennet's next words were, "We'll invite him to dinner. Yes, and the naval gentlemen shall come too. That will help *you* on, Mary."

Mr. Bennet rolled his eyes.

"Madam, have we not had sufficient romance for one evening? Pray cease your matchmaking!"

Mrs. Bennet was under attack. Her spirit bristled at her husband's reproach.

"And would you have your daughters become old maids?"

"Better that, than find they are the talk of all Meryton."

"Whatever can you mean, sir?"

"I refer, madam, to your thespian antics and immodest demeanour with the naval gentleman, boldly displaying yourself before scores of eyes. Quite the coquette, it seems."

He had not meant to upbraid his wife in such a manner nor, worse, in front of his daughters, but it seemed he could not help himself. His family looked aghast. Mrs. Bennet flushed with sudden feelings of insecurity, unsure of her position now. Kitty was thoroughly miserable and Mary, for once, had no moral views to express. The silence that ensued for the rest of the journey was interrupted only by Mrs. Bennet's quiet sniffs into her handkerchief and Mr. Bennet tapping his fingers with scarce-concealed irritation on the coach window frame. Neither of the girls looked at their parents, but stared out into the darkness.

The carriage rattled into the yard and the occupants descended. Mrs. Bennet followed her husband into the house in silence. Hill greeted them with a letter and the news that the Bingleys and the Gardiners had retired for the night.

"Oh, dear Jane. I had quite forgot," said her mother, recollecting herself. It was an effort to speak. "Well, we shall see her at breakfast. So, Hill, please ensure everything is ready, both hot and cold dishes. Thank you for waiting up for us."

Mr. Bennet nodded to Hill and then opened the envelope.

"It's a long letter from Lizzy. Shall I read it to you all before we go to bed?" He was trying to overcome his bitter speech in the carriage and make some amends.

"Yes please," said Kitty with alacrity, eager to restore some familial atmosphere. "May we stay up a little longer, mama?"

Mrs. Bennet was relieved to remain downstairs with the girls present, fearing the evening would end in another marital disagreement and further blows to her new-won self-esteem.

"Hill, dear, would you kindly stoke up the fire in the drawing room? And fetch a little hot wine?"

The mood lightened a little as the warmth of fire and beverage worked their benefits. The family gathered round Mr. Bennet, who read;

'Pemberley, Derbyshire.

July 15th.

My dear Mama and Papa,

We are enjoying calm summer days at present and I trust the weather is as fair for you in the south. It may therefore strike you as a little premature to be considering arrangements for Christmas. The matter has touched me recently as preparations for autumn's chill are already in hand at Pemberley. It would seem the winters are often severe here, so once the harvests are gathered in, the use of the shortening days is to the utmost. My thoughts have naturally turned to my family as the season advances and both Mr. Darcy and myself invite you all to join us for the months of December, January and February. The travelling north in early December should present few difficulties due to inclement weather, while the return journey in early March should be on the edge of Spring. Your farm, Papa, may safely be left with Mr. Tillman until then?

In hope and anticipation of your acceptance of this invitation, I trust you will allow us to offer the use of our carriages? Your party will be quite a large one, comprising not only the family, but perhaps the servants too? As you are aware, we have an army of staff people here, but I presume you will want Hill, Robson and your manservant to attend? It would be my personal pleasure to see them again. They would be a most welcome addition.

I have already invited dear Jane and Charles, who have kindly accepted. Naturally, I am delighted. It will be an especially interesting period for all of us and we are so glad that Jane feels confidence in Pemberley and its staff. Of course, dear Aunt and Uncle Gardiner will be there too, with their children, for the Christmas festivities.

Regarding Lydia and George Wickham, we remain thoughtful. It is still an uncomfortable relationship for my husband. It is possible that they may be invited, but at what cost to Mr. Darcy you may surmise.

We have extended the invitation to some of the rest of our family for the post-Christmas period until Twelfth Night. You may not be aware that Captain Wainwright and his son James are cousins of Mr. Darcy. They had lost touch for many years when they moved away from this part of the county, but we understand they are living very near to you all. If you do not know them already, you may make their acquaintance here.

We shall also invite Charlotte and Mr. Collins, as well as his brother, Charles. This is in acknowledgement in some part to my cousins, but will bring much personal joy to spend time with my dear friend Charlotte again. It will be nearly two years since we have seen each other. In addition we had invited Lady Catherine de Bourgh and her daughter, but upon hearing my family will be here, her ladyship declined our offer, saying her daughter was too unwell to travel far. You may draw your own conclusions from that.

*As you may apprehend, Pemberley
will be a place of some business this
winter, but as Mr. Darcy generously
and often states, "This grand house
was designed for grand numbers."*

*And with that thought, please respond
with a letter of assent, before others
nearer home invite you to their
Christmas—a thought that I could not
bear!*

We both long to see you all again.

Your loving daughter

Lizzy.'

The letter drew forth a ripple of animated remarks.

"Now that's what I call a handsome invitation,"
said Mr. Bennet. "However, I am in some doubt as
to whether we can accept."

"What?" cried all the females.

"Not accept an invitation for a holiday of three
months in that beautiful and gracious home?" cried
his wife.

"How can we take advantage of such an offer
when we are already in such debt to the owner?' he
replied, remembering Mr. Darcy's work in tracking
down their lost daughter Lydia and then giving
every support, financial and actual, to help her
marry George Wickham. Mr. Bennet was also
averse to meeting the naval gentlemen again.

Kitty was too delighted at seeing her favourite
older sisters once more, to be silent in due respect to
her father.

"Why, papa, that debt was discharged at the time of the wedding by Mr. Darcy himself. It would look churlish to reject this invitation to Pemberley. It might be seen as pride and prejudice on your part, as if we held a grudge against Mr. Darcy for being so wealthy. And surely you will want to see your dear Lizzy again?"

This was the arrow that found its mark. Three months with Elizabeth and Jane in that noble house far outweighed any other consideration.

"Of course we shall accept," said Mrs. Bennet firmly. She could see another opportunity to advance the marriage prospects of her daughters with Mr. Collins and Captain Wainwright in the Derbyshire home. They would be together and over some considerable time. As for herself, mentally she was already visiting the apothecary to stock up on the herbs and remedies *she* would need, for a three months' sojourn away from Longbourn.

Mary had been quietly absorbing the contents of Lizzy's letter and feeling torn between the joy of seeing Mr. Collins again and the dampening knowledge that their relationship was a secret, so that there could be no display of her happiness. Mr. Bennet broke up the gathering by rising from his chair. He kissed his daughters goodnight and gave his wife a brief nod. They ascended the stairs together, led by Mr. Bennet who held a candle aloft. The girls ran to their rooms along the corridor. Mr. Bennet gave his wife a stern glance, then turned away to walk to his room, leaving Mrs. Bennet in the shadows.

In her bedchamber Mrs. Bennet reflected on the evening, as she sat alone brushing her hair. Hill had prudently left a candle for her on the dressing table. She gazed at her reflection in the mirror, which was smiling at her memories of the entertaining evening at her sister's home. The images tumbled through her mind: a gracious house, glittering lights, lively music, a crowded ballroom, sumptuous refreshments and, of course, those charades! Such teasing riddles—such ingenious suppositions—what fellowship among the actors—what skills—the accomplished performance by Captain Wainwright—the applause—what merriment!

Her face shone with delight. Then she recalled the events at the evening's close. The carriage home—the cold night—that argument—the cruel accusations—Mr. Bennet's anger—the humiliation in front of their girls—what misery!

The face that looked back at her now showed anxiety and depression: never before had her husband spoken to her in such a wounding manner. She turned to her store cupboard to take out a wine bottle and poured herself several glasses. She had almost been tempted to give it up completely from this evening, resolving to drink nothing but elderflower cordial, but this ending to the day had weakened her resolve. She felt too low to write her journal. With the words of the hymn "Let not sorrow dim your eye" running in her head Mrs. Bennet blew out the candle.

The next morning found the Bennets, the Gardiners and the Bingleys all down by eight o' clock. The atmosphere was lively among the younger people. Mrs. Bennet had passed an indifferent night and looked most unwell. She had been troubled by her husband's disapprobation and found it hard to know how to reverse it. The chatter of the cousins covered her low spirits.

It was Charles Bingley who drew her out by whispering to her as he sat nearest, "Mrs. Bennet, Jane would like to see you after the meal, privately."

"Indeed sir. I shall come at once. I suggest the library. I hope nothing is amiss?"

"I do not believe so," answered Charles in a reassuring manner.

The breakfast was enlivened by discussion concerning the Christmas invitation.

"That will mean new frocks mama," said Kitty. The Gardiner girls all echoed their cousin. Mr. Bennet looked grim in contrast to Mr. Gardiner who smiled and said, "We shall see, ladies. We must all show our best when visiting Pemberley."

Mr. Bennet complained, "We shall have to give that very careful consideration before further expenditure. Much may happen between now and Christmas. That reminds me, Kitty and Mary, there will be both opportunity and necessity to exhibit your musical prowess at Pemberley. You had both better put in a deal of practice. I shall speak to Mr. Chawton about it after breakfast. Indeed, I shall escort you myself to the drawing room to see Mr. Chawton in person."

"Oh papa," said his daughters, torn between delight at their father's oblique acceptance of the

Pemberley invitation and his insistence on witnessing their educational progress.

The servants were ordered to clear the table, as everyone rose. Mrs. Bennet accompanied Jane to the library. Once the door was closed, Jane took her mother by the hand and said in her gentle manner, "Mama, Charles and I have the greatest news to relate. We are to expect a child in January." Her eyes were brimming with emotion.

"Oh, Jane dear! What wonderful news. I am delighted. I half suspected when you went home early from Aunt Philips' home last night. But, Jane dear, will it be safe to travel home from Pemberley after Christmas? The roads may be covered with snow. And what if the carriage was to become stuck? And even if you should manage to reach your own door, the doctor may not. You would be totally alone, far from all of us." Mrs. Bennet became quite agitated. She could feel a sweat rising as her anxiety grew.

"Mama, stop!" Jane laughed. "Do not distress yourself. We are staying at Pemberley from early December until February, so therefore we shall be resident for the whole of my confinement. Lizzy and I have had detailed conversations on the subject and she has excellent staff at Pemberley. There is a doctor in the same village and even the house keeper and midwife who attended Mr. Darcy's mother in her last confinement with Georgiana."

"Oh my dearest Jane. You give me such relief." The tears tumbled from her eyes as she drew her daughter into her arms.

"You are weeping for happiness, I hope mama?"

"Oh yes Jane, yes!"

"Come, mama, let me help you wipe your tears and we'll tell papa together, shall we?"

With their arms entwined, they went in uplifted mood to seek Mr. Bennet and then the family. But Mr. Bennet could not be immediately informed since he was with the tutors. They were in his study discussing financial matters, while Kitty and Mary were practising on piano and violin.

"It would seem I am at present in the embarrassing position of being unable to pay you this month, Mr. Chawton and Mr. Lockhart."

The alarm and anger in the tutors' faces was evident. Mr. Chawton spoke first. He looked anxious.

"This is highly irregular, Mr. Bennet. May we be informed of the time when you are in a position to do so?"

"It would seem, sir, that this is uncertain, I am afraid. There is a choice before us, gentlemen. I can either dispense with your services and send on your salaries when I am able, or you can agree to stay on for another month, when I would hope finances take a better turn."

"And if they do not, then there would be two months' salary owing. Is it likely, sir, that this impecunious state will continue long? I am certainly enjoying my employment here, but cannot afford to offer my services for no return."

"Those sentiments also apply to me, sir." added Mr. Lockhart.

"I cannot at the moment say with any confidence that my finances will be in a healthy state in the immediate future, but the farm wheat yields look promising and if this fair weather continues for another two weeks, we should make a good harvest. The selling of the crop will be a matter for the markets, over which I have no control."

"May we ask then, sir, for a share in the proceeds from the sale, in lieu of immediate pecuniary settlement?" asked Mr. Chawton.

This suggestion took Mr. Bennet by surprise. He looked sharply at the music tutor, who steadily returned his gaze. There was an assurance here that Mr. Bennet had not expected from the young man. His mental astuteness and financial grasp of the situation were admirable, if not a little disconcerting.

"Well, Mr. Chawton, I believe this could be an acceptable alternative. If you and Mr. Lockhart are agreeable to staying on at least till the end of August, then for my part, I find these terms acceptable." A firm handshake sealed the agreement and the tutors departed to their duties, Mr. Bennet to his farm.

It was therefore not until all the family and guests met at lunch that Jane and Charles were able to inform everyone of the expected addition to the family in the new year. Charles made the announcement, smiling broadly as he held his wife's hand.

"It is with the utmost pleasure I can confirm that my dearest Jane is expecting our first child."

Such general delight may be imagined. Everyone spoke at once.

"My dear daughter, this is excellent news," said Mr. Bennet, rising to kiss her. His habitual stern features broke into a smile and the warm glance was extended to his wife. There was, for the first time in many months, a look of mutual joy. It lasted until Mrs. Bennet said, "Of course, I knew before any of you. Jane told me some hours ago." This remark, delivered rather self-importantly, somewhat deflated the joyous atmosphere, since it seemed to be uttered merely to score over her husband and Mrs. Bennet immediately regretted it. But the general mood could not be dampened long as everyone gathered round the future parents.

"Mary and I will be aunts," said Kitty, her face glowing with excitement.

"And we shall be great uncle and aunt," laughed Aunt Gardiner, turning to her husband. His answering smile made Mrs. Bennet feel deeply envious. She thought, "Why do I spoil the moment so often?" She looked at her own husband in the hope of a forgiving glance, but he had turned away. Her remorse was put aside while she joined the group in congratulations. Jane's face was radiant.

"But this will mean you will have the baby at Pemberley, will it not?" said Mary.

"Yes, Mary. We are all settled on that point. I could not bear to hear of all my family together at Christmas and not be there myself," said Jane.

"And it would be unwise to travel home immediately after Christmas, with the baby due so soon," said her husband, looking very responsible.

Mrs. Bennet thought with some remorse, "I remember when Mr. Bennet looked at me in that way once, with tenderness and affection." Her five confinements had each been marked by her husband's careful attention, and this made his present and persistent indifference even harder to bear.

It was Aunt Gardiner who broke into her thoughts with a sudden exclamation, "Does this not mean, should the baby be a boy, the entail on this house would be negated?"

For a full minute, the animated discourse ceased.

"You think there is a possibility that the legal barrier to a female inheriting Longbourn would no longer exist should Jane and Charles have a son?" asked Mr. Bennet of his brother-in-law. "My word, that would change everything." His countenance was suffused with hope at the prospect of such a burden dropping away after all these years.

"Well," said Mr. Gardiner speaking with some deliberation, "it would mean consulting the lawyers to ascertain the exact terms of your father's will. There may be all kinds of legal impediments that could hinder a grandson from inheriting Longbourn. For example, it may state that only your direct son may do so."

"True, true," said Mr. Bennet thoughtfully. "And there may be a clause that could prevent my naming a successor, albeit in the family."

"Oh, that entail! Shall we never be rid of it?" interrupted Mrs. Bennet. "It has infected the whole of my married life. How could your father have been so foolish, Mr. Bennet? It is my poor girls who suffer. I shouldn't wonder if that is why my nerves have been so at odds all these years."

"Oh, mama!" said Kitty. "It's not so very bad for us. And you have been much better of late. Even Mrs. Long was forced to remark on how well you were looking, when we saw her at church last Sunday."

"My dear, do not distress yourself" said Aunt Gardiner. "Your eldest daughters have both made good marriages and will not be a financial burden in the future. And many years will pass before you need worry about leaving Longbourn. Let us enjoy the present. Jane's news is something to delight in, surely?"

Mary added seriously, "Let us take care of the present. The future will take care of itself."

Charles drew Jane's hand closer and pronounced,

"Indeed, Mary. Wise words and well said. We shall enjoy the present."

"Well said, Mary. I propose a toast to the parents-to-be," said Mr. Bennet. He rang the bell for Hill to bring wine and cordials. When they arrived, he said, "Hill, you may stay and share in our good fortune. To Jane and Charles."

"Jane and Charles," said everyone.

"And to the baby, whatever it may be" laughed Kitty.

"Whether girl or boy, it will be wanted and cherished," added her aunt, smiling at Mrs. Bennet.

August 4th

Two matters of great excitement tempered with no little apprehension. The first is Lizzy's invitation to Pemberley. Only think, a winter at the grandest house in Derbyshire! It is both a wonder and a thing to fear. Low spirits overcome the pleasure I should be feeling. I am in awe of Mr. Darcy—such a proud man. I am all amazement that Lizzy should marry a man who thinks so much of himself. I expect it was his ten thousand a year that persuaded her. That fact certainly overcame my initial abhorrence. But it is with some trepidation that I meet him again under his own, very superior roof. As to my staying there, the difficulties of managing my illness in a strange house are already flooding me with embarrassment. Oh to be so far from home when one is suffering!

The second matter is dear Jane's confinement. To think I shall be a grandmother! While worries assail me as to the possible dangers that accompany childbirth, at least I may be of some use in offering advice. The child is certain to be beautiful if it takes after its mother and of genial disposition, after Bingley. It will lack for nothing, being reared in such wealth and affection.

I hope that my illness will not prevent me from taking a full part in family society during my time at Pemberley.

Chapter XII

It was not long after this harmonious gathering that Mr. Bennet felt compelled to speak to his wife in private. With the study door carefully closed, he confronted her with a hand that was full of bills.

"Mrs. Bennet, this situation is untenable. Despite our frequent discussions on the issue of your financial profligacy, you have run up another string of debts. What have you to say to that?"

Mrs. Bennet was somewhat taken aback. She had been, she thought, quite frugal in her expenditure, since their last altercation. Today she felt as though she could not raise her spirits for yet another battle. Her mind seemed to be in disorder. She was caught off guard with any new event and, just as she was recovering, some new twist of fate would push her under the metaphorical water again. The sharp mood at her earlier family meeting had given way to low defeat.

She played for time by saying, "Is this indeed the case, sir? I am at a loss as to your meaning."

But her quiet tone did little to calm her husband.

"These bills, madam. All dated in the last month. I found them in your bureau drawer," he said. "Are you so devoid of judgement that you do not know what you are doing? And so incapable of recollection that you now have no memory of your spending?"

He thrust the bills at her and several fell to the floor. Mrs. Bennet felt overwhelmed by this new assault; she seemed unable to breathe. Her powers of speech deserted her. Staring fearfully at her husband, she awaited his next attack in silence.

He continued, "I shall leave you to consider these at your convenience. Then when you are able to produce some idea of the reason for their existence, you may come to me. I intend to invite your brother to this meeting. With his additional prudent financial advice and fraternal influence, it is to be hoped you may come to you senses, since my admonitions have had so little effect. We cannot, must not and shall not go on like this." Regarding her with no small degree of contempt, he left the study.

Mrs. Bennet went on to her knees to pick up the bills, but found it some time before she could read them. Her sight was blurred by tears and her heart pounded. There she sat for several moments, drying her eyes and gradually gaining control of her breathing. A hot flush swept over her and a feeling of despondency. In some anguish she wiped her sweating neck and brow, then went to her writing desk. She looked about her and realised it was not as she had left it that morning. Slowly her despair gave way to anger. The interior of the desk and all the little drawers were in complete disarray. This was unpardonable. She was affronted and hurt that her husband had been searching her personal bureau without permission. She slammed the drawers shut and banged down the desk lid in fury.

It took two glasses of fortified wine and several drops from the phials in her little carrying case to calm her. Then she adjusted her shawl, slowly gathered up the papers and knelt on the carpet to read them. Using a magnifying glass she began to examine the details. The bills were from a variety of suppliers. The first to hand was an invoice from the apothecary (countersigned by Mrs. Jones) for St. John's Wort, valerian, camomile and carbonate of ammonia.

This surprised her. "But I make my own revivers now," she said aloud. She had spent two whole mornings only that week collecting lavender flowers and seeds to pound into a paste, then mixing this compound with aromatic vinegar. She looked again at the date and saw this was for July last year, not this. "At least this is not outstanding," she mused, for she remembered personally paying this bill to the apothecary in Meryton and he had deducted some of the amount in lieu of her prompt reckoning.

Next were two bills for the Doctor's visits. The senders had told her there was no haste as to payment but Mrs. Bennet had started to regularly save a little from her housekeeping towards the settlement around that time. She searched in her desk drawer and found her journal. A fortnight after the date on the doctor's bill she had made a note: 'Settled both bills from Dr. Jones today.'

"Well, here at least I know I am in the right," she said.

Other bills from the drapers', listing the fabric she had ordered for the girls' dresses, were next in the pile.

"Why, I am sure Mr. Bennet agreed to this expenditure," she said. "I assumed he had already paid them. I kept these merely for the record."

The next bill was for tuition fees.

"Well, there I know I am not to blame, since it was he who contracted the tutors. Though why he has not paid Mr. Chawton and Mr. Lockhart at all this term, is a matter for much conjecture."

The invoices from the various procurers of meat, poultry, fish and game looked to be larger than usual; as did the grocery list of other household commodities, including wine. These were much more comprehensible. The increased expenditure had been justified by the addition of several parties of visiting relatives. She glanced up and found herself looking at her reflection in the glass-fronted cabinet.

"Oh, Mrs. Bennet, look at you. Cap all awry, tear-stained face and so low in spirits. In fact, you could not get much lower." Seeing her reflection hunched over the bills on the study floor, she suddenly realised the comic side of her situation. Here she was, sitting among scattered papers like a poor child in a snowdrift, seemingly paying homage to a cabinet, while only a few days before she had been the queen of the ballroom, with the world at her feet. At this moment, reflected in the glass, her face was like a dissolving water colour painting, whereas in the charade it had been a mask of perfection. If only the captain could see her now! How disabused of his vision he would be!

The captain! Yes, he was coming to dine with them on the morrow. She must gather her wits and forget her troubles. She would need to impress the naval gentlemen. Provisions must be ordered. She would not be gainsaid by a parsimonious, unsociable husband, when her daughters' futures were at stake. Hill needed supervision in the kitchen, the girls would need their best dresses laundered and she must at least smooth the waters with her husband before guests arrived. The rapidity of her thoughts left her quite in the fidgets, but the animation of spirits gave direction to her determination.

*

The next day being Sunday, all the Bennets and their family guests were to attend morning service as usual. The weather was fine, so the walk to church was a pleasant way to pass the time. Mrs. Bennet was resolved to put her husband in a sweeter mood, by forcing a bright smile and asking him about the farm.

"I fear, Mrs. Bennet, these agricultural matters are above your head." With this, he quickened his stride to catch up with the Gardiners.

"Never mind, mama," said Kitty, tucking her arm through her mother's, as she saw the maternal disquiet. "Morning prayers may improve his temper. And isn't it today that Mr. Collins is preaching?" She laughed at the likelihood of their cousin making a fool of himself.

"I had quite forgot, Kitty," replied Mrs. Bennet, as she noted Kitty's smiling countenance. Here, she thought, was positive proof of her daughter's affection for the young clergyman. Nobody observed how Mary blushed.

Inside the building the church was already nearly full. Muted conversation mingled with soft organ music. On entering the family pew, the Bennet party sank to their knees in prayer and, after some minor altercations on the question of insufficient hassocks, knelt in tolerable stillness and made their humble obeisance. This ritual being over, they were free to sit up and take a look round to ascertain who of the good people of Longbourn attended and who were absent. The bustle and greetings, with the rustle of skirts and hymnbooks added to the sound of the organ, covered any whisperings among the congregation.

Kitty's lively observation to her sister that "Mrs. Long's new hat almost overshadows her husband. He has no room to turn his head but is forced by her brim, to slant his face at an angle!" made both girls giggle.

"And see how the long feather is tickling the head of the poor man kneeling in the pew behind," returned Mary.

"Hush girls," said their mother.

Meanwhile the Gardiner children were exchanging comic faces with the younger members of the Lucas family, until stopped by both sets of parents. Further along the pew Jane and Charles glanced fondly at each other.

"Were you very nervous, Charles, on our wedding day, as you stood here waiting for me?" whispered Jane.

"A little," confessed Charles, "for I felt you might not come. But Darcy was a tower of strength and assured me that you would."

Mrs. Bennet noticed the Captain and his son across the aisle. She smiled and, as she did so, she saw her husband at the end of her pew, beyond their daughters, catch her glance. Another error.

The organ changed its playing of Handel's melodic tune to something more triumphal as Mr. Collins, preceded by the great brass cross and a dozen choristers, processed from the rear of the church, down the central aisle.

"This is 'The Arrival of the Queen of Sheba', isn't it?" whispered Uncle Gardiner to his wife.

"I wonder if Mr. Collins specifically ordered it for his grand entrance?" whispered Mr. Bennet, overhearing him.

They suppressed their smiles as Mr. Collins, as majestic as any archbishop, made his stately way towards the transept. He halted and graciously bowed towards the altar, bowed deeply and slowly again to the choristers who returned his bow, then turned and bowed a third time towards the congregation. The good folk of Longbourn were a little disconcerted. Some nodded, some bobbed a curtsey, some stood stock still.

"Too much bowing and scraping." muttered Mr. Jones to his wife. "Old Parson Longley took a minute to start the service; this fellow is taking five. If this pantomime continues, we shan't be eating our lunches till three o'clock."

Mr. Collins was enjoying the moment to the full. He felt empowered. Here were his flock in need of guidance. Here was his stage. He thought he made a commanding figure in his priestly robes. Mary was gazing at him in some awe.

"Dearly beloved," he began in a sonorous tone " We are gathered here in the sight of God"—some of the people were nudging each other—"and in the face of this congregation." Mrs. Jones was whispering to her husband, but Mr. Collins droned on.

"In the face of this congregation, " he repeated with a stern glance at Mr. Bennet who was leafing through his 'Book of Common Prayer'.

"In the face of this congregation," Mr. Collins said emphatically, "to join together—". The congregation were no longer whispering, but openly laughing.

"To join together, this man and—"

Mr. Collins stopped. He blinked. He looked at his prayer book. The congregation's laughter was filling the church.

"Sorry, your reverence, but I don't seem to see no bride or groom," called a voice from the back.

"Er, I, er." stammered Mr. Collins. His face grew scarlet. He looked as if he were drowning.

Mr. Bennet stepped forward. He held an open prayer book.

"Allow me to assist, sir," he said kindly.

With gratitude Mr. Collins took the book and began afresh with the order of Morning Prayer.

"Best laugh I've ever had in church," muttered Mr. Bennet to his brother-in-law when he returned to his seat.

The service rolled on. Mr. Collins' hymn choices were intended to emphasise the solemnity of the religious life, but only succeeded in creating discord where harmony should have held sway. "O let him whose sorrow", "O come and mourn with me awhile" and "How blessed, from the bonds of sin" were among his sombre selections. These caused the congregation to feel merely nettled, but the musicians were in complete confusion, since these hymns were unknown to them. They valiantly sawed, plucked and blew, but, unrehearsed, musical harmony eluded them. The choristers looked in vain for the "kindly leading light' of their choir master; he was too occupied with turning the unfamiliar pages and listening out for the musicians to give much guidance. The mixture of agitation and ire was much in evidence. Reverend Collins sang serenely on, oblivious to wrong notes and whispered resentments.

There was a comforting lull when the time came for the address to be delivered. A grateful sigh arose from congregation, choristers and musicians as Mr. Collins ascended the pulpit. The tumult of battle was temporarily stilled. He raised his hand in the best sign of blessing he could display. Practice in front of his bedroom mirror had made this perfect.

After a glance to the roof so long, that the congregation all stared upward too and a prayer of deep humility that begged his maker to bless his immediate efforts, he began his sermon.

"My theme for today is Love. That great evangelist Saint Paul said in his letters to the Ephesians, chapter 5, verse 25, 'Husbands love your wives'."

At this, Mrs. Bennet nodded at Kitty and turned her head to Mr. Collins, then back to Kitty, while slowly winking. Kitty frowned and shifted in her seat. Then Mrs. Bennet stared at Captain Wainwright and, catching his eye, nodded at Mary.

Mary caught the look and saw where her mother was indicating. She found herself staring straight into the captain's eyes, to her intense embarrassment. Deeply mortified, Mary fervently hoped Mr. Collins had not seen this mime-show.

It was Aunt Philips, seated nearby in a side aisle, who was watching all this silent interaction and, grasping that her sister was linking two couples completely incorrectly, shook her head. But Mrs. Bennet did not take the hint and continued to intertwine the gazes of the four unwilling participants until the end of the address.

Mr. Collins ceased after two hours, feeling pleased with his work. Hoping that it had fallen on fertile ground, he made his majestic way down again from the pulpit.

The striking chords of "Love Divine, all loves excelling" sprayed out from the organ and the congregation struggled to its collective feet, some personages being awakened from their slumber by shakes and nudges. With the musicians, choristers and organist all familiar with the Wesley hymn, the church was filled with confident sound. The collection bags sped along the pews like hot potatoes, to be gathered up by the church wardens and sidesmen at the end of each line with patience and a firm stare to shame any parishioner trying to avoid a donation. Every coin gathered in, they walked up the aisle. Upon reaching the front of the nave, they stood in a black-gowned group like so many crows and waited. A united bowing followed. They dropped their collection bags on the vast silver plate held out to them by Mr. Collins. His deep bow to the church officials, imitated with varying degrees of servitude, was repeated, until he felt the ritual had been given its due of sufficient length in its solemnity. Then, with a flourish of wrists and a swirl of robes, Mr. Collins held the plate high and walked with noble strides towards the altar. Holding the plate aloft for dramatic effect, he gave several prayers of thanks, ending, " Glory be to the Father, and to the Son and to the Holy Ghost. Amen." Finally the collection plate was slowly lowered on to the holy table.

An episode of three pieces sung by choristers followed, during which the priest raised his eyes heavenward and mouthed the words, while the congregation were at liberty to admire the floral arrangements and polished brass. "I am on the flower rota with Lady Lucas next week." whispered Mrs. Bennet to her neighbour.

A further twenty minutes of intercessions followed. The knees of the elderly members shifted on their hassocks and the smaller children bobbed up to see what was happening, then were pulled down by their elders with ill-concealed whispers. Many were the minds that strayed to practical concerns in their daily lives, beyond the church service, not least the thought of the Sunday lunch.

Mr. Collins announced the final hymn as, "An innovative work that will surely please the mature ladies of our parish." His choice was, "How blest the matron who endures," and his smirking glance at Mrs. Bennet indicated, at least to him, the nobility of the older woman. He considered this matter to show some delicacy in the pursuit of acquiring the benison of his future mother-in-law. On gaining his *prie dieu* once more, he gave her a telling glance. Mrs. Bennet was surprised and puzzled, but had little time to consider it further as the congregation rose to do battle once more with yet another new refrain.

"And they call this progress," muttered Mr. Philips to his wife.

The intercessions, which brought the service to a close, were led by Mr. Collins kneeling at his prayer desk, which by providence or other means, had been placed in a spot under the great east window. Through the yellow stained glass sunbeams streamed, pouring a rich golden halo on the bowed head; an effect that was not lost, he hoped, on his parishioners. Here before them was a vision of glory, a man transfigured. In the silence following the prayers (the one 'for priests and pastors' being singled out for special emphasis) soft organ music played; at his behest it was the tune from "Love divine, all loves excelling," reminding the congregation of the final lines—

Changed from glory into glory,
Till in heaven we take our place;
Till we cast our crowns before Thee,
Lost in wonder, love and praise.

The sound died away. He remained kneeling. None could accuse him of unholy haste. Ancient knees in the pews were starting to protest. Children shuffled, impatient and hungry. At last Mr. Collins rose to give the final blessing. His features displayed divine benevolence. His hand raised in blessing echoed the time-honoured pose of the administering angel. Here was his flock. He was their shepherd. All was as it should be.

The thundering recessional music, 'Bach's Toccata and Fugue', emphasised Mr. Collins' heightened demeanour as he walked behind the choristers, down the aisle to the church door. Glances from the congregation in each succeeding pew as he drew level, followed by their mass kneeling as he passed by, were to his mind like sheaves of corn bowing down in Jacob's dream.

*

Out into the sunlight, Mr. Collins shook hands firmly with everyone. If he held Mary's hand slightly longer than anyone else's, it went unnoticed.

"There, Kitty," said her mother "what more proof do you need of Mr. Collins abiding attention? A whole sermon on husbands loving their wives and the hymn on love divine; a compliment to you, I am sure."

Kitty strode on in silence. Mr. Bennet looked thoughtful and at least allowed his wife to hold his arm, as they ducked under the lych-gate: a semblance of forgiveness and conjugal felicity. The service, in one way or another, had lifted all their spirits.

"A Divine Comedy!" was Uncle Gardiner's verdict, while his sister attached a more emotional interpretation. The dining room looked beautiful when they returned, thanks to Hill's careful preparations and the flowers Jane and Aunt Gardiner's children had gathered from the garden the previous day. Kitty and Mary had arranged them that morning. A delicious smell of roasting lamb drew everyone to their chairs. The naval gentlemen and Mr. Collins soon joined them and lunch was served.

Captain Wainwright began by saying, "My son James has some news to share with you."

James looked up from his lamb chop to announce, "Thank you father. I have been offered a promotion on board HMS Shannon under captain Philip Broke. I board ship on Thursday at Greenwich, so must sadly take my leave of you all today."

Aunt Gardiner looked at Kitty. If Kitty felt heartbroken, she did not show it.

"Congratulations young man!' said Mr. Bennet. It pleased him to think there was one less suitor to keep his eye on.

"I shall accompany him to the port," said the captain. Mrs. Bennett looked to see if Mary was saddened at the departure of her future husband. Aunt Philips stared at her sister, but to no avail.

Still Mrs. Bennet chattered on, dropping hints about marriage and betrothals. Mr. Bennet noted how much meat was consumed by all the men around the table and accounted the cost of such victuals. For one moment in his life he was pleased to have had only females in his house all these years: young men took some filling. He was resolved to hold no more such feasts, at least until the farm yields were known. He also noted the gallantry with which Captain Wainwright treated the ladies: witty compliments, touching attentiveness in passing dishes, appreciative remarks, all flowed in a constant stream from this gallant sea dog.

"Flatterer" thought Mr. Bennet.

The conversation turned to their all meeting again at Pemberley for Christmas.

"How generous Mr. Darcy and Lizzy are!" said Aunt Gardiner.

"So much to consider when preparing our luggage," worried Mrs. Bennet. "Only think how much we shall need for so long a stay."

"Will there be games, mama?' asked one of the Gardiner children excitedly.

"Well, that will be likely at Christmas, don't you think?" answered his father.

"I must reply to Lizzy's letter concerning the date we are to leave Longbourn," said Mr. Bennet . "And when will you be arriving at Pemberley, sir?" Mrs. Bennet asked Captain Wainwright.

"Around the 27th is likely to be the date I shall hove to" smiled the gentleman. There was general laughter at this nautical reference.

"And you, Mr. Collins?" Mrs. Bennet asked.

"It is my preferred plan to visit from the 28th. GW and WP," joked Mr. Collins, a little self-consciously, not to be outdone in proclaiming his profession. This answer received puzzled looks around the table.

" GW and WP? What does that mean, sir?" piped Mr. Gardiner's smallest daughter.

"God Willing and Weather Permitting," answered Mr. Collins heavily, rather irritated at having to explain.

Polite smiles followed.

The entry of the desserts and their consumption occupied everyone's attention for the next hour.

"May I press you to take a little more of this dish, sir?" asked Mrs. Bennet of her gentlemen guests.

"Well, I have partaken of two helpings ma'am," said the captain, "and any more would mean purchasing new breeches. My retirement has given me the rounded figure of a land-lubber."

"Delicious, ma'am," added Mr. Collins. "I am particularly in favour of your apple pie." As Mrs. Bennet served him a generous helping, she said, "Good apple pies are a considerable part of our domestic happiness, sir."

Mr. Bennet was calculating how many more meals could have been had in the following days if his wife had sent away the dishes after one helping per person. Mr. Gardiner, sensing the tension, drew his brother-in-law into conversation on farming matters, while his wife spoke to Mrs. Bennet and the girls about their progress under the new tutors.

Jane noted her parents' estrangement and endeavoured to engage the children's attention with more light-hearted matters. She spent a little time in talking to them and thinking how she could amuse them after lunch.

"Mama, dear, do you recall a game we played as children where we made ships of paper?"

"Indeed I do," said her mother. "We called them Nelson's Navy and gave them names of the fleet."

"Did you get them to water, ma'am, or were they merely for display in the nursery?' asked James.

"Ah, there sir, we had the greatest amusement, for we collected horse chestnuts, then took boats and chestnuts to the pond. The little ships were set afloat on the water. The chestnuts were our cannon balls and we bombarded the ships as they bobbed by." Mrs. Bennet smiled at the memory.

"Aunt Bennet, if we are finished, may we get down from the table, please? And shall you help us to make the ships, Aunt Jane and Uncle Bingley?" asked the Gardiner children with the greatest of eagerness.

"Indeed you may," Mrs. Bennet smiled. "There is plenty of paper to be had in the kitchen drawer, so ask Hill to help you. You may have more difficulty in finding horse chestnuts as it is still too early for this year's crop, but I believe Robson keeps some stored from last year in the cellars. They are useful in deterring spiders if placed in the corners of rooms."

Laughing, the company broke up. The children dragged off their not unwilling Aunt Jane while Mr. Collins, Captain Wainwright and James paid their compliments to their hosts and brought the meal to a close.

*

With the farewells over and the guests gone, Mr. Bennet went in search of his wife. She was rather expecting him to compliment her on such a fine dinner. Instead, he upbraided her angrily as to its cost.

"Could we not have had just two meats, rather than four, if we are also indulging in fish, game and poultry? And all those puddings! To have had trifle would have been sufficient, without the almond pudding, apple pies, blancmange and tarts."

Mrs. Bennet grew red with anger and this spilled over into tears. It was Jane who came upon her crying alone in the hall and who attended her to her room.

"There, there, mama, just sit down. Here is your handkerchief. May I ask what is the trouble?"

Mrs. Bennet sat for a few more moments crying and dabbing her eyes. She longed to unburden herself to her daughter but felt torn between loyalty to her husband and fear of losing Jane's respect. Rather than berate her husband in front of their eldest, she tried to overcome her present feelings and asked, "Dear Jane, could you fetch your mother a drink?"

"Why, of course, mama. Would you prefer tea or water?"

"I think a little wine would restore me better. Could you ask Hill for some madeira?"

Jane patted her mother's shoulder and went in search of the wine. While she was gone, Mrs. Bennet went to her own supply in her cupboard and poured out a large glass for herself. She drank it quickly, replaced the decanter, consumed some fragrant fennel seeds to mask the scent, and wiped her mouth. The warmth of the wine made her feel more relaxed and ready to face the world once more.

On Jane's return, she managed a smile.

"Here you are, mama. A small glass of madeira and a fresh handkerchief. Are you able to tell me what is troubling you now?" she asked gently. Jane held her mother's hand as she sipped the wine and felt her forehead. It was very hot. She regarded the flushed cheeks and noticed a sweet smell of herbs in the room. It was clear all was not well. These emotional fluctuations between anger and tears were more marked in her mother than Jane had ever witnessed before. Mama had always been a woman of strong spirit; given to passionate opinions and a degree of self-pity when she felt events too much for her. But these changes of temper displayed in outburst of tears and current lassitude made a disturbing contrast to the hostess at today's meal and the lively woman who had performed with such exuberance at the charade evening.

"Oh, just minor matters. Ladies' ailments, dear. Perhaps I am feeling my age."

"Just lie down, mama. Take some time to rest yourself. You have been so busy looking after us all, it is not surprising you are a little weary."

"Perhaps you are right. I'll have a sleep. I fear I can do little else. I feel quite spent."

Jane placed a shawl round her mother and quietly left the room. She then took the bold step of entering her father's study and engaging him in conversation.

"Dear papa, I know you have your concerns about the household expenditure, and rightly so. But mama is not entirely in the wrong. The dinner today was in order to show how welcome she wanted Aunt Gardiner's family and our other guests to feel.

She is also deserving of some sympathy, papa. Her condition is a daily and nightly struggle of survival and I for one recognise how bravely she is dealing with it. She needs your support and your affection. I would not speak, but I see the distress she is undergoing and how cool your relationship has now become. Please help her, father. As for the finances, this letter from Lizzy may come as a welcome intrusion."

She gave the paper into his hand and watched as he put on his glasses and stood near the window to read.

> *'Pemberley.*
>
> *August 15th.*
>
> *My dearest Papa,*
>
> *This brief letter contains a money order drawn from my private account. It is an order that will be repeated every month. There is no protest that will change this arrangement. Mr. Darcy has given me a separate account to dispose of as and when I may. He is fully cognisant of this arrangement and totally supportive.*
>
> *You are in no way allowed to mention this when we meet at Christmas; a fatherly embrace for me and a cordial handshake for him will suffice. The household expenses will be the main use for this sum. I have taken the step of awarding a regular, though lesser*

amount, to be paid to mama, for use on her personal medical care. Aunt Philips and Kitty will see she uses this wisely.

Mr. Darcy and I look forward to welcoming you all to Pemberley at Christmas. Our wishes are that you will be able to leave Longbourn on December 1st. Please confirm if this date will be convenient for you and we shall send our carriages at that time.

Till we hear from you, we send you our loving thoughts.

Your affectionate daughter

Lizzy.'

Mr. Bennet dared to look at the money order and gasped. To say he was overwhelmed would be to understate his emotions at such tidings. He knew not whether to laugh with relief, weep with emotion, or sing with gratitude. Such bounteous kindness! Such a degree of thoughtfulness! He was rendered lost for words.

While Mr. Bennet was digesting this extraordinary good fortune, his wife was now awake. Kitty and Mary had interrupted her sleep to see how she was faring.

"Mama, we have brought you some tea. We hoped it might revive you."

"Revive me? To let me sleep on would have been preferable," Mrs. Bennet sharply replied. Then seeing her daughters' crestfallen faces, she made an effort to sit up. "Very kind of you dears. I am sorry I am not myself at present."

Her tone became softer as she said, "Now Kitty dear, you know that Mr. Collins is not in the vicinity much longer. His sermon made plain his sentiments towards you. This public display of his intentions seems to be a firm declaration of his feelings. I shall discuss the matter with your father, and remove any obstacles, if some remain. Thus your path will be smoothed. My intention is that we have Mr. Collins here for tea this very week and I shall ensure there arises an opportunity where you and he may be alone."

Kitty was torn between furious confrontation and silence. She chose the latter. There were other considerations. Mary remained in quiet contemplation and was only moved to speak when her mother turned to her.

"Pemberley will be a real opportunity to advance your relationship with Captain Wainwright, Mary. The season of Christmas always puts people in an amiable mood. I am sure the captain can be captured!"

"Mother, perhaps you are mistaken in supposing the captain to have any interest in me."

"Nonsense! As a mother with three married daughters, I know about such matters. *You* are far too young to understand."

"And yet not too young to become a wife," thought Mary, seeing it was useless to argue. She must hope that Mr. Collins and her father would come to an agreement as to when the betrothal could be made public. Perhaps this might occur at Pemberley?

September 3rd

Yet another clash with my very unreasonable husband! I am incensed that he should dare to search through my private papers. A woman's bureau is sacred. This act has rendered me violently angry. As to the bills, he is completely in error. If I were not so brought down I would storm into his library and upbraid him with the very bills he threw down so contemptuously in my room. No matter. I shall merely ignore him for the present, for I am much too caught up in pursuance of marriage prospects for Kitty and Mary.

Here I am at least a little successful. From today's service it is apparent that Kitty will not be long in remaining single. Mr. Collins has made his intentions very clear indeed.

As for Mary, the captain was attentiveness itself at our table. The very happy coincidence that he and Mr. Collins will be at Pemberley this Christmas will unquestionably mean there will be wedding bells in the New Year.

Chapter XIII

Mrs. Bennet regarded herself in the mirror. Two matters were demanding her immediate attention: the first being her relationship with Mr. Bennet, the second, her own state of health. Her husband, she perceived miserably, had distanced himself completely. The avoidance of his wife in society and at home caused her grave disquiet. Matters of domestic finance and male visitors were the focus of his disapprobation. His demeanour in each case was one of scarcely contained anger. It was only on these matters that he connected with Mrs. Bennet at all. Otherwise he assumed indifference. Whence had the former Mr. Bennet gone? That affectionate father and witty husband, whose wry sense of humour had once lit her every day, had vanished; replaced by a man of severe and chilling countenance who scarcely could bring himself to look at her. She could not comprehend the degree of ire he exuded when confronting her with bills, which were not in all cases justified. But with Lizzy's recent and welcome generosity, these should no longer be an issue. However, his barely disguised animosity towards Captain Wainwright was bewildering, since he still seemed to be unaware of the naval man's potential as a son-in-law. In fact, the captain had been informally banned from the house, Mr. Bennet having insisted to his wife that the naval gentleman was not to be invited to dinner again.

As for her own state of health, Mrs. Bennet considered all the symptoms that had haunted her during the two years of her menopause. Her husband's collective term for them as "your nerves" had cloaked a lengthy list of disparate sufferings, each of which had brought her low. Of her forgetfulness, tremblings, flutterings, spasms, head pains, heart beatings and unrest, she wondered which of them were the most troublesome, and which of these symptoms had abated, since applying to the apothecary and his wife. The forgetfulness was irksome but was becoming less frequent, provided she kept pen and paper to hand. Her head pains had lessened in severity and the palpitations, though disquieting, were bearable, since she had resolved to stay calm whenever she felt her heart start to flutter. Where formerly she had been alarmed at the onset of the sudden rise in the pace of her heart, she now felt able to control her reaction by sitting quite still and breathing slowly, thus enabling her to regain some composure. "Altogether," she mused, "I believe feelings of desperation are not the first response to these symptoms. What was it Mrs. Jones advised? Ah yes! 'Less alarm, more calm'. There's something in that!"

As to her sleep, though erratic in pattern, this had now improved since the taking of the apothecary's preparations and her own revivers. She was finding, to her delight, that she had more periods of vigour and was less often prone to feelings of lassitude. The *chaise longue* in her room had seen little of her in the last two months and indeed she now kept less to her room than in the whole of her marriage. On her better days, the animation she experienced had rendered her more positive about herself and well disposed towards others. She noted wryly that this resulted in a not altogether admirable propensity for the increase in conversation that many would regard as trivial, but which had always been a feature of her nature. When in this mode, she felt herself to be happy and able to look kindly on others' foibles. Ah, the ease of forgiveness when one is in the best of health! In addition to the restorative of improved sleep, she found her memory and mental powers in general were not so troublesome. Of late, there had been no incident of misplaced items in bedroom wardrobes or forgotten facts whereby her daughters could call her to account.

Still, the sudden onset of hot and then cold sweats was frightening and caused her distress, especially in company. However, their lessening frequency she gratefully acknowledged, was due Mrs. Jones' advice on clothing, cooling tinctures and soothing balms; these enabled her to "manage" those formerly overwhelming symptoms. And now that the damp airs of autumn provided cooling mists and soft rains, she felt able to face life with more tranquillity.

It was probably the rapid changes in her moods that still caused her most concern, she reflected. When in a neglected condition (fancied or real) she felt unable to be her usual lively self. At such times, the world looked grey, and prospects of an upturn in her fortunes, bleak. She knew that she was bitter, snapping fiercely at those closest to her, as if some beast possessed her and her will was not her own. Sometimes she felt a surge of energy and surrounded by supportive friends; at these times her world was safe, her esteem high and her lifted spirits radiated to everyone around her. The most disturbing feature of such differing emotions was the frightening speed of their alteration. Without warning, her smile would be replaced by a frown, and her warm sympathetic feelings would be washed away by an icy torrent of harsh words, whether she would or no. She was aware immediately of such uncalled-for anger, seeing the reactions in the faces around her and the withdrawal of their smiles. At such moments inner despair swept over her. How ashamed she felt of *this* Mrs. Bennet. How often she wished her words unsaid. When alone in her room recalling these moments, tears of lamentation and regret were her sole companions. At such times, she seemed marked for misfortune.

Mrs. Bennet looked again at herself in the mirror; today the lines on brow and cheek were etched deeply while her once sparkling eyes were dull and adorned with dark shadows. She felt her looks had fled with her bright behaviour. She sighed, then faced the image before her. A steady gaze brought her to a recognition that was tinged with a degree of hope. "All in all, there *is* an improvement in my health. There *is* more control of my condition. With time and patience I may be able to conquer my illness." She glanced at the wine glass and bottle on her table. "And when all else fails, I can rely on my private restorative," She told her reflection with a smile.

It was in this situation that she heard the front door bell jangle, followed by Hill's voice welcoming a visitor. The stranger soon was no longer a mystery as Mrs. Bennet recognised the voice of Aunt Philips in the hall. She had come with a view to cheering and heartening the family. Mrs. Bennet swiftly hid the bottle and glass. A few minutes later, the sisters were in each other's presence and fell into easy conversation.

When the usual pleasantries were over, Mrs. Bennet could not contain her delight at the financial assistance so generously offered by Lizzy and Jane.

"Did ever a mother feel so cared for?" exclaimed Mrs. Bennet. "I am no longer beholden to Mr. Bennet for my personal needs. I cannot tell you how unshackled that makes me feel."

Mrs. Philips smiled and did not reveal her own part in the forwarding of these financial arrangements. She merely shared her sister's joy. Just observing the improvement in her sister was reward enough. Then the latest family news was raised, discussed, carefully deliberated over and opinions confirmed.

"Yes, dear Jane is well in her confinement and prospers," smiled Mrs. Bennet, "and with the generosity from Lizzy, the tutors are continuing with Mary and Kitty."

"This is good to hear, sister. And what of their progress?"

"Both are improving in manner and skills. Mary is much less prone to preaching; she allows herself but four days out of seven to hand down her morality to the rest of us."

"I take it that this must include Sundays?" smiled her sister.

"Of course," laughed Mrs. Bennet, "but on Sundays she gives us the benefit of double doses. It's good for our spiritual health, she says."

"How is dear Kitty doing?"

"Her musical prowess, like Mary's, has progressed in a very satisfactory way, as has both girls' French and Drawing."

"And her general deportment?"

"Ah, there is a cause for congratulation. Kitty is much more tractable than formerly. In society there is a happy air about her that is very pleasing to me. Her former irritable nature has abated and is replaced by constant affability. Even Mr. Bennet has remarked that there is less giddiness in her than formerly."

"To what do you attribute such a change?"

"I am uncertain, but I would hope in some part it is due to her forming an attachment to a young man as well as her gaining from her education."

Aunt Philips forbore to comment on the young man, but enquired about her nieces' progress in music.

"And the girls' skills will be displayed at Pemberley, will they not?"

"Indeed. Mr. Bennet has already heard their musical pieces and says that with a little more rehearsal, the girls will not disgrace us when they exhibit at Christmas."

"Tell me how you and Mr. Bennet are now, dear sister."

Mrs. Bennet made no reply, but went to her store cupboard and drew out a bottle of Madeira and two glasses. She poured out the golden liquid with a sad smile. It was not the face, but Mrs. Bennet's actions that caused her sister to feel consternation.

"My dear, do you not take water with your wine? Those glasses look to contain rather large portions for a lady."

"They are taken from the cabinet in the dining room where the port decanter is kept with glasses for the gentlemen. Why should I not have as much liberty as my husband and his friends? As to watering the wine.. no, I never add water, since diluted the wine has little effect."

Mrs. Philips tried not to show her alarm. Instead she asked gently, "And do you often take wine?"

"As often as I need," said her sister abruptly. "Here, take this glass and join me in celebrating my empty marriage." The bitter grimace that accompanied this statement alarmed her sister even more than the size of the glass. In reaching across the *chaise longue* to accept the proffered drink, Mrs. Philips' foot caught against some objects beneath. The sound could only be that of clinking glass. She looked straight at her sister, who averted her eyes. Mrs. Philips stepped back and bent down to observe for herself. She reached under the seat and pulled out bottle after bottle. Her first feelings were those of astonishment.

"Oh sister! How long has this been going on?"

"Do not question me! I know what I am doing. I am not a child. It is a trifling matter only." There was a wild and desperate look in Mrs. Bennet's eyes. Her sister had never seen Mrs. Bennet so defensive nor so estranged from the girl and woman she had known for over forty years.

"Leave me alone! Nobody can help me. At least I can find solace in this." She turned away from her sister and stared at the wall, still nursing her glass of wine. Mrs. Philips did not move.

"Go away!" Mrs. Bennet's voice rang out harshly.

There was a silence. Neither sister moved. The silence continued for a few moments. Eventually, out of curiosity, Mrs. Bennet looked over her shoulder. Mrs. Philips was kneeling down and holding out her hands. "Come, my dear, come here to me. You are beloved by us all. These troubles will pass in time." She lent forward, and Mrs. Bennet stared, bit her lip, then suddenly put down her glass and, in a torrent of tears, embraced her sister. They held each other for some time, and when the sobbing subsided Mrs. Philips asked, "Is it The Change that is still causing you so much distress, my dear?"

Mrs. Bennet shook her head.

"Is it something to do with Mr. Bennet, perhaps?"

Mrs. Bennet coughed and caught her breath. She nodded and slowly sat upright. By wiping her eyes and breathing more deeply, she struggled to regain some degree of composure and at last was able to breathe more evenly and look at her sister.

"Oh, I fear that this is where I suffer far more than from my ailments! Mr. Bennet abhors me! There is coldness, suspicion and disapproval whenever we find ourselves alone. In front of others he plays the amiable husband, but in private there is no improvement at all," said Mrs. Bennet.

"I have seen a little of your troubles these past few months and noted you seem to spend much time apart. I am sorry to see you so unhappy. The evidence here displays how deeply that unhappiness goes." She glanced at the bottles. "Believe me, this is not the answer. Your menopausal symptoms will not lessen by imbibing, my dear. And as for your marriage, secret drinking will not help you towards a solution. Can you see that?"

Mrs. Bennet stared around her at the bottle-strewn floor. A wave of shame ran over her. How could she have allowed this to happen? Doubt followed shame. "Is it possible to stop this habit, or is it too late?"

"It's never too late."

Their conversation was interrupted by Kitty calling up the stairs, "Mama, Aunt Philips, may I bring you some tea?" The sisters heard Kitty's footsteps coming close.

"Oh, what shall I do? I must not let the girls see this."

"Quickly, sweep them under the bed." They were just in time. Kitty entered as the two women were resuming their places on *chaise longue* and sofa.

"Welcome my dear," said her aunt. "Yes, two cups of tea would be most refreshing. Could you bring them here with some of Hill's excellent scones?"

"Of course, Aunt Philips."

As soon as Kitty left, the two women faced each other. Mrs. Bennet begged, "Oh please take all these bottles away. And those in the cupboard too. I will not be so tempted if they are gone."

"Better than that, my dear, put them all in the linen basket. It is essential to your recovery that *you* take this action. It will be a moment of the utmost importance, sister, for it will mean a decisive disengagement from your dependence. This may take all your courage, but I am convinced you are strong enough to act on this advice. For my part, I shall find an opportune time to carry them downstairs and hide them in the cellar. I shall later dispose of them. No-one will be any the wiser. I am happy to do this for you, but on the condition you abstain from all wine. Will you promise me this?"

"But what if, in a moment of weakness, I should lapse?"

"The fact that you have no easy access to the means of temptation will prevent your immediate reversion, dear. I am sure that your respect for those closest to you and your own health will alert you to the dangers of surrender to this harmful habit. I trust your judgement in such a circumstance. Now can you take the first step?"

In answer, Mrs. Bennet picked up each bottle and buried it among the laundry in the linen basket. She hoped her current resolve would not be tested too often. With that done, she said, "Such relief! I hope this is truly the end of such a practice. However," and here her face grew sad, "the distance between my husband and myself will not be so easily breached. There is no cure for broken wedding vows."

"Come, come, sister. We must do what we can to repair the separated strands. I have already thought of a plan, which may take you forward. The lack of financial impediment, thanks to Lizzy, will aid us here."

"I fear no amount of money will save this marriage."

"Listen, sister dear." Mrs. Philips took her hand and said brightly, "There are some new supplies come to Meryton stores which I insist on your seeing: dresses, bonnets, boots. All are delightful. You are to view this as a start to your campaign in recapturing Mr. Bennet's heart. You first did that at an assembly when you were but 18, the time where Mr. Bennet first saw you. I could tell he felt immediately in danger. He never looked at another woman that evening. I feel sure that sentiment is not lost, merely buried. We must give it new life! Come, put on your cloak and walking shoes. We'll set off as soon as may be."

"I do not have the heart to covet new gowns. I fear my days of adornment are over. If Mr. Bennet has no interest in me, then I have none in myself."

"Nonsense, nonsense!" replied Mrs. Philips and, despite the protests, bundled her sister into shoes, gloves and cloak.

"No, really, I assure you, I have no wish to waste money. No energy to walk out today."

But there was no denying her sister and, despite the light rain, the couple reached Meryton in fine spirits. They joined the other damp but eager women who fingered the new brocades, examined the latest dresses, slipped on the new leather boots and tried the most handsome hats, cloaks and bonnets. The conversations and movement of fabrics rose from the ladies like a cloud of butterflies.

"This shade of harebell blue will compliment your eyes," said Mrs. Philips, holding up a beautifully cut gown. "Try it on at once, with these matching shoes and hat." The latter proved to be a very dainty "fancy" of blue velvet studded with tiny cream flowers. Mrs. Bennet was not inclined to object and disappeared into a changing booth. After a few minutes, and feeling slightly self-conscious, she stepped outside the crimson curtains to show herself to her sister.

Several other ladies ceased their searches of the fabric tables and dress racks to look at her. There were glances of admiration rather than the censure Mrs. Bennet had feared. Mrs. Long was the first to speak, albeit reluctantly.

"Why, Mrs. Bennet, that gown seems to be just your colour."

Mrs. Jones added, "I quite agree with Mrs Long, and will add that the fit is excellent."

"Ah yes, madam," said the proprietor bustling forward, "It is the way the material is cut across the bosom. A very flattering line, if I may say so."

"We'll take it," said Mrs. Philips quickly.

"The shoes and hat, too," she added, for she could see that the approval of others might lead to the items being purchased by them, if the sisters wavered. It was not long before they had selected gloves, fans, two other day gowns in worked muslin, a silk pelisse and three Indian shawls, while for travelling, a sumptuous velvet hooded cloak was added to the collection. Or rather, Mrs. Philips selected, Mrs. Bennet concurred.

"After all," said Mrs. Philips, "Lizzy directed me to ensure you spent that allowance on yourself."

"You give me fresh life and vigour! I am indebted to you for your kindness," she said, as they walked to Longbourn together.

The new apparel, when tried on later in the quiet of her own room at home, filled Mrs. Bennet with growing confidence. She stood in front of her mirror. The garments gave her figure a dignity and enhancement that belied her customary stance. Her reflection showed a woman who had started to renew her courage and a flame of self-belief. She hoped the purchases would enhance her progress in regaining her husband's affections. The prospect of wearing such lovely things and of being in Derbyshire among her family again was a cause for excitement and enlivened her spirits. Perhaps when Mr. Bennet was in Lizzy's company once more, he would soften towards his wife. Her logic extended to the hope that once this situation occurred, he would look on her with a more kindly eye and if she appeared in her finery, she might win him again. After all, he had once remarked of her in comparison with her daughters, "Mrs. Bennet you are as handsome as any of them."

She decided she would not reveal the "new" Mrs. Bennet before Pemberley, but would pack away all these treasured garments, saving the cloak, lest her self-conviction vanish like the late autumnal mists that hung across the lawns.

*

Bags, hatboxes, trunks and general luggage were
piled on top of the two carriages waiting on the
Bennets' drive, that crisp December morning a few
weeks later.

"Surely no more, Kitty, I beg you!" called down
her father from his place on the carriage roof. Kitty
was handing up three or four more boxes, with
several still on the gravel drive below. Mary stood
waiting with one modest bandbox and a small bag
of religious books.

"But I have been as prudent as I can, papa, I can
assure you," laughed Kitty.

Mrs. Bennet, from her seat inside the coach,
poked out her head to speak. "There is a little more
room inside if we place the hatboxes under our
feet."

"That space I had marked for my own luggage,"
replied her husband.

"Whatever for? Your chest of clothes is already
stowed above us."

"My books are yet to be put in."

"Books?" she laughed incredulously and looked
into her husband's face.

"Books? Has not Mr. Darcy the largest library in
Derbyshire? "

"He may not have the copies that I favour."

"Mr. Bennet, you are too precious! I had thought
we might be spending a little more time
together at Pemberley, once you were dragged away
from your study here, where you bury yourself
every day. Surely you can leave behind a few
dreary, old texts?"

Stung by her reference to his beloved volumes as "dreary", he said sarcastically, "Madam, since you care nothing for literature, you can exercise no intelligence in the matter. Your taste in great writing runs only as far as the frivolous novels of the circulating library, and those you do choose, are of the shortest length you can find. I come across them in use as door stops or buried under your cast off clothing. They are often overdue by a whole month. It is my firm belief that you only borrow books at all because you need a knowledge of title and author, pretending to the world you have more wisdom than you actually possess."

Mrs. Bennet's face reddened. The servants looked away in some embarrassment.

"Are there so many of father's books that we cannot find a small space for them?" said Mary, in an effort to make peace. "If you hand them into the carriage, papa, I shall tuck them under my feet."

Mr. Bennet went indoors and returned struggling with a large portmanteau.

"Oh papa!" Mary gasped.

"Think of the poor horses!" said Kitty.

"Mr. Bennet, you can hardly upbraid your girls for their luggage when you intend to take that," said his wife.

Mr. Bennet paused to reply in ungracious self-defence, then suddenly burst into loud, hearty laughter. "You are all in the right. The library at Pemberley will furnish every book I could possibly need for a life-time. Come Hill, Robson, we'll stand about in the cold no longer. I shall return the books to the house and then, let's be off."

Mrs. Bennet smiled and as he was about to join them in the carriage, said, "Take it not amiss, sir, but I suggest you travel with the servants. That way you may take a few of your most precious books, the load of people will be spread more evenly between the carriages, and we shall each enjoy more space."

Her perception and generosity astonished him.

"Why, that is an excellent idea and one I shall accept with gratitude."

He relished the thought of such unexpected freedom from the hours of female chatter that would lie ahead on the long journey to Derbyshire. He could read at his leisure and would also be able to discuss farming matters with his manservant.

"That thought does you credit, madam," he added graciously. "I am indebted to you."

He turned to the coachman with a smile. "Drive on, James. Follow up there, Thompson, as soon as I'm aboard."

The carriages jolted forward. With rugs covering their legs and their hands deep in muffs, the three Bennet ladies settled for the journey.

"How fortunate to be transported to Derbyshire in such a fine conveyance," said Mrs. Bennet.

"How generous of Mr. Darcy and Lizzy to loan it. An act of true benevolence," Mary added.

"If we urge James to quicken the pace, we may even catch the Gardiners, who left a full half hour before us," laughed Kitty. With this observation she leaned out of the window and eagerly called up to the driver, "God speed, James! Make all haste to Pemberley!"

December 1st

Since I last wrote in my journal, there have been weeks of varying fortunes. I have gone from growing confidence, through elation, and finally to indecision. As we leave for Pemberley tomorrow I have forced myself to pick up quill and ink once more and so make amends for my tardiness.

Surely it cannot be that there is no entry since September? I find no excuse for this omission. In my defence, some days have been so full there has scarce been time to breathe! But as the days have shortened and the year draws to a close, I am impelled by guilt as well as necessity to set down the more important business of my Longbourn life.

Firstly, to write of my condition. There is much to be grateful for. I am relieved to note Mrs. Jones' wise counsel and remedies have soothed my nerves and aided my return to health. I have not taken a drop of wine since October and feel the better for it. However, I am not yet completely cured of my illness. It is my quickening moods that most bring me down. The sharp words fly when least I expect them and often spoil the family harmony. There is much shame in such utterances. 'Prevention is better than cure' I frequently think when such speeches occur and I am determined to conquer this unworthy fault. Perhaps all this care has benefited myself in one respect; I believe my figure is less full than in the summer. True, my face has a haunted look, but then I cannot claim to be the beauty I was, after twenty-three years of marriage.

Another matter is the continuing coldness of Mr. Bennet. His affability is in evidence when with visitors but at home, with me, he is a stranger: I can gain neither his affection, nor his interest. He appears to be a lodger in his own house. I am saddened and angry by turns, and make no headway. Will he change when we reach Pemberley?

Sister Philips has heard my marital concerns with her usual patience. Kindness itself! Indeed, she keeps me from being more spiteful than I should be without her. Of course, we love to gossip. Tell me a woman who does not? And she has been the means by which my spirits have been lifted this past month. Firstly she made me see the folly of my private drinking. This was a hard moment for me; but I acknowledge that my increasing reliance on wine was not helping with my health. Giving it up has not been easy, but I persevere. Secondly, I have received from Lizzy an unexpected pecuniary gift. This is to be used for the purchase of new clothes. What times my sister and I have shared in the shops at Meryton! For so long I have gazed through the draper's windows and coveted the dresses there, but through dear Lizzy's help, I have walked in, head held high, and mingled most happily with other wealthier ladies of Meryton. Sweeping past Mrs. Long at the hat counter, and registering her complete surprise, was worth all the tea in China. Even her barbed comment, "Are you sure you have sufficient funds for this establishment, Mrs. Bennet?" could not detract from the experience. A triumph!

"Clothes maketh the woman," to adapt a phrase. It should not be so, but it is. Fine feathers make fine birds and my new plumage has made me feel a different creature.

The past week has seen indecision upon indecision. It is all very fine owning new clothes, but which should

I take and which leave behind for our expedition?

I am sorry to say I dithered and dallied until I grew quite distracted and had to lie down for a full half day. Around my room every thing in my closet and drawers was strewn across bed, chairs and dressing table. Kitty came in and screamed when she saw her mother lying among the flotsam. I think she believed I had become completely demented!!

And in a sense I had.

Chapter XIV

As the carriages rounded the drive that led from Pemberley Woods, the occupants saw the beauty of a Derbyshire winter extending on every side. Frost-covered fields lay like white carpets as far as the eye could see. The clear anatomy of Pemberley's great oaks rose majestically from the ridge ahead, standing like gaunt grey figures against pewter-coloured skies.

"Will there be a white Christmas, papa?" asked the youngest Gardiner, his eyes wide with wonder.

"If those clouds are to be believed, it is more certain than not," his father replied.

The horses gave of their best in the long haul to the top of the hill, gradually ascending for half a mile. Then, gaining the summit, they were checked for a few minutes to recover. On looking out, the passengers found themselves at the top of a considerable eminence, gazing across to Pemberley House, which was situated on the opposite side of a valley. It was a handsome, cream, stone building, standing well on rising ground and backed by wooded hills. In front, a stream flowed into the large lake, where two swans were mirrored in the still water.

Upon seeing the carriages approach, the great front doors were flung back and Lizzy, closely followed by her husband and Georgiana, his sister, came eagerly forward to meet them. Lizzy's welcome was easy and unaffected, her father observed, despite the magnificence of this noble setting. The servants quickly followed, bearing thick capes and rugs with which to wrap the chilled passengers as they stepped down.

"Dear Lizzy!" called Kitty, as she ran into her sister's arms.

"Dearest Kitty!" replied Lizzy, with the warmest of embraces. Here at last was her own, very dear, family. Kitty was prepared to be more formal with Mr. Darcy, but he would have none of it and gathered her up in a brotherly hug.

"Mama!" called Lizzy on catching sight of Mrs. Bennet. "How good it is to see you!" She took her mother's hands in hers and looked her up and down. She longed to say her mother looked well, but despite Mrs. Bennet's elegant costume—a deep plum velvet cape and matching hat—she could not utter an untruth. Noting her mother's lined face and tense jaw, Lizzy felt grave disquiet. Mrs. Bennet, though slimmer than when last with her daughter, looked very pale, and there were heavy shadows under her eyes. Lizzy had heard from Jane that their mother was going through a difficult time with the change of life, but did not think it would show to such a degree. She squeezed her mother's arm and resolved to give her the best Christmas that was in her power. Then she turned to her father.

"Papa, how truly wonderful to receive you here!" she cried. Mr. Bennet beamed at his favourite daughter. He felt happier than he had for months, just being in her company again. Mr. Darcy shook his hand in so cordial a manner that there was no denying the genuine warmth of his welcome.

"Come in sir, come in!" he said and all was bustle and laughter as he ushered the Bennets, the

Gardiners and their servants into the great house. A crackling fire lit the large vestibule, giving life to the space. Garlands of holly, ivy and mistletoe adorned the walls and a glass bowl of Christmas roses decorated the central oak table. The guests were more than a little overawed at such wealth and grandeur, as they gazed upwards at the tall windows, porticos and imposing portraits. A sweeping staircase led from the hall, and down it came Jane and Charles, holding out their hands. Their happy faces revealed the sincerity of their welcome and reflected the couple's inner contentment.

"Splendid, splendid!" laughed Mr. Gardiner, his warm voice echoing in the high-ceilinged room. The august surroundings lessened in formality as hosts and guests voiced their mutual delight in being together again. When the salutations were completed, which took rather a lengthy period, there being so many to exchange, Lizzy laughingly broke in, by saying, "We must save our sharing of news till later. Come, let us show you to your rooms, where you may refresh yourselves. As soon as you are ready, pray join us the drawing room where hot punch is waiting."

Led by the servants carrying ewers of steaming water and towels, the party made their way up the wide carved staircase to the landing. Lizzy, with smiles, showed each of them their rooms, then scampered downstairs to organise some hot mince pies and small savouries. Darcy was at the drawing room table before her with sleeves rolled up, adding hot wine, oranges, sugar and herbs to the steaming bowl.

A short time later, all the children ran down the stairs and were the first to arrive in the drawing room, followed by Kitty and Mary. They eagerly made short work of the various dainties laid out on the crisp white linen cloth. Mouths either consumed or shared news. The warmth of the Darcys' welcome, appreciated by every guest, filled the room. It seemed that only Mr. Bennet and his wife were not on speaking terms. Once the adults had dined (Mrs. Bennet being the only one who seemed to lack appetite), they were free to roam about the house while the evening meal was prepared. Lizzy took this opportunity to take her father aside.

"Papa, I am somewhat concerned at mama's appearance. She looks most unwell. Jane tells me she has been receiving some care from the apothecary and his wife, I believe, but are you not alarmed?'

Mr. Bennet felt uncomfortable. He was uncertain how much Jane had revealed about his marriage.

"Well, papa? Am I mistaken in thinking mama is unhappy and suffering a great deal?"

"Lizzy, you are aware that for many years your mother has suffered with her nerves. After my initial husbandly concern in our early-married life, I realised that to pay them attention only resulted in her greater dwelling on them. The time of her life where she is now is a natural phase. From what I have gathered from others, the symptoms are certainly unpleasant. I admit that these have caused her some degree of distress, but Nature's ills must be endured. These nerves are best ignored."

Lizzy frowned. While recognising the truth in much of her father's words, she nevertheless believed that the distancing of Mr. Bennet from his wife was a sorry matter; one which would harm the pair, perhaps permanently. She had realised that her parents' relationship had not always been a happy one; when he had first heard of her preference for Mr. Darcy, her father had warned her, "Let me not have the grief of seeing *you* unable to respect your partner in life."She had hoped that with the easing of their lives in seeing three of their five daughters married, her parents would be growing closer, but his cold manner in delivering his views alarmed her. There was an austerity in his countenance when he spoke of his wife that was new to Lizzy. It was with painful recollection that she recalled warning her father to take some action in preventing Lydia's visit to Brighton and he had not intervened. The consequence of that failure had caused the family a tumult of trouble. Since that time she had thought that Mr. Bennet had resolved to take more responsibility in family matters. Lizzy had never been blind to the impropriety of her father's behaviour as a husband. While living at Longbourn she had endeavoured to forget what she could not overlook, and banish from her thoughts that continual breach of conjugal obligation and decorum which, in exposing his wife to the contempt of her own children, was so highly reprehensible. His present indifference to her in society was improper and bordering on the uncivil.

Moreover, while in the privacy of Longbourn, Lizzy had learned from Kitty in her letters that Mr. Bennet was frequently violent in his conversations with their mother. Lizzy had believed these quarrels to be magnified by Kitty, but seeing her father and mother under Pemberley's roof, she recalled those words and the emotions evoked from her own decisions to take no action, it not being her place to do so. But she had never felt so strongly as now. Here at Pemberley she was mistress and she resolved to ignore the circumstance no longer; she would speak to her uncle and aunt.

*

The delights of Christmas-tide were not to be denied. The gaieties of the season were evident in every part of Pemberley. In the great kitchens servants, under Lizzy's watchful eye, set about their tasks with alacrity: the preparation of several dozen dishes, pastry making, mixing of puddings, the bringing in of logs, roasting meats, the chopping of herbs and onion to make the stuffings, cooking of sweetmeats, baking of cakes, steaming of wild fowl, shelling nuts, making marzipan, jellying fruits and crystallizing ginger kept them all busy for a week. Under Jane's calm supervision, the children and young people created gifts for the family, which were stored away till Christmas Day; while the gentlemen, in thick boots and great coats strode across the frozen meadows with their guns in search of game for the festive table.

Mrs. Bennet found it a relief not to be in charge of the housekeeping and was at liberty to rest, stroll the spacious grounds, listen to Kitty and Mary practise their pieces and write to her sister Philips. Lizzy, knowing of her mother's necessity of constant company, quietly saw to it that either Aunt Gardiner, Jane, Kitty or Mary were engaged to spend time with her at some point in the day.

Mr. Bennet was enjoying his time in his son-in-law's extensive library, and it was here that the Gardiners found him.

"Dear brother, we would be obliged if you would let us tell you of our concerns," began Uncle Gardiner. Mr. Bennet was not entirely surprised at their visitation, as there had been the mention of Uncle Gardiner's views recently by Lizzy, regarding the troubles of the Bennet marriage. The Gardiners' serious nature in approaching him again, gave Mr. Bennet some unease.

"Pray forgive this intrusion on such a personal matter," added Mrs. Gardiner, "but we hold you and Mrs. Bennet so dear that we feel we must speak."

Mr. Bennet looked resigned. He did not really believe there was so very much amiss. Lizzy's financial assistance had removed the major worry. Why, having now a personal allowance, which his wife was free to spend as she pleased, how could any woman be unhappy?

"Lizzy has told us of her alarm at her mother's deterioration since they last met. Aside from her ill health, there is a danger to which you seem oblivious," said Uncle Gardiner in a voice of concern.

"And what could that possibly be?" asked his brother-in-law.

"While we were enjoying your hospitality at Longbourn, we could not help but notice the relationship between yourself and Mrs. Bennet to be somewhat strained. There is a definite coolness between you. While you may be satisfied with a life bound by books and agriculture, my sister seems decidedly unhappy. I understand that she is at a vulnerable time in her life." Here Mr. Gardiner glanced at his own wife and held her hand.

She continued, "In case you are wondering otherwise, Mrs. Bennet has not confided in us. Her loyalty to you is total at present. But from personal observation, we believe she feels sorely neglected. Your remaining daughters will soon leave home and the two of you will be left alone. She has been a faithful wife to you, sir, for many years. She has cared for you and your daughters. She is deserving of your care now. This should be a time when older married couples draw closer. If you are treating her with such cold civility as at present, how do you think this situation will develop?"

"I cannot answer that, since I am not a fortune-teller," Mr. Bennet laughed, aiming to ease the tension and deflect further criticism. "Mrs. Bennet is merely suffering from her nerves. Her condition is largely the result of an over active imagination. It is all of little consequence."

His face appeared to affect nonchalance, but mentally he had to own he was a little disturbed. The bell sounded for dinner and interrupted them. Without waiting for more words from his brother-in-law, Mr. Bennet hurried away, leaving the Gardiners to shake their heads.

After dinner Mr. Bennet withdrew to the refuge of the library. Here at least he would find some respite from over-anxious relatives. However, despite the abundance of so many fine examples of literature, he found he was unable to concentrate on any. His mind returned repeatedly to the subject of his wife. Was her condition a cause for genuine concern? Did she really feel neglected or was this a symptom of her fancy? Was he actually guilty of not caring for her? Furthermore, did she no longer care for him?

That night his restless thoughts pursued him even in his sleep. In his dreams his wife had grown young again and looked much as the first time they had met. He saw her from a distance across a ballroom, which was thronged with couples. She was dancing with a handsome officer resplendent in his scarlet regimentals and they were laughing together as the set progressed. His dream-self felt extremely anxious and he awoke to find he was in a sweat, with the bedclothes wrapped around him.

Mrs. Bennet was sleeping in the adjoining bedchamber and clearly in no similar state of agitation, for he could hear her gentle snoring through the wall.

"Perhaps I am being foolish," he murmured to himself. "She is as she always was, a creature who seeks attention. I am certain her nerves are the cause of her current condition. Though I will allow she has perhaps been more anxious in recent times than I remember. But I will not own I have neglected her. I am no different from what I have always been. I have often chided her on indulging her feelings of self-pity, in the hope of distracting her from herself. There at least I can take some pride as a husband."

He fell silent, feeling better. But the images of Lizzy and The Gardiners came again before him. These were people whose opinions he valued more than anyone's. Were they so wrong? He fell again to recalling his dream and the picture of his wife in the officer's arms. Reason told him that this was an absurd fear. Could she be attracted to any man other than himself?

"Now *that* is very unlikely," he said. "She is past forty, nearer fifty in fact. Who would want her? Why, she is always so unwell and so much in her room, where would there be opportunity? She has scarce the energy to eat her meals, let alone pursue another romance. It is all nonsense." The notion of Mrs. Bennet leaping hand in hand with a lover, along a primrose path, accorded him such an image of absurdity that he chuckled aloud. Why, she would be so weighed down by her bag of potions and tinctures, she would be unable to walk, let alone dance!

*

To the delight of young and old, the first snowflakes of winter began to fall a few days later. It was Kitty who was looking through the window when she noted the curious behaviour of the two smallest Gardiner children.

"Why, Mary!" she called to her sister as she sat sewing. "Whatever do you think they are doing, do you suppose?"

Mary looked up and saw the children sticking out their tongues to the sky, then licking their lips. Their sudden leaps of excitement were understood when specks of snow multiplied and whirled about them, as they ran and caught each elusive flake. The joyful surprise that lit up their faces and displayed itself over their whole bodies in a variety of capers and frisks, was evidence of their utter pleasure.

"It's snowing! It's snowing!" they shrieked, and ran up to the sisters at the windows to wave their arms in delight.

"Perfect! We shall come and join you!" Kitty shouted.

The change in the weather had everyone talking, and the servants joined with Mr. Darcy and the other gentlemen in the hauling of logs to stack the great fireplaces of Pemberley.

With the bustle and preparations for Christmas and general distractions of a full household, Mr. Bennet meditated on his wife no longer. He felt certain there was little need to be anxious. He resolved to make the most of the many diversions to be found in and around the estate. He immersed himself largely in male company: hunting in the fields and woods surrounding Pemberley and when bad weather kept them indoors, billiards and cards or his beloved and solitary reading filled the days. Mr. and Mrs. Bennet met at the dinner table, but with so many people at each sitting, they scarce exchanged words.

Lizzy particularly noted this barrier and saw to it that her mother was entertained with walks around the shrubbery accompanied by other family members, pointing out the beautiful holly hedges, conifers all laden with snow and the frozen ponds where frosted reeds rose from water like glass. With rare winter sun sparkling in silver slants across the landscape, there was much to uplift the spirits. The children's antics in the snow provided Mrs. Bennet with a great deal of entertainment, particularly the snowball fights that not only the Gardiner children but the Bennet girls undertook. On more than one occasion, Mr. Darcy and Mr. Gardiner joined them, while even the reticent Georgiana was persuaded to participate when she saw how much fun Lizzy was having.

Inside the spacious house was a feast of ideas to puzzle or amuse: several musical instruments, including a grand piano, backgammon, cards, books, games and enough portraits in the Long Gallery to entertain and admire, especially when the master gave a guided tour of his ancestors. At quieter moments Mrs. Bennet found Jane often sought her company, asking her advice or opinion on the care of infants. These conversations occurred in the spacious sitting room while they were engaged in making small garments for the new baby.

"Mama, with five tiny ones all brought successfully into the world and reared to adulthood, you are to be regarded as a veritable fount of wisdom!" Jane laughed.

"Ah, Jane dear if your little one turns out half as amiable a child as you were, the rearing will take care of itself," smiled her mother.

Visits from neighbours and friends occurred frequently enough for the houseguests to cease from their labours or play, to assemble in the salon. For Kitty and Mary the delivery of letters was a regular delight. These missives were purportedly from acquaintances in Meryton and Longbourn. The content of the letters was reported only in vague and general terms and few paid these much attention.

December 10th

Pemberley quite overwhelms me! The estate is magnificent.

Never have I seen so many fine views, lakes, hills and ancient trees. Bingley tells me the woods are full of game, and Mr. Darcy—I dare not write of him more familiarly, even in my journal—relates the rich acreage and yields on his agricultural land. Even in this wintry weather, there is much to be seen and admired as I take my walks in this beautiful countryside.

As for Pemberley's interior, there is such ample evidence of history and wealth I can scarce write a half of it. Why, the portraits alone are worth a fortune! The plate at dinner, the chandeliers, the windows dressed in the finest of fabrics! All is grandeur and elegance.

Yet Lizzy makes us all welcome and with no show of condescension. Now,

*that is what I call good breeding!
Perhaps some credit may be due to
her upbringing?*

*Jane comes frequently to me for
advice on child rearing. She was such
a mild-mannered girl from her
infancy that there was little need of a
firm hand from her parents. However,
if I am to be credited with something
of her good fortune, then it shall be
praise for bringing about her
marriage to Bingley. Had I not sent
her to Netherfield on a day that
promised rain, she would not now be
in her delightful and enviable
position. Even the Longs and Lucases
of this world must acknowledge my
adroitness. Now if Kitty could get Mr.
Collins, and Mary, Captain
Wainwright, then shall I be satisfied!*

*As to Mr. Bennet, he is further from
me than ever. Shooting at game in the
frosty fields necessitates him coming
into the drawing room at the end of
the day to warm by the great
fireplace, but there is no warming of
spirit towards me. When summoned to
dine, he is assiduous in his avoidance
of me and never sits near. At dinner
he laughs and jokes with those
around him, never glancing in my
direction. I am shut out. What others*

make of this I cannot surmise. All I know is that I feel humiliated.

Chapter XV

Christmas Day was full of excitement and joy; with the children waking early, the scramble to be down for morning prayers, then the luxury of a substantial breakfast, before the whole household walked out together on Pemberley's well-laid paths. Crisp morning light favoured them as the bright sun stood like a silver guinea in a blazing blue sky. Despite the freezing temperatures, the group walked with huge pleasure, declaring they had never seen a Christmas scene so beautiful. Their voices rang out in the clear air.

Christmas dinner was a long affair with several courses and many dishes, each a delicious example of the cook's art. The goose and plum puddings were perhaps the most admired, being borne steaming into the room by the cook herself, amid much applause. Conversation flowed from end to end of the table and several participants proposed speeches in praise of the meal.

Looking round the happy table, Mr. Darcy said, "This is much the merriest Christmas I can remember at Pemberley. My dear wife Lizzy has made me the happiest of men and together we welcome you all. Our joint hope is that you share our joy, and may this Christmas live long in all our memories."

Lizzy met his eyes as a toast was called and felt that she could not be more content. It was only when her perceptive glance fell on her mother that she felt the grief behind Mrs. Bennet's strained smile. Lizzy looked to where her mother's gaze fell—it was on the convivial Mr. Bennet.

"They shall leave Pemberley a truly united couple," was Lizzy's silent wish and she resolved to affect that consequence to the best of her ability.

A few days later came the arrival of "The lesser guests," as Mr. Bennet observed. First were Charlotte and William Collins. After them came Charles Collins and Captain Wainwright. The former was all grave politeness, and the latter, blustering charm. Their assimilation was seemingly without awkwardness, apart from Mr. Bennet's silent observation, "So shall Pemberley witness a fine display of rhodomontade from this pair of covert coxcombs. The one does so by overt humility, the other by exuding a superfluity of naval gallantry." While as often as she came across Kitty, Mrs. Bennet would drop heavy hints about the advantages of matrimony. This was not met with the daughterly deference that she expected.

"Indeed, mama, you surprise me. When one sees daily the example of a certain older couple, it maybe the case that all marriages are not made in heaven. Or if they are made there, they do not always remain so."

(It may be as well to point out that Kitty had not been in receipt of a letter for several days and was feeling particularly unhappy.)

This utterance caused her mother to sharply reply, "Such shocking disrespect! Kitty you are to go to your room until dinner!"

Though satisfied that she had taken control of the situation, Mrs. Bennet frowned after Kitty departed and felt the bitter truth of her daughter's remark.

Captain Wainwright could not help overhearing the raised voices as he walked through the hall.

"A sudden squall, ma'am?" he said, seeing Mrs. Bennet in the doorway. "I trust there will be calmer waters ahead."

"Forgive me, sir, I had no wish to offend the ears of others, but in the rearing of daughters a mother sometimes has to retain the upper hand."

"True, ma'am, though troubles are not limited to parents of the fairer sex. The behaviour of sons can necessitate a firm hand, too."

"And have you heard from young James recently, sir?" she asked.

"Yes, ma'am, we have received intelligence that HMS Shannon is off the Azores and shortly to join the remainder of the fleet."

"And do you miss the sea, sir?"

"To be truthful, ma'am, I do, but have schooled myself to seek other distractions. I am an active soul and find myself most content when with other people, engaged in an interesting project. In fact, knowing I was to enjoy the hospitality of a Pemberley Christmas, I fell to pondering on a venture which might make some small reparation for all Mr. and Mrs. Darcy's kindness, while I am here."

"You intrigue me, sir. May I know your plans?"

"Well, ma'am, they are not yet fully formed, and one should never leave dry land without charting a course, but I have gone some leagues in preparing the way to suggest an amateur theatrical. May I ask you, ma'am, if I am not presuming too far, to venture your opinion on such an enterprise?"

"Why, sir, of course I can only speak for myself, but I would welcome such a diversion. It would be an opportunity for invention and amusement. I am sure others in the house would agree."

"Your approval means a great deal to me, Mrs. Bennet," said the captain. He caught her hand and kissed it in a theatrical manner and both burst into laughter.

"But sir, do you have a certain play in mind or are we to invent one? "

"Indeed, ma'am, we shall be certain of success with the ready made drama I have in mind. I recently saw Oliver Goldsmith's new comedy in London and thought it capital. Do you know the work? It is called 'She Stoops to Conquer'."

"I have heard of it, sir, through my sister who resides in the city. I should very much like to read it. Do you have a copy of the drama?"

"Several!" rejoined the captain. "Do take one to your room and, when you have read it over, I should be glad to learn of your thoughts. I feel the play would furnish us with several characters suited to our company. We could perform some of the scenes and amend the script as the need arises."

"Should we mention this enterprise to anyone else, sir?"

"I think it judicious to keep it to ourselves at this time, dear lady. But I shall, on the strength of your response, privately consult Mr. Darcy as to his opinion."

"Mr. Darcy!" she exclaimed. "I cannot imagine he would so unbend as to take part."

"Perhaps you are right, Mrs. Bennet, but as guests in his house, perhaps he should be approached before anyone else don't you think? Meanwhile, we'll keep this venture to ourselves, shall we?"

With a conspiratorial wink, the captain bowed low over her hand. She felt strangely light-headed and lest she said more, departed, taking the play script to her room. He mulled over their conversation for a short while then quickly departed to find his host. As a naval gentleman who responded with alacrity when circumstances demanded action, the captain eagerly sought out Mr. Darcy in his study.

"Ah, sir, is it a convenient moment to converse with you?"

"I am at liberty and therefore at your disposal, Captain Wainwright," said Darcy with a smile.

"Thank you, sir. I should like to sketch out a proposal that I hope will find your favour."

"Speak on, sir. You will find a ready listener in me."

Captain Wainwright described his venture, and found to his surprise that Mr. Darcy was asking questions in some detail. The captain thought his host would reject the proposal out of hand, since it might smack of frivolity or be unwelcome to his taste. Or if the plan was found acceptable, then he expected a man of such standing, as master of Pemberley, to give his general approval, then dismiss any further involvement, expecting the captain to proceed with it alone. Instead, the more the plan was revealed, the more eager and more thorough the questions became.

"So if we are to perform 'She stoops to Conquer'," said Mr. Darcy, "have you ideas for casting among our household? Have you seen the play in performance? Do you require costumes, a stage set and musicians? Will the dining room be space enough? Or shall we need some larger area? The barn has been used before, in my father's time. We could appoint wall brackets for torches and candles for the stage. How long have we to rehearse? Have you appointed a Director? Who is to act as Prompter?"

The captain was rather taken aback at Mr. Darcy's knowledge of amateur theatricals. Before he could answer, Mr. Darcy eagerly went on, "I confess, sir, I have seen the play in London and thought it very fine. It was the talk of the season last year. If you have not yet appointed a director, may I offer myself?"

"Why, sir, nothing would delight me more. From this moment, you are the Director. I have only confided in Mrs. Bennet, and she is to give me her opinion of the play after she has read the script. When she hears of your support, she will most certainly approve, and the venture will be on the slipway."

The gentlemen shook hands and agreed to meet with Mrs. Bennet after dinner, to take the project forward.

*

"The great honour has fallen to me of taking overall responsibility for a forthcoming entertainment," said Mr. Darcy to the assembled company the following evening at dinner. His whole manner was one of theatricality and his usually serious features were curved into a genial smile.

Mr. Bennet whispered to his neighbour, "I am all astonishment. Is this the same son-in-law before whose very eyebrow I cowered? Certainly, Lizzy has improved him."

"In short, with your agreement, we hope to stage a shortened version of the play currently so popular in London, 'She Stoops to Conquer'."

This was met with immediate general delight, everyone having at least heard of the play's unprecedented success. Then the elation slowly ebbed as each listener realised the full import of 'we'.

"But, sir, we are utterly unskilled," said Mr. Collins with a nervous look. He did not add that he had no wish to look an utter fool in public.

"Fear not," said the host "Some of us have seen the play and know what it involves, and several of us are not without experience in the field of amateur dramatics."

"I once took the part of Bottom at school, sir!" called out the eldest Gardiner boy. This was received with laughter. Before the mirth could descend into good-natured teasing, Mr. Gardiner came to his son's rescue, stating, "I for one shall be pleased to offer my services in any capacity."

His wife squeezed his arm and added, "You may also count on me, Mr. Darcy. I have a little experience myself, and shall accept any position, whether it be a speaking part or assisting with the costumes."

"Excellent!" said Darcy. "I should like to add that the whole idea is not my own, but the imaginative suggestion of my friend, Captain Wainwright."

Mr. Bennet muttered to himself, "Trust that cockscomb to want to show off his pitiful talents."

But Mr. Bennet was alone in his desire to dampen the venture. Despite personal modesty, everyone felt that an amateur theatrical would lighten the darkest days of the year. The questions arose from every part of the room.

"When shall we perform?"

"How often shall we rehearse?"

"Are we to audition?"

"Shall there be an audience?"

"Will you need musicians?" (This request was from Mary, who was confident in her musical skills, but trembled at the thought of any acting.)

"People, people," laughed Mr. Darcy, "All in good time. Captain Wainwright has the scripts to hand and we shall rearrange our chairs in a circle, then have our first reading."

The scraping of chairs on the polished boards created some confusion, but all were eventually settled and every countenance was turned expectantly to the captain. Mrs. Bennet could not but admire his easy confidence; an admiral regarding his flotilla could not have appeared more content.

"I have assigned the roles randomly to start with. Be assured, all will have a turn at reading today.

From the most experienced sailor to the lowest powder monkey here." This brought a few smiles. "Before I begin, however, I hope you will accede to my request that we name Mr. Darcy as Director?"

"Here, here!" said Mr. Gardiner and Bingley together.

"Seconded, sir!" laughed Mrs. Gardiner and Lizzy.

Mr. Darcy took a bow. With a nod from Captain Wainwright, Darcy continued. "For those who are not familiar with the play," said the new director, "the plot is briefly this. It revolves around a comic misunderstanding between Mr. Hardcastle and two young men named Marlow and George Hastings. The latter have been sent by Sir Charles Marlow to visit Mr. and Mrs. Hardcastle, their daughter Kate and the stepson Tony Lumpkin, none of whom have met before. When the two friends stop at an alehouse they meet Tony, who does not reveal his identity, but who resolves to have a joke at the visitors' expense. Tony tells them that their destination is a very long way yet, so they had best stop overnight at an inn called 'The Three Pigeons'. Marlow and Hastings take his advice. The inn is in fact the home of the Hardcastles.

"Young Marlow's character is complex: he is shy around 'proper people.' particularly well-bred, pretty young women, but crudely behaved in lower-class company.

"On arrival at the 'inn', Marlow acts abominably. He enrages the mild Mr. Hardcastle, who cannot abide these London people. But it is Kate who decides to turn the tables on the young man. She pretends to be a servant, to see this young man for herself. So, dressed as a barmaid, 'she stoops to conquer'. The rest of the plot will be unravelled as we progress. The Captain and I have edited Mr. Goldsmith's script to create a shorter version; one that can be rehearsed and then performed over the next five weeks."

There was immediate discussion among his listeners, but by holding up his hand for quiet and an encouraging smile, Mr. Darcy regained their interest as he read the list of characters.

"The Dramatis Personae are as follows:

Mr. Hardcastle
Mrs. Hardcastle
Kate
Tony Lumpkin
Charles Marlow
George Hastings
Sir Charles Marlow
Constance Neville, Mr. Hardcastle's niece
and there also are several servants.

"Just for the play reading, I shall allocate the roles, changing them as we go, so that everyone's voice is heard and we shall all understand the plot," Darcy concluded.

With a few minor stumbles, the play was read through. It was found to provoke many chuckles as the story was revealed. Everyone could see the comic potential of the piece and enthusiasm grew.

"A very satisfactory start," said Darcy. "The captain and I shall be announcing our cast tomorrow."

A private meeting of the two gentlemen took less than an hour. The parts almost selected themselves. The only question mark was over the role of Tony Lumpkin.

"Young Gardiner is keen enough, but being only twelve years old, he lacks the maturity, I fear. His voice is only half-broken and may cause him embarrassment in performance," said Darcy.

"Could the part be played by a young woman?" said the captain.

"A novel idea, whom did you have in mind?"

"I had thought of Miss Kitty Bennet. She is confident enough and could be taught to walk and act like a roguish young fellow."

"Not impossible," said Darcy. "Let's ask Hill to fetch her."

Kitty was soon found. She was at her writing desk. On hearing Hill knock she quickly covered her paper and listened to Hill's request.

"I shall come at once," she replied, and in less than three minutes had joined the gentlemen. On hearing their proposal, she was a little taken aback.

"May I consider this over the evening, sirs? I can give you my reply tomorrow."

Although this response was not ideal, the director nodded, and they began to turn their attention to rehearsal schedules, practice rooms, props, costumes, overture, sets, programmes and all the other minutiae that must attend a play.

Kitty had not been idle after leaving the room. She had another suggestion for Tony Lumpkin, and one that would surprise everyone. Yesterday she had received a letter from Mr. Chawton, stating that he would be in Derbyshire, visiting his uncle in Lambton. This was only two miles from Pemberley. He wished to call on Kitty, and his first thoughts were to make this visit a covert mission, but Kitty had other ideas. She quickly wrote the following note.

> *'My dear Edward, please come*
> *immediately. I shall be waiting for*
> *you at the entrance to Pemberley*
> *Woods, nearest the gatehouse. Kitty.'*

The note was terse but the effect was profound; Edward Chawton, intrigued and not a little concerned, wrote an affirmative reply, which the messenger took back at once.

On receipt of his letter, Kitty donned her cloak and slipped silently out of the house. She had not waited long before she saw him through the trees, and in a moment he had dismounted and drew her to him.

"Kitty, dearest, are you in some trouble or danger?"

"Neither, Edward. How good it is to see you. Your letters have not made up for our separation. But I must tell you why this meeting has been of some urgency." She felt nervous at what she was about to say, but believed it to be her only course.

"Are your feelings as you have written so often in your letters, Edward?"

"Dearest Kitty, have no doubt on that score. As long as I live, I shall never devote myself to another woman."

"Then here is my plan. Pemberley is to put on a play. There is nobody in the house suitable for the role of Tony Lumpkin."

"Tony Lumpkin?" Edward laughed. "You make him sound a buffoon."

"He is indeed, for he is a rogue and a comic character. You would play him admirably."

"Thank you, my sweet!"

Kitty laughed. "Edward this is all a device to gain acceptance with my family. My mother still has hopes of my marrying Mr. Collins."

"Never," said Edward, looking concerned.

"Do not alarm yourself. I know he no longer has designs on me since I rejected him. Besides, he is now being pursued by Mary. With our family staying at Pemberley until the end of February, we must make the most of the opportunity to meet. But first we need to gain Mr. Darcy's confidence. I suggest you call tomorrow morning as soon as we have taken breakfast, and say you are staying in the neighbourhood and are calling to pay your respects. You will be invited in and in the private meeting with him I shall endeavour to casually drop into his study and when the conversation turns to our Christmas play, shall propose you as the ideal fellow to play Tony Lumpkin. This will ensure your open and frequent access to the house."

"A bold plan. I shall try it, Kitty. We can but hope that Mr. Darcy does not send me about my business, backed by the powerful bodies of his henchmen."

December 28th

At last I have the liberty and energy to write my journal. Such a busy time!

Never was Christmas Day managed in so grand a manner! Mr. Darcy spared no expense in providing the most bounteous hospitality. I cannot begin to list all the delights of the Pemberley celebrations. We sampled an abundance of delicious foods at every meal and in between there were fancies and dainties laid out on every small table, lest anyone might feel the slightest pang of hunger. I was tempted to imbibe when I saw the array of champagne and fine wines placed on the table, but I feared even a small glass might stir up the cravings again. Instead, I took quantities of water which in Elizabeth's exquisite crystal glasses, twinkled as brightly as any sparkling wine.

Despite the many thoughtful and pretty gifts I received from the family, I find I cannot be totally happy since among the pile of presents I looked eagerly for one from Mr. Bennet. A second careful search did nothing but confirm there was none. Rather than make a public show of the omission, I chose to feign ignorance. I took some interest in others unwrapping their parcels, and was keen to see how my husband regarded my gift to him. This was a rather splendid brass-handled magnifying glass. My hope was he might acknowledge this gesture as a support for his private reading in the Longbourn library. He opened the package without reference to the label and when his eyes fell on the glass his face suffused with delight. I felt warmed by his response. When he looked for the label and saw my hand, he became thoughtful, then a little embarrassed.

Later, I found a small parcel on my bureau. It was from him. Though late, I was touched. But I was soon disabused of my kindly feelings. The contents were napery; in short, six linen napkins. How was this to be regarded? More a present for a housekeeper than a wife! An insult indeed!

It is fortunate that the children drew me into a game of riddles in the drawing- room, and then challenged me to a game of cup and ball. Valuable distractions. They discovered that Aunt Bennet was not to be defeated so easily. I won seven games of the ten.

A belated Christmas gift addressed to "A nymph worthy of adoration" was pushed beneath my door as I was writing this journal. It contained a slim volume of love poems and, in the frontispiece, the signature of the captain, with a request to read Shakespeare's eighteenth sonnet:
'Shall I compare thee to a summer's day?'

Upon studying this verse, I was not only struck by its beauty, but was overcome by its candour.

'But thy eternal summer shall not fade,
Nor lose possession of that fair thou ow'st.'

What am I to make of this? The lines are of so direct a nature, and seem so personal to myself, since it was delivered to my door. Is it merely a reassurance to the older woman? He may have witnessed my discomfiture when opening my Christmas presents.

Or a declaration of love? Am I to pass it on to Mary? If the book is meant for her, then why give it to me? Perhaps the captain is thoughtful that love poems directly from himself to

Mary would be a breech of decorum and he is asking me to act on his behalf? This betokens a respectful and proper behaviour, which is to his credit.

Then again, perhaps it is a gift of no particular significance?I am at a loss to understand its import. I can only wait for some further sign.

To report on possibly the best moment of the week, the company at Pemberley have agreed to act a play! It is Oliver Goldsmith's 'She Stoops To Conquer'. I am absolutely delighted! It is a highly comic drama. I read the part of Mrs. Hardcastle. A contentious and challenging role that amuses me mightily. A woman who says what she thinks. I should love to play her!

Mr. Darcy and the captain are to announce the parts tomorrow. Until then I must be patient. But the truth is, I can scarcely wait!

Chapter XVI

Everyone gathered in the drawing room. There was much chatter and laughter. Captain Wainwright and Mr. Darcy were seated at the large table. Darcy picked up his notes and stood before the assembled persons. The room grew quiet.

"Welcome to you all, the play has been cast and there will be understudies too. Those who are not selected for a role will be involved as musicians, backstage crew, or servants in the Hardcastle household.

"The cast is as follows:

Sir Charles Marlow: Mr. Gardiner."

"Thank goodness," whispered that gentleman to his wife, "not too many lines to learn, or time away from country pursuits."

"Mr. Hardcastle: Captain Wainwright.

Mrs. Hardcastle: Mrs. Bennet."

"I do not much like the sound of that alliance," muttered Mr.Bennet. He had been to Mr. Darcy last evening to protest that he wished no part in such a foolish venture, but had been persuaded to act as an understudy.

Constance Neville: Kitty Bennet.

George Hastings: Charles Bingley,

Kate Hardcastle: Lizzy.

Marlow: myself.

Tony Lumpkin's friends will be played by our manservants. Understudies are as follows:

Mrs. Hardcastle: Mrs Gardiner.

Mr. Hardcastle: Mr. Bennet.

Sir Charles Marlow: Mr.Collins.

Marlow: Tom Gardiner.

Kate: Emma Gardiner.

Constance: Mary Bennet.

The prompter will be our excellent housekeeper, Mrs. Reynolds, the most patient lady I know.

As to our costumes, Mrs. Gardiner, Jane and Hill are to undertake those positions. Georgiana and Robson will oversee stage properties, assisted by the younger members. The stage set will be the work of any able person. Mary will be in charge of the musical interludes, assisted by Mr. Collins."

"Poor Mary," thought Mrs. Bennet, "but I shall use the opportunity to get her to forward Kitty's renewed interest in Mr. Collins."

"You have not yet mentioned Tony Lumpkin," said Mr. Gardiner.

"He is not forgotten. We have found the perfect actor to step into that role. Last seen in Longbourn, I present no less a talented person than—" Here Darcy drew back the long curtain at the drawing room window to reveal Edward Chawton.

There was a surprised gasp, followed by applause. Only Kitty was seen to blush, though her mother thought this was due to the natural embarrassment of a pupil suddenly seeing her tutor in an unfamiliar place.

"Capital!" declared Mr. Gardiner.

"Hear, hear!" called his wife. Edward Chawton bowed to the assembled company and took a seat near Kitty.

"Thank you sir, and my best wishes to all the actors in their new roles," said Mr. Darcy. He picked up a heavy pile of papers. "To continue.

Here are the play scripts and rehearsal schedules. You will see where we have shortened the speeches. We shall read through the amended texts to see how they work. Please suggest any new ideas as we go along. The captain and I are no Mr. Goldsmith, and it is not easy tampering with the work of a genius written for professional performers, so I trust the narrative flows for our company of amateur actors.

"You will see from the schedules there will be an opportunity to rehearse with your fellow actors each morning. During that time, each scene's performers will be called-for, as they are needed, to join me in the library. I hope you will know most of your words by a week tomorrow. With the cuts the captain and I have made, this should not prove to be too difficult." His listeners looked doubtful, but he smiled at them encouragingly. "I have every confidence in you. If there are any problems, please speak up and we shall do our best to solve them. Are there any questions?"

"Yes, Mr. Darcy. Will there be an audience, or are we acting only for ourselves?" asked Edward Chawton.

"Well, that depends how rehearsals progress and what people think. Shall we look at this matter after we have run through every scene?"

Charles Bingley voiced a concern, "I think I may be speaking for most of us, Darcy, when I ask if five weeks will be sufficient? What I mean to say is, shall we be ready in time?"

Several others nodded at this request. It was one thing to enthuse about an entertainment as a winter diversion, but quite another to find oneself being organised and rushing towards a deadline, where one's frailties might possibly be exposed to an audience. Darcy resolved to keep a paternal eye on his flock and constantly assure them of their abilities. There would be no undue pressure to present the play unless he felt they were ready and could do Goldsmith's work justice.

*

The next week was to see Pemberley's corridors paced by wraith-like figures, scripts in hand, murmuring to themselves. Every room was full of actors and understudies who stumbled through their lines, trying out different styles of delivery with varying degrees of success. Mary took over the violin and on the pretext of hearing his lines, and her practice, she and Mr. Collins were able to spend time together legitimately.

Alone in her room, Mrs. Bennet began her acquaintance with Mrs. Hardcastle. "Now, what may I deduce about this lady in the stage directions? It says in Act I the room is 'old-fashioned', crowded with comfortable furniture and a blazing log fire. She is 'busy with a piece of embroidery', but throws it down with 'impatience'. Ah, it is clear she is dissatisfied. Her words to Mr. Hardcastle are angry, 'You may be a Darby, but I'll be no Joan, I promise you'. He sounds a stay-at-home gentleman, whereas she craves company. How very like myself and Mr. Bennet! But, is he kindly towards her?" She read on to where the couple disagreed over her age: 'I'm not so old as you make me. I was but twenty when

Tony was born. Add twenty to twenty and make money out of that.'

Mr. Hardcastle's reply, 'Let me see; twenty added to twenty makes just fifty seven!' made Mrs. Bennet laugh.

"Well, the similarities are remarkable! His put-downs are so like Mr. Bennet's. They seem always to be quarrelling. Never in amity. She is certainly a lady of swift temper, but with that husband, is it so surprising?"

She wondered about her feelings towards Tony Lumpkin, her son: 'a poor boy' who was 'always too sickly to do any good. Anybody that looks in his face may see he's consumptive'. Mrs. Bennet felt for this lady. Was she herself not as fond of Lydia? But her husband's rejoinder set a reality on the matter, since as soon as he remarks, 'He sometimes whoops like a speaking trumpet', Tony halloos loudly backstage and Mr. H. says, 'O, there he goes—a very consumptive figure, truly!'

"Ha: ha!" laughed Mrs. Bennet. "Why, how blind she is to her child's faults!" She could not wait to read the next lines to learn more. Mrs. H. defended her son by saying, 'He coughs sometimes'. Only to be met with 'Yes, when his liquor goes down the wrong way'.

Mrs. Bennet noted how Tony described his mother's tempers as: 'She fidgets and spits about like a Catharine wheel'. "How violent she is! But she seems also to suffer by being greatly misunderstood, for even when she is sincere in her mortification at the theft of her niece's jewels, she is not believed. That's just like my husband! He does not believe me when I am low with The Change!"

She spent the next few days reading her lines aloud, while walking around the room, addressing her words to imaginary actors. She was beginning to understand the appropriate intonation, but was unsure of gesture and facial expression. Darcy was little help in this direction. When rehearsing with him and the other players, the director's major concern was with positioning his actors, so rather leaving the characters to their own devices where interpretation of text was concerned. Despite her best efforts in front of the mirror, Mrs. Bennet was feeling a distinct lack of self-possession.

"I remain Mrs. B., rather than Mrs. H.," she thought.

*

Her next rehearsal alone was influenced by a conversation she had overheard at dinner that evening. Pemberley had been visited by a personage of some eminence, Lord Graham, who had recently been travelling in Europe.

"It is with much pleasure I can speak of my time with Queen Maria Carolina and her husband Frederick, whilst in Naples. Their hospitality was most generous. As to entertainment, we were asked to witness the most charming performances by Lady Hamilton."

The mention of the latter caused much excitement around the table. Some gazed at the speaker with no little disdain, others with curiosity. English society was fascinated by Lady Hamilton;

she had been living openly in a *ménage a trois* with her husband and Lord Horatio Nelson for some time. After Trafalgar, she had continued to reside in Italy and remained a figure of intrigue.

Mr. Collins struggled between his awareness of his place as a guest and his convictions of his calling. Self-regard won the battle over self-restraint. He stood up and with a smile as respectful as it was insincere, said, "While paying due deference to your lordship's position, as a man of the church I feel it incumbent upon me to express my righteous indignation. It is beyond my comprehension that anyone could condescend to see such a woman. (I cannot in any circumstance, refer to her as a lady). Her reputation is tainted and her liaisons are not fit for respectable society," said Mr. Collins.

"My dear sir, I can assure you that Lady Hamilton is admired wherever she goes. She moves in the highest circles. Moreover, her friendship with the queen has been politically useful to our country."

"Yes, yes. All very interesting," Mrs. Bennet interrupted. "But what of her performance, sir? We are all impatience to know." Everyone else at the table seemed more in agreement with Mrs. Bennet's curiosity than Mr. Collins' censure. Lord Graham noted the eager faces around him and continued.

"Well, madam, I for one was prepared to be sceptical when I heard how praised it was at court. But having seen it myself, I can say with some truth, I was utterly enthralled. It was all done with the utmost decorum and offended nobody's sensibilities. She is a lady of exceptional beauty, as may be deduced by the many times she has been painted by famous artists all over Europe. However, this would not be sufficient to entertain an audience for over two hours, if she were merely lovely to behold. No, her brilliance as an actress is unique. She has developed a performance that she calls her 'Attitudes', a form of mime art. These are a *melange* of postures, dance and acting."

"Attitudes, your lordship?" Kitty queried.

"They are a kind of silent tableaux. She stands in a tall black box surrounded by a gilded frame, lit by her husband standing by with a lamp. Her long, chestnut hair flows over her shoulders and she wears softly draped tunics in the ancient Greek style. Lady Hamilton adopts the pose of a classical figure from Greco-Roman mythology, or an emotion. She is able to change from grief to joy and from joy to terror so rapidly and so effectively, we were all enchanted. She seemed to float from one image to the next, and always with great dignity and poise. I cannot tell you how alluring the performance was, so gracefully was it portrayed. Gesture, facial expression and movement were all exquisitely communicated, with delicacy and precision. After each pose, Sir William Hamilton asked the onlookers to guess the character or emotion. Apparently, she has over two hundred of these 'Attitudes'. A gifted woman; we were all in awe of her. The whole evening was a sensation."

During this tribute Mr. Collins averted his gaze to show he had no interest in such a testimony. He was under social obligation to stay seated, but closed his eyes in contemplation, giving his thoughts to more lofty matters. He hoped by so doing that others might be drawn to follow his example, but with questions from all sides to Lord Graham about the subject of his discourse, Mr. Collins' nobility remained unobserved. He was more than a little dismayed to find on opening his eyes to glance at Mary, that she too was listening with seeming eagerness to the speaker. She coloured as soon as she felt Mr. Collins' stare upon her and looked down at the tablecloth. Mrs. Bennet was particularly engaged by the speaker and, while careful to avoid the appearance of too little impropriety in questioning so distinguished a personage (she had begun to recognise the wisdom of moderation), was engrossed by every pronouncement. Her animated features and concentrated gaze betrayed her desire to absorb as much intelligence as she could.

The interesting information about Lady Hamilton had given Mrs. Bennet much food for thought. She found herself looking hard at her play script to elicit the 'attitude' of Mrs. Hardcastle in each of her speeches. Anger, joy, contempt, fear, patience, sorrow and many more were evident. With each in mind, she stood before her mirror. Once she had identified the mood, she set face and body to display it. She then stood still, holding the pose, and regarded herself with a critical eye.

"Ah, so in sorrow I droop my shoulders a little. My face becomes mournful and my eyes look down. Capital! It will all need much working on, but there is promise in this beginning. Thank you, Lady Hamilton. You have shown the way!"

*

Next morning, in the conservatory, Edward, as Tony Lumpkin was declaiming to Kitty in a strong agricultural accent;

"Why, gentlemen, if you know neither the road you are going, nor where you are, nor the road you came, the first thing I have to inform you is, that — you have lost your way."

He was enjoying the country bumpkin style of Tony and, having quickly mastered the lines, was starting to enlarge upon the part, by lolling over the couch or putting his feet up on a stool, while miming drinking from a large pewter mug. His usual manners were swept aside for those of an ill-mannered rustic. Kitty was trying hard not to laugh while she read the lines of the servants. And the scenes between Tony and his cousin Constance were proving highly amusing to both, since they involved a great deal of argument. This intimate situation enabled their own relationship to explore and develop in a manner impossible to imagine from their normal daily encounters as tutor and pupil at Longbourn. Such is the legitimacy and licence of play rehearsal.

In Darcy's library the episodes between Mr. and Mrs. Hardcastle were progressing in a very lively manner. Mrs. Bennet and the captain found they had a close understanding of spouses quarrelling, and were exploiting their sparkling exchanges with bold gestures and improvised action. The captain had seized on the husband's sullen attitude and his verbal sparring with his discontented wife. As Mr. Hardcastle he muttered sourly,

"I wonder why London cannot keep its own fools at home. In my time, the follies of the town crept slowly among us, but now they travel faster than a stagecoach. Its fopperies come down, not only as inside passengers, but in the very basket."

Mrs. Hardcastle railed in a scornful voice, "Ay, your times were fine times indeed; you have been telling us of them for many a long year. Here we live in an old rambling mansion, that looks for all the world like an inn, but that we never see company. Our best visitors are old Mrs. Odd-fish, the curate's wife, and little Cripplegate, the lame dancing-master: and all our entertainment your old stories of Prince Eugene and the Duke of Marlborough. I hate such old-fashioned trumpery."

Hardcastle replied triumphantly, "And I love it. I love everything that's old: old friends, old times, old manners, old books, old wine; and, I believe, Dorothy (taking her hand), you'll own I have been pretty fond of an *old* wife."

This insult caused Mrs. Hardcastle to register an expression of extreme rage. She reacted with some energy by miming a well-timed clout at her husband's ear, which sent the captain spinning. The blow had caught them both off-balance and they fell on to the sofa and from there to the carpet with much laughter. Mrs. Bennet felt she had not had so much amusement in years.

It was at this moment that Mr. Bennet opened the door. He was seeking a book that Darcy had promised to lend him. What confronted his astonished gaze, was his wife and Captain

Wainwright together sitting on the carpet, their faces red with laughter and their arms entwined.

Mr. Bennet was shocked beyond speech. He stood rigid with tension. The couple scrambled to their feet, adjusted their clothes, and were about to explain their behaviour when Mr. Bennet turned away in fury and slammed the door.

He went to his room and sat on the bed, agitated and with thoughts prickling like holly. He stood up, walked to the window, then walked back again to the bed. He took up his book from the bedside table. He tried to read, but the words blurred together. He realized he was crying. But was it with rage or sorrow?

Across the hall, Mrs. Bennet was alone. She had left the rehearsal soon after her husband, excusing herself to the captain. Her feelings were in turmoil. That Mr. Bennet had found her in such a situation was unfortunate. That he had drawn the wrong conclusion was wounding, but the thought that he might believe she was deceiving him, after all these years of utmost loyalty, was mortifying.

"Such an unlucky coincidence!" she told herself, "Surely he cannot believe I am misleading him? Have I put our marriage at so very great a risk?"

Other thoughts came pouring in. She turned from despair to anger.

"It is not all my fault if we are at odds. He has neglected me. He is over-suspicious and he is utterly wrong about Captain Wainwright. I am merely rehearsing my part in a play, and I am furthering Mary's cause. Does he not want our girls to be married?" She stared at her reflection. Despite the circumstances of an open rift with Mr. Bennet, the face that looked back at her was one of health; this surprising situation was due to the enjoyment she was having here at Pemberley. The welcome she felt from Lizzy, the intimacy she was experiencing with Jane, the pleasure of living in a beautiful home with no cares to weigh her down, were all contributing to her general well-being. She observed, that since she had been in Derbyshire, she had gradually been experiencing better sleep too. There was little doubt that the northern air was refreshing after the less beneficial atmosphere generated by the spiteful old ladies of Meryton. In addition, the diversion of rehearsing 'She stoops to Conquer' was an inducement in assisting her to look forward to each day.

"If only Mr. Bennet would join us! He would see me in a different light. Surely he wants me well? I am a different woman altogether now from the poor creature who dwelt so miserably at Longbourn."

January 4ᵗʰ

"The play's the thing!"

What it is to long for something and then gain it. I am to play Mrs. Hardcastle! I cannot pretend that I shall perform to the same degree of brilliance as a London professional, but there will be no lack of spirit!

The gallant captain is playing Mr. Hardcastle. How may art and reality be compared? My stage husband and

Mr. Bennet? The characters in the play are not dissimilar, since Mr. Hardcastle is a man of dampening demeanour, who sees society as an evil wherein the unwary may be trapped. And what of the two men themselves, the captain and my husband? They are far apart in my view; Captain Wainwright is a gentleman who knows how to please. He has a way with words and women that is very captivating. Our rehearsals are times of the greatest amusement where we rail at each other in the most sportive fashion. I forget my personal troubles and enjoy the world of theatre where all is liveliness and art. The silence of my husband proves a poor comparison....

The arrival of Mr. Chawton surprised us all! Produced like a conjuring trick at the casting meeting. My reservations as to his thespian abilities have vanished since I saw him rehearse with Kitty. A fine voice and an admirable Tony Lumpkin, it would appear.

Later.

And now honesty demands I record a moment of acute embarrassment. Mr. Bennet came suddenly upon my rehearsal with the captain and found us both fallen upon the carpet. Humiliation! A complete act of innocence, but, seen from Mr. B's perspective, it may have seemed like marital betrayal. How am I to make amends?

Chapter XVII

Mr. Bennet had now been a full hour alone. He had calmed his anger enough to think more rationally about the situation. Was his wife deceiving him? Did he care?

To the first question he had no answer, to the latter he was forced to admit, he did.

Hadn't Mr. Gardiner warned him of the likely dangers where a wife is neglected? How foolish he had been! He owned that her weak understanding and illiberal mind had been a bar to real affection very early in their marriage, but where other powers of entertainment are wanting the true philosopher will derive benefit from such as are given. His reflections on the time they had shared together sharpened his mind to consider Mrs. Bennet's present worth. This woman had raised their five daughters, kept his house on very little income and her ignorance and folly had amused him all these years. Yes, and irritated him too, but did he not also have his faults, and had she not always been quick to forgive his foibles? He was forced to admit that his own character was not one to be easily understood, let alone provide an easy companion. Mr. Bennet recognized that he was an odd mixture of quick parts, sarcastic humour, reserve and caprice. A marriage of twenty-three years had been insufficient to make his wife understand his character, but she had been closer to him for longer than anyone and had accepted all his faults as well as his virtues. He recalled she had credited his wit in an early conversation on the pride of Mr. Darcy when first that gentleman had been encountered at the Meryton Assembly, "I wish you had been there, my dear, to have given him one of your set downs". He smiled. Did not this betoken at least some knowledge of his complicated character?

His conscience asked did she not deserve his support now she was apparently unwell? He had been told by Kitty and Jane how low their mother was feeling, and he had disregarded that at Longbourn. And here at Pemberley the kindly Gardiners had tried to help him see the warning signs, and his own dear Lizzy had felt certain enough of her mother's illness to speak to him. How foolish he had been, such prejudice he had shown! He had displayed no compassion, no understanding, no solicitude; he had not behaved as a husband ought. And all along there had been a handsome and gallant naval officer probably courting his wife behind his back, while he, Mr. Bennet, had retreated to his books and let it happen!

Was it too late to win her affections once more?

He decided to set aside his pride and seek the advice of those who had warned him. His only hope was they would not turn from him now, just when he needed them.

*

"Another satisfactory morning of musical harmony," laughed Mary, resting her hands from the violin. "It is all coming along well, don't you think, Charles?"

"Indeed Mary, we are perfectly in tune. With only two more weeks rehearsal, we are more forward than I expected."

At this moment, the door opened to reveal the three younger Gardiner children with their Aunt Jane, all eager to begin their own pieces. They were to perform two songs in the interval and these still needed further practice.

"Come, sit here Jane, you look a little tired," said her sister kindly.

"Oh no, I am quite well, Mary dear. It is such a pleasure to be with the children. All good experience you know—my own rehearsal for when Baby Bingley makes its appearance," she smiled.

"How long will that be, Aunt Jane?"

"Soon, Emma, only three or four weeks we believe. Then your patience will be rewarded."

*

In the library, they were rehearsing in earnest. Darcy and Lizzy were thoroughly enjoying Goldsmith's entertaining script as Marlow pursued the disguised housemaid, Kate.

Darcy stared into his wife's face saying, *"Yes, child, I think I did call. I wanted — I wanted — I vow, child, you are vastly handsome!"*

Lizzy backed away with a coquettish look and in a country accent said, *"La, sir, you'll make one ashamed."*

Darcy took hold of her hand. *"Never saw a more sprightly malicious eye. Yes, yes, my dear, I did call. Have you got any of your — a — what d'ye call it in the house?"*

Lizzy pulled away and replied sternly, *"No, sir, we have been out of that these ten days."* Darcy, taking both her hands in his, said roguishly, *"One may call in this house, I find to very little purpose. Suppose I should call for a taste, just by way of trial, of the nectar of your lips; perhaps I might be disappointed in that, too!"*

Lizzy's harsh response was given forcibly, *"Nectar! Nectar! That's a liquor there's no call for in these parts. French, I suppose. We keep no French wines here, sir."*

Lizzy broke away to say in her own voice, "Do you think I am playing Kate too sternly, or is she flirting with Marlow?"

"An interesting point, Lizzy, though she already has formed one opinion of him, as an inarticulate and bashful young man when he thought her to be a lady of his own class. In this scene, where she appears to be a bar-maid, she may now be truly shocked at his openly passionate manner."

"So you think he really is deceived?"

"Absolutely. He is emboldened by her present status; you will recall when they first met she had her face hidden by her bonnet, and he dared not raise his eyes to her."

"You have been doing your homework," laughed Lizzy. "I am glad you did not display such unrestrained behaviour when you were first with me alone at the Rosings."

"Who knows how I would have behaved if you had given me any encouragement?" Darcy smiled.

"Perhaps it was just as well that I did not, then, but gave you the time to think again and try another tack?" she smiled, her fine eyes sparkling.

They were both laughing now at the memory of Darcy's first proposal and how it had all eventually been resolved. Privately Lizzy was astonished that this so-called "unbending gentleman" had changed, and all to the good. She felt as well as knew she was happy. If only her parents could be so.

*

With the performance so close, everyone doubled their efforts in rehearsal; the pressure of the date that loomed so fast induced feelings of excitement and anxiety in equal measure. Jane, Mrs. Gardiner and Hill were attending to costumes while the final rehearsals were taking place.

"Can you stand still just a moment longer, mama dear, while I pin up your hem?" asked Jane, as Mrs. Bennet trailed across the improvised stage.

"Be aware of that beam overhead, everyone!" called Darcy, as above him Mr. Gardiner and some of the men servants were erecting a stage curtain.

In front of the actors, Mr. Chawton warned, "Be careful with those long gowns, ladies; we are going to put the candles into these footlights and, once they are lit, please act at least two feet further upstage."

"But then we shall be knocking over the scenery," said Kitty.

"Wouldn't oil footlights be better?" asked Uncle Gardiner. "They would not need trimming so often, and with five wicks each would give more light."

"We only have candle footlights," Darcy firmly replied.

Mr. Collins added peevishly "And how are we to see over your footlights if we are in the orchestra pit?"

Darcy looked puzzled. "Orchestra pit? What do you mean, sir?"

"Aren't the musicians having a pit to play in? I think you are leaving it very late, sir, to employ your constructors."

"There will be no pit," said Mr. Darcy abruptly.

Mr. Collins fell silent for a moment, then said, "Well sir, may I ask where are the musicians to play?" He believed that the musical items were of far greater importance than the actors. Mr. Darcy's initial response was to give Mr. Collins a sharp and crushing rejoinder as to the very minor role of music compared with the glorious words of Mr. Goldsmith, but marriage to Lizzy had taught him to moderate his tongue when provoked. He even managed a placatory smile (marvelling at his own self-restraint as he did so) and replied, in a firm voice, "That sir, is all in hand."

Darcy spoke with confidence, but he privately thought, "Tiresome man! I had quite overlooked the musicians. I'll ask Lizzy about that; she'll produce a solution."

Mr. Collins appeared mollified, and ever mindful of the rank and gratitude he owed to his host, thanked and re-thanked Mr. Darcy who bore the parading and obsequious civility with admirable calm. If he did shrug his shoulders, it was not until Mr. Collins was out of sight.

Georgiana entered the library, leading the Gardiner children, who were bearing stage properties: books, tankards, jewel case, fans, cushions. Behind them came two stout young men aiding Captain Wainwright with sofas, chairs and small tables.

"Your end down a bit, Jackson," said the captain, as they manoeuvred the largest of the pieces.

"Right you are, sir."

To show his feelings of resentment at being overlooked, Mr. Collins struck up his violin and, recognizing the tune, the children began to loudly sing their piece. The combined effect of unpractised voices and the off-key notes of the violin were irksome. The sound cut right across the heated exchange that Mr. and Mrs. Hardcastle were having on stage. As Darcy was about to reprimand the musicians, the carpenter began hammering nails into the beam above them, while Mr. Chawton was walking among the cast with a naked flame. He was paying no attention to the candle, but looking at Kitty. The flame was just about to catch the hair alight of one of the little girls.

"Stop! Stop! *Stop*!" Darcy shouted. "This is complete confusion! Please, everyone, stand still, stay where you are and listen to me."

Darcy was finding all the unseen pitfalls of a first-time director.

"Never again. Never again," he muttered to himself.

*

"Do you intend to invite guests solely from the village or further afield, sir?" asked Captain Wainwright. He had assigned Mrs. Bennet to enquire among the cast how they regarded the idea of an audience. She had taken up the challenge with alacrity, and where there was doubt or modesty she had persuaded, flattered and encouraged. In a very few days she had a full list of approvals to show Mr. Darcy.

"I believe we might see upward of twenty persons in our audience, sir, if we ask our acquaintances from the immediate vicinity as well as those from Lambton. There is a large house party at Davington Manor, and Lady Groombridge has several relatives residing at Dene Hall. They may welcome a diversion. Of course, the weather could deter some of them from travelling, if it changes."

The past week had seen a thawing of the snow and the air had taken a milder turn. Though wet underfoot, a carriage would have little difficulty in reaching Pemberley.

"As for the prospective audience, we may write invitations, and they could be delivered this week," said Darcy, wondering just how he could fit in the hours this would take.

Mrs. Bennet asked, "May I offer my services to oversee the writing? Jane has a very fair hand, while Kitty and Mary have improved under the tutelage of Mr. Chawton. Perhaps they might submit a sample for your approval?"

"A good idea, Mrs. Bennet. With several writers the task will be completed before one can tie a sailor's knot," laughed the captain.

Mrs. Bennet smiled and sat down at the bureau to make a list of guests and addresses, dictated by her son-in-law.

"There are many people in Lambton, both old friends and acquaintances, who may wish to view the amateur theatricals at Pemberley. They will come perhaps as much out of curiosity as a genuine interest in the play. A few may come to laugh at us, but I hope they leave laughing with us," he said.

*

During one of the lunch intervals in the last weeks of rehearsals, Mr. Gardiner amiably commented to the director, "Let us trust the weather stays fine, so we have a full house, Mr. Darcy. We should not want our admirable production to go unseen." His optimism throughout rehearsal had been infectious. If Mr. Darcy was the driving force, then Uncle Gardiner and his cheerful wife were the axle grease that smoothed every rough obstacle in public.

But it was Mrs. Bennet who was the confidante of every actor, whenever private solace was needed or advice sought. On hearing of a minor trouble, Lizzy would send the actor to her mother with the encouraging words, "Mrs. Bennet will advise you."

It was therefore with some amusement that Mrs. Bennet found herself being consulted upon a myriad of subjects: on stairwells, in corridors, near doorways and in other quiet places.

"Aunt Bennet, I have a sore throat. What if I should lose my voice?"

"Dearest mama, were you troubled from sleeping when your babies were soon to be born?"

"Ma'am, I should value your advice on behalf of my son James. He has written to me asking for new silk stockings. I wonder if you know of a supplier?"

"Ma'am, I'm in a fair mess as to the sorting of the costumes, but daren't tell Mr. Darcy."

"Mama, what am I to do with my complexion? It is so reddened from the cold."

"My dear sister, I am experiencing some strange symptoms of late: hot sweats, sleepless nights. Do you have any advice?"

"We're sorry to put you out ma'am, but Jack, Ned and I wonder if you could spare a few moments to 'ear us lines? We're fair moithered with the larnin' and don't want to be letting Mr. Darcy down."

"Mrs. Bennet, ma'am, would it be too much trouble for you to show me how to do the children's hair? They twist about so much, that every time I pin it up; it falls down."

These constant queries made her quite forget her own problems. Though she wistfully longed for *any* request from her husband, there was only silence in that direction.

*

To the cast's mingled consternation and delight, almost all the recipients of the invitations had written to say they would attend.

"Shall we really be ready on time?" said Mr. Collins anxiously, at the next assembled cast gathering.

"I am sure you will all reach a standard of performance that will entertain an audience. You will do Mr. Goldsmith's comedy full justice," said Mr. Darcy, more confidently than he felt. He kept his misgivings to himself, as he recalled the strange sounds he had witnessed emanating from the music room. Also, he was more than a little anxious at the servants still needing so much prompting and the curtain, though now erected, would not run smoothly and a vigorous tug would cause it to fall down frequently and completely.

"All minor impediments," Lizzy would tell him, but he was losing much sleep over the whole business. To reassure himself, he would sometimes visit other rooms, without notice, where the actors not currently under his direction were rehearsing. He felt, in the main, that the Captain and Mrs. Bennet would confidently carry the play, and that the performances of other protagonists were making significant if rather slow progress. It was the understudies who were showing a fragility that did not bode well. Mr. Collins, as understudy to Charles Marlow, displayed a diffidence at odds with the eminent man of maturity that the role demanded. The clergyman stooped rather than stood erect, and though his vocal delivery was sufficiently loud (his pulpit experience notwithstanding) he rushed his words. His mastery of his lines was far from complete, and his habit of standing with his back to the audience caused Mr. Darcy to reprove him so frequently that at one point the director was driven to physically turning the actor to face the (imaginary) audience.

"There, Mr. Collins. *That* is where you should be directing your lines."

"Oh, my dear sir. A thousand, thousand apologies. It seems in remembering the lines, I am unable to think of my movement at all."

"Shall we try again, sir?" said Darcy, as patiently as he could manage. He silently hoped that Mr. Collins' thespian talents would not be called upon.

On other occasions it was Mary, understudying Constance Neville, who necessitated Darcy's forbearance. She was often disposed to interrupt her speeches, and ask for clarification of the script or to offer her observations on its moral implications. Matters came to a head when the cast of understudies was having its final rehearsal.

"Does Constance really believe her aunt is keeping the jewels for herself? And why does she pretend to be in love with Tony Lumpkin when it is very clear she is attached to George Hastings? I cannot believe in such deception, Mr. Darcy. Indeed, to make such a pretence of love on the stage is quite beyond me. I see no reason for it and to try to persuade an audience of it is futile."

It was in vain that Darcy explained the conventions of contemporary comedy and the clever humour of Goldsmith's script. He pointed this out to her in a letter Goldsmith wrote to Samuel Johnson when prefacing the play: 'It may serve the interests of mankind to inform them that the greatest wit may be found in a character, without impairing the most unaffected piety'.

"No, no, Mr. Darcy! I see nothing to smile at in such duplicity. The theft of the jewels, the imbibing of too much liquor and the quarrelling between the couples, to my mind are not fit subjects for laughter.

Such behaviour is reprehensible. Please do not ask me to undertake any role in this play. I am willing to play the violin for the performance but that is as far as I am prepared to go."

Mary's virtuous speech inspired little religious imitation in her listener other than a private prayer that Kitty would remain in her customary good health.

January 18th

How time has flown since the first day of rehearsals! The whole business of making a play has amazed us all. Costumes, music, set, lighting, properties, seating and I know not what. To think we believed all we had to do was learn Mr. Goldsmith's lines!

The stage is now in place and we all have had our first experience of "treading the boards." How grand that sounds! But pride comes before a fall, and this evening there was a half hour of such chaos that I feared Mr. Darcy would be moved to cancel the whole venture. How can one rehearse while carpenters hammer nails into beams, naked flames are set up with no regard to safety and costumes are being fitted? As to the swelling self-importance of some who regard the music as of far greater significance than any other aspect of the play, I trust a sharp rebuke from the Director will soon be forthcoming.

One strange but happy occurrence is the softening of Mr. Darcy towards myself. He has become almost affable! There has been a new and not unwelcome respect. This began with his approval of my suggestions concerning the invitations. His former stiffness was replaced by a smiling countenance; an event so rare that I can still scarce believe it happened. In truth, the sole reason must be that a sort of madness has seized all those connected with the play and the poor man (that I should ever call him that!) has been so overwhelmed with tasks that he is glad of any help, no matter whence it comes.

There has also been a growing seeking of my company by various members of the cast. It seems they want advice and comfort from "The Menopausal Matriarch" (as I call myself in private, being the 'mother' of Kate Hardcastle and Tony Lumpkin). At first I thought it a self-deprecating title, and wondered how others viewed the oldest woman in the cast, but it seems that far from being an aged personage of little use, I am regarded as a woman of experience, whose knowledge is welcomed from the youngest upward.

However, I must beware of arrogance—a shortcoming I have known all my days, but not recognized till now—though regrettably too quick to point it out in others, alas.

Well, Mrs.B, this journal has become something of a confessional. Am I on the road to improvement? Where will it end?

The only fly in the Pemberley ointment is still Mr. Bennet. He remains as taciturn as ever, but I shall not give up Mrs. Hardcastle. It is far too amusing. After all, he has not expressly forbidden me to act. Besides, it would let Mr. Darcy down if I were to withdraw now. As to my understudy, Aunt Gardiner, what a sudden encumbrance it would be for her. For while I have the utmost confidence in her willingness to step in, I am all too aware of the burden this would place on her at the present time, since she has recently entered that most telling stage in her life, which I am now so gladly leaving. No, I cannot betray such a loving and generous lady, who has been so good to our family and so approving of myself.

It is a strange thing to observe, that I appear approved of by everyone at Pemberley, except the very person whose opinion I value the most.

Chapter XVIII

Two weeks later the Dress Rehearsal started well: lines needed little prompting, the costumes, make up, set and lights were all correct and the overture sounded splendid. Standing at the back of the auditorium, Mr. Darcy, with sleeves rolled up and arms folded, appeared to be without strain or anxiety. The velvet curtains drew back smoothly to reveal a room in the Hardcastle house, where its owners were standing and looking angrily at each other across a room of shabby but comfortable furniture. Mrs. Bennet was resplendent in red taffeta with green underskirt and a feather in her hair. Her husband was more plainly dressed, in brown velvet jacket, breeches and a tri-corn hat.

Mrs. Hardcastle, hands on hips, glared at her husband, declaring resentfully,

"I vow, Mr Hardcastle, You're very particular. Is there a creature in the whole country but ourselves that does not take a trip to town now and then, to rub off the rust a little? There's the two Miss Hoggs and our neighbour Mrs. Grigsbv, go to take a month's polishing every winter."

She looked very disgruntled. He met her gaze with an equal dislike and sarcastically replied,

"Ay, and bring back vanity and affectation to last them the whole year."

The audience of understudies was paying this arresting opening their fullest attention, while in the wings, the scene was causing so much merriment that the prompter had frequently to hush the watching cast.

It was at the point of Mrs. Hardcastle's attempted ear-cuffing that the catastrophe came; in aiming to dodge the 'blow', Captain Wainwright took a step backwards and fell awkwardly over the table, twisting his leg under him. Something cracked. It was not the table.

The captain's anguished cry made everyone rush towards him. Darcy was first to help.

"Step back, everyone. Mr. Gardiner, send one of the men for the doctor." The captain gripped his ankle, which was swelling rapidly. Despite the sharpness of the pain, he allowed Mr. Darcy to straighten the leg a little, then lift him on to a sofa so as to lie in a more comfortable position. Kitty had run for cold compresses, which she and Mrs. Bennet gently applied to the swollen limb. Lizzy and Hill placed a blanket on the invalid, while Mr. Bingley administered some brandy. Captain Wainwright, white with pain and shock, closed his eyes. It was a terrible moment for everyone.

The physician arrived within the hour, having found the roads from Lampton passable. His presence restored the onlookers to a semblance of calm. After a thorough examination of the unconscious captain's ankle, the doctor stood up and regarded the group of worried actors.

"Well," said Doctor Jacobs, "the poor fellow is best left asleep. His ankle is broken and will need to be set. May I have two men to hold him down should he awake?"

Mr. Darcy stepped forward and before Mr. Gardiner could offer, it was Mr. Bennet who said firmly, "I'd be honoured to assist, sir".

*

It was another two hours before Mr. Darcy joined the company to say, "The worst news is that Captain Wainwright will be unable to perform."

Everyone looked shaken. All these weeks of preparation and for naught!

"But," Darcy continued, "the good news is that Mr. Bennet will play the role of Hardcastle instead." There was a shocked silence. Mrs. Bennet's eyes were the widest. Her husband? He who had scorned the very idea of acting? The man who had shut himself away and only attended rehearsal on compulsion? Would he master the lines in time? Would his performance let them all down?

"Better than no Hardcastle at all, I suppose," was the general conclusion. At least the play would go on. Their anxiety was of brief duration, though his wife's disquiet was not so short-lived. She allowed herself to dwell on the matter momentarily when discussing the change of stage partner immediately after Mr. Darcy's announcement, but then resolving to turn her thoughts to *that* particular problem when they should be in rehearsal together. At those times, she vowed she would try to keep her doubts to herself and raise her spirits, being aware that the company would be needing a confident pair of protagonists if the play was to succeed.

*

The weather remained mild and the prospect of an audience was now a reality. In the two days between the dress rehearsal and the performance, responses to the invitations were many and positive. By servants on foot, gentlemen on horseback, or ladies in carriages, the letters were delivered to Pemberley. Mr. Bennet's view was akin to that of Mr. Hardcastle's, '*I cannot think why these country houses cannot keep its own fools at home*' though he kept this thought to himself. He was struggling with his lines and was feeling more than a little apprehensive at the thought of a large crowd of strangers witnessing his possible discomfiture. Why ever had he agreed to be an understudy?

But Mrs. Bennet was delighted at the thought of real society coming to see the play.

"Only think, Mr. Bennet! Lady Groombridge herself and Lord Harford from Davington Manor, both bringing large parties. Then there are all those people from Lampton! How pleased I am! Kitty and Mary will have an opportunity to....."

Her husband could bear her raptures no longer and went to read over his script in the quiet of his room. But his wife was in a tumult of joy and would not let her spirits be dampened. She gathered the latest bundle of replies and took them to her host's study, where she came across Mr. Darcy talking to the captain.

"Only fancy!" exclaimed Mrs. Bennet. "So many more than we expected or even hoped for. We shall need far more than the twenty chairs we already set out in the library."

"Indeed ma'am, we may need to consider a new venue for the performance if the guests continue to multiply," agreed Captain Wainwright, who was taking an interested if somewhat less physical part in the proceedings from his position on the *chaise longue*. He continued, "How many are planning to come aboard, Mrs. Bennet?"

"Well, sir, there are ten from Dene Hall, eight from Davington Manor and the numbers from Lampton are still coming in. Even if those who have not yet replied are unable to come, there are still five families who are definitely attending. In addition, we cannot overlook the people at Pemberley who are not involved in the play."

Darcy looked thoughtful. The extra chairs would need finding, but he felt confident this could be done. However, to take down all the set, curtains and staging. then transport them elsewhere, would involve hours of work and time was now very short. The whole venture looked under threat. He surmised "There could be upwards of forty or more. The library simply is not large enough."

"Shall we take another look and get the servants to bring more chairs?" suggested Mrs. Bennet. Mr. Darcy privately felt yet another assessment would be futile and was resigned to some inevitable overcrowding. However, he could think of no better plan at the moment, so agreed.

From Darcy's study to the library was a short walk, but for the incapacitated captain, it necessitated calling for three men to push the *chaise longue* on its brass wheels slowly so as not to jolt his newly-set leg.

"Are you all right, sir?" asked Darcy, seeing the naval gentleman wince as they turned a corner.

"Worse things happen at sea, Mr. Darcy, much worse."

As they moved along the corridor, young Emma Gardiner ran past, singing one of the songs from the play.

"That gives me an idea," said Mrs. Bennet. She looked into her reticule and drew out a list. She stopped to read it, then began counting. Mr. Darcy and the captain were intrigued.

"Well, ma'am," said Captain Wainwright, "are we able to weather this storm? Is there blue sky ahead? Enough to make a sailor's pair of trousers?"

"Wait till we see the library and I shall let you know," she replied.

The room was already set out with twenty chairs and it was clear that an additional fifteen, let alone twenty, could not be accommodated. She noted that the first row of chairs had been placed ten feet back from the stage in anticipation of the musicians. She also observed that the stage did not reach from wall to wall, but had a few feet either side in front of the velvet curtains and space to accommodate the offstage actors in the wings behind. Moreover, there was a small minstrel's gallery set at the audience end of the library. Mrs. Bennet, under the frankly curious gaze of Mr. Darcy and the captain, walked around the area in front of the chairs, counting under her breath, then left the library to ascend the stairs to the gallery. From this vantage point she called down, " If we move the four musicians up here they may view all the action below. I then believe it entirely possible to accommodate another twenty persons in the audience. We could place cushions on the floor in front of and around the sides of the stage for the children, and add some chairs for the adults. What do you think, Mr. Darcy?"

Without immediate reply, the master of Pemberley paced out the area surrounding the stage, then joined his mother-in-law in the gallery. After a thoughtful pause, he smiled and said, "I believe you may well have solved our problem, Mrs. Bennet. There is sufficient space for two rows of ten cushions immediately in front of the stage, and ten chairs may easily be spaced at the sides of it for adults or taller children. All will have an excellent view. And I believe even Mr. Collins will be satisfied by his elevated position."

"Yes!" laughed Captain Wainwright from below. "Mr. Collins will do well from his perch in the crow's nest."

"Come, I shall seek out those cushions and extra chairs, without delay. Thank you Mrs. Bennet. An intelligent and practical solution. I am in your debt." He gave her a brief bow of acknowledgement, then hurried away to find the housekeeper and put the new plan into immediate effect.

It was with no little astonishment that she received this remark. Mrs. Bennet had long been in awe of her son-in-law's superior mind, wealth and social standing, so to hear such praise unstintingly given, and to be spoken to as if on equal terms, was as surprising as it was pleasing. As for Mr. Darcy, he now recalled, with some shame, that he had once said of Lizzy and Mrs. Bennet, 'Miss Elizabeth Bennet a beauty? I should have soon called her mother a wit'. He had uttered these words to entertain Miss Caroline Bingley, when recalling an early meeting with the Bennets. His embarrassment at that recollection made him glad the women who were now his wife and his mother-in-law had never heard them. He now reflected how hasty and ill-judged that comment had been. His dearest Lizzy was now to him the loveliest creature in the world, and as for Mrs. Bennet, she grew in his estimation every time they met. Darcy privately admitted that the relatives on *his* side were not without fault; his aunt, Lady Catherine de Bourgh, for all her breeding had shown a marked lack of civility in her visit to Longbourn two years ago, when commanding Lizzy to promise she would never be engaged to Mr. Darcy. How much worse this was than Mrs. Bennet's imprudent remarks in society; such utterances, though ill-considered, sprang from a mother's wish to better her daughters' fortunes, whereas his aunt had been determined to bend Lizzy's will to her own, with little regard for the young woman's feelings or her nephew's. Lady Catherine's infinitely more privileged position should have secured her good manners. While Darcy felt the responsibility of his own situation and a duty to less fortunate members of society, his aunt believed deference from others was her due. Her sole contribution to society was that of condescension, and where challenged she used her rank to overcome opposition. In comparison, Mrs. Bennet he considered was the lesser offender, and by some marked degree. However, his duty towards each lady was as limited as etiquette would allow, without appearing uncivil.

In the first twelve months of his marriage Mr. Darcy had believed the distance between Longbourn and Pemberley a very satisfactory one, reflecting that to dwell in the vicinity of Lizzy's mother and the Meryton relations would be far from desirable. So far, previous visits had been of fairly short duration, occurring only when business caused the couple to travel south. To his relief, only Kitty and her father had been twice to Pemberley in the summer months, Mary staying at home with her ailing mother.

Out of love for his wife, he had agreed to the notion of a lengthy winter stay from the Bennet family, though he privately feared that such prolonged intimacy would not improve the relationship with Lizzy's mother. His initial strategy was to avoid her presence in the house as far as civility would allow; not a difficult undertaking given the number of rooms and the capacity of the country estate. To his surprise, Mrs. Bennet's necessary proximity when engaged with the play had caused the master of Pemberley to re-consider. Over the past few weeks her support, on and off the stage, had proved invaluable. He recognized with a rueful smile his own pride *and* prejudice, but was heartened to realize these difficulties had been slowly dispersed in the growing familiarity during the Christmas season and its activities.

Captain Wainwright looked at Mrs. Bennet with renewed respect, and said, "You own a wise head ma'am. I add my congratulations to Mr. Darcy's on solving the seating problem. We shall soon have everything ship shape."

"Oh, it was very little, sir, a simple idea. Before Mr. Darcy returns with the cushions and extra chairs, perhaps I should occupy myself in looking again at the letters of reply to make a more exact reckoning. Would you be so kind as to assist me, captain?"

"Always willing to be of service to a lady, ma'am." With this, the two sat close and began their task.

*

There was to be no hindrance from the weather when the day of performance arrived. On pulling back her bedroom curtains, Mrs. Bennet saw the morning was one of palest blue skies and thin frost on the fields. She looked at her colourful costume hanging outside the wardrobe. Until the Dress Rehearsal she had felt supremely confident in her role while playing against the captain. Every practice had developed their skill and understanding of the lively relationship. Then came the accident. All had changed.

When first the notion of having her real husband play her stage husband was made fact, it filled her with apprehension. The long history of his neglect and unkind remarks on 'her nerves' had had the effect of undermining belief in herself and trust in him. His increasingly distant attitude at Pemberley had not lessened her anxiety. To find herself in a position where she would play opposite this man, who had become a cold stranger was now a serious threat to her developing confidence in her acting ability. It had been easy to play the capricious wife to Captain Wainwright's Hardcastle. All then had been frivolity and light. The raillery between them had lifted her spirits and self-regard. In contrast, Mr. Bennet was a man who made her feel ill-at-ease. In short, she feared him.

The rehearsals with him had been arduous; a duty rather than a pleasure. He had been reserved and distant; *she* had reflected *his* restraint and Goldsmith's sparkling exchanges became weighed down in stiff formality. Where *he* was heavy in word and action, *she* was dull and lifeless. Where the scenes between the captain and Mrs. Bennet had flowed from the first rehearsal, with little interruption to advise, Darcy was finding it necessary to intervene at almost every line. The original couple had improvised in gesture and stage business, rendering the lively script visually rich, with few suggestions from the master of Pemberley. While it was not reasonable for him to expect such polished accord now, it was with difficulty that he disguised his dismay at the lack of lustre before him.

"Allow me to intrude, Mr. Bennet. When Mrs. Hardcastle asks you to 'allow the boy a bit of humour,' your response needs to show sarcasm when you reply, 'I'd sooner allow him a horse-pond!' His following expansion of this theme should reveal his growing scorn, as he goes on to say: 'If burning the footmen's shoes, and worrying the kittens, be humour, he has it.' At this point, you, Mrs. Bennet, should be starting to show signs of defending your son, so that when he relates the anecdote, 'It was but yesterday he fastened my wig to the back of my chair, and when I went to make a bow, I popped my bald head in Mrs. Frizzle's face!' you will be ready hotly to respond with your indignation. You need to show anger in face, voice and body.

"Your line, 'Am I to blame?' may be delivered as roundly as you like. This droll quarrel should clearly indicate the tension between the couple, and remind those in the audience of the real incident that happened to Goldsmith himself when with Lord Clare at Gosfield. You will recall how it was Lord Clare's daughter who played this trick on the playwright while he was asleep. Thus, this early dialogue should heartily amuse, but will only do so if the lines are delivered with spirit between the two of you."

Darcy's growing inner perturbation at the pallid exchanges left him feeling his abilities as a director were sorely deficient. After an hour, he suggested the couple work at the scenes alone, as he was needed urgently elsewhere. Mr. Bennet initially believed this sudden and unexpected opportunity to be solely with his wife might allow him to begin to overcome their estrangement.

He had some belief that all was not entirely lost, but was alarmed at his own inability to summon the necessary words, and Mrs. Bennet was not at all relaxed in his presence.

While he had the excuse of still needing the script, and scarce raised his eyes while rehearsing, she delivered her lines with indifference, while staring at the space above his head.

*

In her room, later that day, she reflected on the final rehearsals with a strong degree of agitation.

How would this mutual distrust display itself tonight? Was there a way out, even at this late stage? Was she to repine? To mentally and emotionally relapse into her former self? The lady who veered from lamentation to bitter words in a heart beat? A sudden sweat ran over her. Were those wretched flushes about to assail her newfound composure? Should she take to her bed and let down everyone in cast and audience?

Waves of self-doubt tumbled though her mind. Every passing moment added to her misgivings. She was at a crossroads. The bell to summon one of the housemaids was close by on the dressing table. She could send a message to Mr. Darcy, telling him of her incapacity and the necessity of using an understudy. So much easier to surrender to her despair, than spend the hours of today becoming more and more tense, and then give a poor performance; which would be recalled forever by those who witnessed it. Such humiliation!

No-one else could make the decision; it was in her hands alone to either be the victim of her condition, or to surmount her troubles. To give in now she felt would be to accept the menopausal Mrs. Bennet as permanent. It would confirm her husband's life-long opinion of 'her nerves'and would seal their marital divide forever.

Perhaps she should seek out some fortifying beverage? It had been four months since she last drank from those secret bottles at Longbourn. She had partaken of a single half glass of wine with her

Christmas meal, but had refrained from more, fearing she would be dragged back to those sad times. But in these present circumstances, perhaps just one? It might give her the confidence she sought. She felt an old longing come over her, and could almost taste the madeira in her mouth. She took a step towards the door. She stopped. She saw again the bottles on her bedroom floor and her sister's saddened countenance. No, she could not hurt her dearest friend and relative again. Biting her lip, she sat down.

Despite her resolve, she still felt an extreme of anxiety at the thought of performing with Mr. Bennet. Her trepidation looked for solace; she picked up her journal and read her comments about her husband. And his remarks of her. Were they justified? Was she so undeserving of his esteem? Was his Mrs. Bennet a mere cipher, a figure of little importance that shared a house with him but had little real impression on his life? Nothing other than an irritation at best, and at worst, a figure of contempt?

"Who is the real Mrs. Bennet? Is she victim, or victor?" She thought again of Lady Hamilton's "attitudes". As she repeated "victim" her image assumed an air of dejection, with dulled eyes and dispirited figure. Her very surroundings appeared dismal, with shadowy draperies to the bed behind her and darkened closets standing gloomily against the bedroom walls. It was a moment of inner turmoil.

Something made her look at her costume. It emanated confidence. She touched the bright fabric and its glowing colour reflected on her fingers. Looking up, she caught sight of herself in the mirror and asked, "Would it be so very difficult to rage against a husband as Mrs. Hardcastle does?" Her face became energised, and she shouted, "Indeed not! Mrs. Hardcastle is a woman who feels wronged, as I do when my husband is unjust. I shall not let Mr. Bennet's neglect or suspicion bring me low. I shall express my frustration in *her* violent speeches. For too long I have suffered from self-pity. Tonight I shall hide this weakness and become a person other than myself. Mrs. Bennet may be re-invented, at least for one evening. Let the old Mrs. Bennet lie sorrowfully in her bed, let the new rise up and play the grand dame that Mr. Goldsmith has so brilliantly created." She peered again into the mirror and questioned her reflection.

Another glance at her dress decided her.

"No matter who this tormented creature may be tomorrow, tonight she *is* Mrs. Hardcastle."

With this resolve she tried on her costume, revelling in the rustling taffeta and the bobbing feather. In putting on the clothes of Mrs. Hardcastle, she assumed her character. She drew herself up into a firmer posture and took a deep breath. She felt a new vitality flow through her.

Striding back and forth across the room, then suddenly coming to a halt to glare at herself in the mirror, she ran through her lines, directing them forcibly at the invisible Mr. Hardcastle. With the flick of her fan. and then using it to point at her imaginary husband in the mirror, she became increasingly animated. The feeling of power was immense. She relished this sense of control. Why, if Mrs. Bennet was a woman of mean understanding, little information and uncertain temper, Mrs. Hardcastle was a formidable female with a lively wit, confident manner and never at a loss for words. Where Mrs. Bennet drooped, Mrs. Hardcastle flourished.

"Mrs. Bennet," she told her vibrant reflection, "if you can conquer your condition in private, you may conquer again tonight in public." Her cheeks glowed. Her eyes sparkled.

"Leave Mrs. Bennet to weep; Mrs. Hardcastle will make the world laugh.

February 2nd

An up and down fortnight!

The actors are in command of their lines and the set is complete. Mr. Collins continues to irritate; I believe he sees himself in a bishop's mitre at the very least. Kitty glows with an inner light. Her vivacious manner will be called upon to enliven Mr. Collins in a future partnership. Though Mary utters her pious platitudes as often here as at Longbourn, the rest of Pemberley's inhabitants are lifted in spirits, and all due to the play. Mary may become more cheerful when married to Captain Wainwright. He continues to entertain me, though some may find his continuous cheerfulness irksome.

I suspect that both my daughters often arrange secret assignations within Pemberley's extensive interior. Mr. Bennet may privately rail about the necessity of chaperoning them—to my mind unnecessary—but I do not see him exerting himself to seek out their company, despite his words. Too busy reading in Mr. Darcy's library! At dinner last night he informed the whole company that he had read at least twenty-five novels since he arrived. He began to list them, but I found myself yawning and had to turn away.

February 3rd

Disaster at the Dress Rehearsal! The captain has broken his ankle! Was there ever such misfortune?

February 4th

Mr. Bennet is to play Mr. Hardcastle!!! The performance is tomorrow night. I am not at all certain what my sentiments are regarding this change of partner. We went over the lines together this morning. To my utter astonishment, he appeared to be practically word-perfect! However, his manner is so unlike the captain's, that we did not get into the feeling of the piece at all: stiff formality and wooden movement, with scarce a word to me that was not Mr. Goldsmith's. I could make allowance for bashfulness had we been newly introduced, but we have lived together over twenty years!

After one rehearsal with me, Mr. Darcy spirited him away for extra coaching in private. I hope it is not in vain. They have been closeted together for much of the day.

Mr. Darcy emerged only to discuss the seating arrangements. It appears we have many more audience members than we first expected. A solution occurred to me, which I suggested to Mr. Darcy. He looked a little doubtful, but when we put the notion to a practical test by means of moving the musicians aloft and filling the new space around the stage with cushions and extra chairs, the result met Mr. Darcy's approbation. His subsequent gratitude, and the warm manner in which that gratitude was shown, has removed any of the previous coldness between us. For the first time since we made acquaintance, I am able to understand why Lizzy is so happy with the master of Pemberley.

February 5th

*The great day has dawned!
Pemberley's first theatre company
will be displaying their talents to a
sizeable audience this very evening. I
cannot believe that the time has come
for the Derbyshire production of "She
Stoops To Conquer". Will our efforts
prove a success? I am trembling with
excitement at the thought of
performing such a wonderful play!
My fellow actors have all worked so
hard. It is like being in a second
family. It is time to leave my journal
as the bell is summoning everyone to
breakfast ....*

Noon

*A crisis of confidence this morning. In
the hope that at last Mr. Bennet and I
might be reconciled, I was
determined, on this day of all days, to
do my utmost to engage him at
breakfast. I dressed myself with more
than usual care. However, he was not
to be seen. I can only conclude he still
wishes to avoid me. This knowledge
has left me in a state of utter
wretchedness.*

*How can I perform with a husband
who is no more than a cold stranger?
I am a woman who thrives on*

approbation; without it I am totally reduced in self-esteem.

The greatest dilemma raged for an hour in my mind. Could I overcome my anxiety, or would I give way to those former tremblings, palpitations and flutterings that so dragged me down before? Would all the support from friends and family be wasted? The clamour of cowardice grew to terrifying heights as I wrestled with my fears. What if acting with Mr. Bennet should prove the worst public and personal catastrophe of my life?

I was about to yield to this overwhelming feeling of self-doubt, and was at the very point of sending Mr. Darcy my resignation. It seemed I could not escape my emotional imprisonment.

But salvation came in the unlikely form of drapery; to wit, Mrs. Hardcastle's dress. How it heartened me to see such a bold colour, while in my darkened state. It cried 'courage' to me and the embers of hope began to glow. ...

Here was a new Mrs. Bennet, if only I would seize her! Reason told me there was nothing in my way, if I could but will myself to move forward.

Just one touch of that beautiful fabric was enough to restore me to health. How absurd I sound as I read this page over! How overly dramatic! But it is no more than the truth.

Whether Mr. Bennet and I are permanently estranged or no, I at least shall play my part to the very best of my ability.

Come what may, I shall look forward to this evening, forget my self-absorption, and do my best by Mrs. Hardcastle, Mr. Darcy and, above all, Mr. Goldsmith!

Chapter XIX

The last hours before the guests were expected were full of action and incident. Mr. Darcy was overseeing every aspect of the final preparations: assisting Mr. Gardiner with the curtains, soothing the nerves of the musicians, ensuring the prompter had script and chair, helping the Gardiners' eldest to master the sound effects of horses' hooves (two pieces of wood), checking costumes and props, seeing that the footlights all held candles, the set was correctly placed and the actors all calm. Last but not least he needed to find the time to rehearse his scenes with Lizzy. He had noted the quiet bearing of Mr. Bennet during their scenes, and wondered if he needed more rehearsal, but felt he would only add to his father-in-law's anxiety if he suggested too much instruction at this late stage. He had, he hoped, given some useful words of direction, which would be sufficient.

By six o'clock the library was ready, the actors going over their lines for the last time and the servants standing by to welcome the guests. Everyone looked out from the great windows on to the drive, where the first carriages were coming through the gates, their lamps flaring in the darkness. Some guests arrived by hack chaise. Those who had walked from the village were in groups, with lanterns held aloft, and their figures smothered in heavy winter clothing to keep out the chill night air.

Once across the threshold of Pemberley and into its well-lit vestibule, the visitors' anonymity disappeared as they divested themselves of their thick outer garments and responded to the warmth emanating from the great marble fireplaces. Servants bore away their capes, hats and cloaks and showed them to the library. There they found an impressive theatre: neat rows of chairs faced a stage where red velvet curtains hung and footlights flickered. A programme of Dramatis Personae and details of the play were neatly laid on every seat. Above the auditorium hung a highly decorative chandelier whose candles glowed in curved gilt branches. With every wall lined with books, and the gallery already showing some activity in the shape of two servants putting out sheet music, there was much for the audience to see and discuss as they waited.

Behind the scenes, in various darkened corners, the actors were murmuring their words, adjusting their costumes and wishing each other well, exhibiting every sign of anxiety, which contrasted severely with their enthusiasm for being awarded a role only a few weeks ago. They looked at each other in mutual perturbation. Public excitement was tempered by private disquiet.

"Have you got your fan, mama?"

"I have, but why is your jewel box on stage? Shouldn't it be on the properties table?"

"Where is my riding crop, Kitty?"

"Your wig is on sideways, Mr. Gardiner. Allow me to adjust it."

"Write your words on your cuffs, if you fear for your memory."

"Lizzy, dearest, can you help me with my cravat?"

"Is it time to go up to the gallery, Mr. Darcy? Oh dear, I seem to be without my sheet music. Mary, have you taken it? Oh, yes, pardon me, I had quite forgot, Mr. Darcy; you told us it would be placed by the servants in readiness. But what of my viola? I'm certain I had it this morning. Oh, yes, that is in the gallery too. You told me it would be. How foolish of me. Do you happen to have a piece of resin about your person, Mr. Darcy? I fear I am in need. Is it too late to send a servant to Lampton to purchase some? Oh, it seems there is a piece here in my pocket. My profuse apologies, Mr. Darcy."

While individual anxiety grew, the collective belief in the venture dwindled, and the cast asked each other:

"Will the play be well-received?"

"Will they be disappointed?"

" What if they do not understand the jokes?"

"A triumph or a tragedy?"

They could hear the audience arriving and, by peeping through the narrow opening between the curtains, could see them taking their seats.

"There's the bishop and his family. I hope they won't think it all too ungodly," whispered Mr. Collins to Mary.

"Isn't that Lady Groombridge?" said Lizzy to her husband.

"It is, Lizzy. Widowed so young; it is good to see her and her daughter here tonight."

"Ah, there are the Dixons. Oh, and those people from Lampton who live in the old bakery."

Mr. Darcy quietly called the cast together on the darkened stage. They huddled in a group around him, awaiting reassurance and encouragement.

"You all look splendid!" he began. They turned and gazed at each other as if for the first time. Indeed it was hard to recognize some of them, the art of costume, hair-pieces and stage make-up having rendered their everyday selves into Goldsmith's characters. They smiled at each other and felt that they now at least looked the part.

"These weeks of diligent rehearsal have reached their culmination tonight. You do not need a long speech from me. I have every confidence you will each play your part splendidly. The audience will be thoroughly entertained. Cast any anxieties aside. Just go out there, enjoy yourselves and make me proud of you." With these heartening words ringing in their ears, the cast shook each other's hands and went to their separate posts.

A moment's wait till all was ready then, in the wings, Mr. Darcy struck his staff loudly on the floor three times to signal the play's commencement. All chattering ceased on both sides of the curtain and the Pemberley Performance of Oliver Goldsmith's 'She stoops to Conquer' began.

Mr. Collins on viola, Mary and young Emma on violin and Georgiana on flute, struck up the opening bars of the overture. They were seated on elegant gold chairs in the gallery. With such an elevated position, even Mr. Collins was satisfied.

The curtains drew back, revealing a large room with comfortable furniture and two figures stiffly posed in anger. Mr. and Mrs. Hardcastle were at odds.

Mr. Bennet as Hardcastle was so magnificently withering in his exchanges with his nagging wife in the first scene, that those who knew the couple well, thought it art imitating life. The bitterness was palpable, and their watching daughters feared it was too near the truth, but everyone else found it highly amusing. As they left the stage, the Hardcastles received a spontaneous round of applause.

Lizzy and Darcy won the audience's admiration with their portrayals of Kate and Marlow. To see the two sides of the hero; bumbling and reticent before "Miss Hardcastle", then lecherous and rough with her, as the supposed barmaid, was very entertaining. Kitty drew another round of applause by her sharp-tongued quarrelling with her cousin Lumpkin. Chawton was in his element, using his fine singing voice to the full. His 'inn song' was encored, and so much so, that after the third verse, he invited the audience to join him.

"Let school-masters puzzle their brain,
With grammar, and nonsense, and learning,
Good liquor, I stoutly maintain.
Gives genius a better discerning;

Let them brag of their heathenish Gods,
Their Lethes, their Styxes, and Stygians;
Their Quis, and their Quses, and their Quods,
They're all but a parcel of Pigeons.

Toroddle, toroddle, toroll!"

The audience stamped their feet in time and clapped to the echo as he finished.

*

As each act unravelled, the confidence of the cast grew. There was that certain 'group spirit' that exists with a theatrical company who trust each other completely. Any slight slips were covered immediately by another actor, line 'feeds' were generously given and taken, the dramatic pauses were a masterpiece of timing and by the final curtain the cast knew they had surpassed every expectation. Their faces glowed with exertion as they faced their cheering audience. Pride and relief swept over them.

Mr. Collins in the gallery stood up to take his bow, a mixture of self-importance and humility. He turned to Mary, Emma and Georgiana, who rose and curtsied. The applause seemed unending. Curtain call followed curtain call, actors and musicians bowing and curtseying, until Mr. Darcy raised his arms for silence.

"Thank you, one and all. Some of you may be wondering why there has been no epilogue, as in Mr. Goldsmith's original script. In fact, we have one, written by a member of the company. You will know that Mr. Bennet took on the role of Mr. Hardcastle just two days ago. As well as learning his lines, he has written an epilogue especially for tonight. It is of a rather personal nature, and is dedicated to his wife."

Darcy waved Mr. Bennet forward. He turned slightly towards Mrs. Bennet in the line of actors, swept off his tri-corn hat, bowed to her and the audience, and without use of a script began.

"Our life is all a play, designed to please,
'We have our exits and our entrances'.

Well, having stooped to conquer with success,
Kate gained a husband wearing no grand dress.

Dear Mrs. Bennet, wife of twenty year,
Has fallen out of love with me, I fear.

The fault is mainly mine, I must confess.
My books have been the cause, I must profess.

From wife and world I've shut myself away,
Ignored this lady both by night and day.

She, poor creature, has endured much pain,
Which, brutally, I treated with disdain.

When she but needed tender loving care,
And looked for me, I took myself elsewhere.

It was in vain my daughter and my brother
Gave dire warnings; could there be another?

I laughed at such a notion, thought them wrong
To say she could to someone else belong.

Until one evening, searching for a book,

Went to the library, there to take a look.

The door when opened, gave on such a sight,
It changed my world completely, from that night.

My fury knew no bounds, I fled the room,
And sat alone, tormented, sunk in gloom.

Did I still care? I asked myself that night.
The truth was—yes I did—with all my might.

From those I trust, I learned that she'd been true,
Ne'er looked at other men, as some girls do.

And that the distance twixt us was so great,
I'd best do something quick, before too late!

What was a man to do? How win her heart?
For we had drifted now so far apart.

Fate intervened, by breaking Wainwright's leg.
And I stepped in to play his part instead.

So here I kneel in front of you, dear wife,
Ashamed and sorry, offering you my life.

I too have borrowed clothes to conquer you.
Will you forgive me, let me start anew?"

There was a deep hush in the room. Fifty pairs of
eyes looked at the kneeling figure of Mr. Bennet,
then turned to gaze at his wife, who stood
transfixed, centre stage, unable to utter a syllable. A

mixture of astonishment and agitation held her captive. There were many minutes before she could truly comprehend what she had heard. She could not have felt more surprised if the Royal Naval fleet in the English Channel had sailed over her, and the late Admiral Lord Nelson had jumped out to offer his hand. To be publicly spoken of in such a manner! And by the most reticent of husbands! He, whose previous communication to her in society had been but utterances of cold civility, while in private, his demeanour had been one of indifference unless provoked by matters of financial consideration, where he had then assumed a violent dislike, leaving her in a most pitiable state. Until now, his every word and action had seemed to be those of a man bent on increasing her vexations. Yet here he was, kneeling patiently at her feet, silently beseeching her to forgive all that was past and to say 'yes' to a new life together.

At length she recovered sufficiently to take a cautious look at him, in order to ascertain his true and present nature. She stared into his eyes, not daring to believe he was sincere. His familiar face showed such uncertainty, that she felt herself longing only to forgive him. All the former bitterness between them melted away. One more moment, and then she found her voice. With softened tones she said, "Oh, yes, Mr. Bennet, yes. Nothing could make me happier". And throwing all modesty and etiquette aside, she drew him up to give him a long and heartfelt embrace. The audience applauded. Under cover of the noise, he whispered, "My dearest Cassandra, I love you. Now, and always."

Lizzy moved across the stage with the greatest celerity in order to be the first to congratulate her parents. She had never felt closer to them. It was only Darcy standing in front of the couple that lowered the applause. They drew apart, but stood hand in hand, their faces shining.

A cough from Mr. Chawton broke the quiet.

"I should like to be the first outside the family to congratulate you both." He shook their hands and while they were wondering at this, Kitty ran from her place in the line to add her congratulations. Before anyone else moved, Mr. Chawton turned to Kitty and, to her immense delight, went down on his knee and said, "Dearest Kitty, in front of your honourable parents, I shall dispense with tradition and ask *you* first for your hand in marriage. Will you honour me with your affirmation?"

Kitty beamed at him and not worrying if her parents should disapprove, said, "Yes, Mr. Chawton, yes!" The audience were unsure if they should applaud or hold back, in case the parents objected. Mr. Bennet looked surprised, and began to say, "Well this is all a little sudden; perhaps when you are twenty-one, Kitty _"

"Nonsense, nonsense, Mr. Bennet! Of course we approve," interrupted Mrs. Bennet. Her sudden shift in allegiance from priest to pedagogue left him open-mouthed. To herself, she reasoned, "Better a husband in the hand than two in the bush". To put her thoughts into action, she shook the tutor's hand, saying, "Mr. Chawton, you have proved yourself such an able tutor to Kitty, that we may safely give her to you for a life-long education."

"Oh, thank you mama, thank you." Kitty looked at her father, but he was in no mood to spoil the moment, merely adding this fatherly injunction; "At present you have my blessing on a betrothal, Kitty. You will continue your studies with Mr. Chawton. When you have learned sense, as well as sensibility, you may seek my approval for your marriage. I have little doubt that this will not be too long delayed."

"But what of Mr. Collins? Now who will have him?" asked Mrs. Bennet in a whisper to her husband. She had learned much from her experiences at Pemberley, where discretion in expression was prized more highly than volubility.

Mr. Collins had been observing this whole 'epilogue' with fascination, and it filled him with confidence. His own satisfaction at the musicians' performance, in front of the bishop, had given him the resolve to lean over the gallery balcony and speak to everyone below.

"One and all. Your most sincere attention please, I beg of you. It is with great humility and self-abasement that I stand here tonight."

"Not another sermon," groaned Kitty.

"—that I stand here tonight. I have something momentous to declare."

"Spit it out, reverend!" called a rough voice from the back.

"Ahem, yes; well, it's this. I would like to ask for the mand in harriage, I mean a partner in Holy Matrimony…"

"Get on with it, Reverend."

"—Oh, drat it; Mary dear, will you make me the happiest of men?"

Mary looked at her feet with embarrassment. Her heart was full, but what if her mother objected? After all, she had wanted Mr. Collins for Kitty. She dared at last to look down at Mrs. Bennet, and saw a face of utter astonishment. Mr. Bennet seemed only slightly surprised. He said, "Well, if Mrs. Bennet has no objections, neither have I". He motioned the couple to descend, kissed Mary, then shook hands with his two future sons-in-law. He privately thought, "Mr. Chawton's head for finance will be an asset when dealing with the family accounts, while Mr. Collins will prove a very useful fellow as far as church services go. Moreover, each will provide me with enough amusing material, musical and clerical, to write a book." For, now he had composed his Epilogue, Mr Bennet felt a real talent might be unfolding. Why, he could invite Mrs. Bennet to contribute; a joint venture to cement their new relationship. A story 'about three or four families in a village setting' would be just the thing. Now where had he heard that before? Mrs. Bennet's ear for news in Meryton and Longbourn would do nicely. His wit and her worldliness…

He was pulled from his reverie by his wife whispering, "Mr. Bennet, what about the captain? This is a triple blow for him."

"What can you mean, my love?"

"You know, he was so predisposed to Kitty. First his leg, then the play, and now the loss of a potential wife."

They turned to look at the captain, lying on a *chaise longue* where he had been propped up to see the play. Downcast? Not a bit. He was smiling.

As eyes turned in his direction, he said, "Am I disappointed? 'Tis a bit of a setback to have a broken ankle; but as to the play, Mr. Bennet made a far better job of it than I could ever have done. He and Mrs. Bennet's quarrels were so well acted they'd have given those London folk a run for their money. As for love, well, a lady here present has already accepted this old seafarer as her shipmate." He pointed at Lady Groombridge, who was seated nearby.

"We'll sail through rough weather and smooth together, won't we, ma'am?"

Lady Groombridge left her seat in the audience to take up a chair next to the captain. She held in her hand a book of poetry, which looked to Mrs. Bennet's eye disturbingly familiar. A second glance confirmed that it was twin to her own Christmas gift. For a moment she was vexed, then with a smile she realised how blind, partial, prejudiced and absurd she had been while under the spell of the captain's gallantry. She held her husband's arm all the tighter and he met her gaze with an enquiring look.

She whispered, "Mr. Bennet, notwithstanding your own brilliance in verse, I think we may sum up this evening by a quote from Shakespeare: 'All's well that ends well', don't you agree?" He nodded, and both joined in the laughter.

There were more congratulations, as the audience were now mingling with the actors and musicians:

so many good wishes and warm laughter that the room resounded like a beehive. Suddenly the bells of Pemberley chapel pealed out, a glorious and joyous cascade of sound.

"Whatever is happening?"

"It must be for the success of the play tonight."

"Is it to signal the end of the evening?"

"Or another great military victory?"

Opinions were varied and numerous. A young man with a red, excited face, and wearing attire that was less formal than he usually showed in society, entered quickly from the hall. His shirtsleeves were rolled up, his cravat undone. He had run down two flights of stairs and had hardly the breath to speak. His face was smiling broadly. All he could do was point to a figure behind him; it was Mrs. Hill carrying a small bundle. A quick gasp and Bingley was able to draw breath enough to cry,

"May I present you with—my son."

"A boy!" screamed Mrs. Bennet, darting across the room. Her joy burst forth in the greatest animation of spirits, her eyes sparkling with delight. She reached out towards the newest visitor to Pemberley. Then, gently lifting the tiny infant into her arms, she held him to her. The most tender emotion and deepest love showed in her countenance. She slowly turned round to face everyone.

"As a grandmother and matriarch of the Bennet family, may I offer some advice? To my daughters, when you have children, let your girls marry or remain spinsters, as they choose. To your sons and daughters, when you make your wills, include NO ENTAILS, please!"

February 5th, midnight.

A final entry. Further recording of my state would seem superfluous, as matters have taken so favourable a turn.

Life could have no happier outcomes; dear Jane has safely given birth and I have a fine new grandson. Mary and Kitty are betrothed, albeit to different gentlemen from those I had planned. Darcy and Lizzy appreciate and care for me. And my final good fortune is that the play was a complete success (even my own attempt at acting was well-received).

My menopause seems finally to be over. Despite all the horrors I suffered in its duration, I have learned much from it. In daring to step outside the trap of my fears and don a mantle of confidence, it may truly be said I have 'stooped to conquer'.

As for my marriage—well, as I put down my goose quill and close this journal, the last face I see before extinguishing the candle, is that of my dearest Mr. Bennet, smiling at me from our pillow.

4352033R00204

Printed in Great Britain
by Amazon.co.uk, Ltd.,
Marston Gate.